HAWG

by STEVEN SHREWSBURY

"If I'm going to die," Andrew said with a smile, holding up two hand grenades. "It isn't going to be pretty. I've spent a lifetime gathering up this stuff and playing soldier, sweetheart. Now, it's time to fuckin' fight."

While Micki wrung her hands, she looked back at the direction the roar came from. "Give me a gun."

Andrew focused on her face, then looked at her shaky hands.

The bellow of the beast resounded in their ears and she screamed, "You have to give me a gun! I'll kill myself before I let that thing have me again."

Andrew took a sawed off shotgun, showed her where the safety was, and instructed her to get in-between the crypts. "Get in, hon. I'll go along the outside side. I doubt Hawg can fit into the gap. If he tries, just blow his fucking face off."

She nodded, squatted down and grabbed Andrew's arm as he started to back away from her. "You afraid?"

Andrew half smiled and winked. "Shittin' my pants, sweetheart. I'll change later."

He crept around the side of the Solow crypt like he was out on maneuvers again. As the Harley roared, obviously in motion, Andrew wondered if he unconsciously put himself away from the high explosives in his own crypt. He stepped out, scooped up the trigger switch grip and started to back up for cover.

Andrew stopped for a moment as he saw Hux swing around into view in the distance. The ass end of his Harley fishtailed, but the biker grinned as he acted. Not twenty yards behind him leapt Hawg into view, moving on his all fours. Up on hind legs for a moment, the beast bellowed and dropped down, in hot pursuit of the laughing biker.

Andrew shook for a moment, enough to rattle his teeth, but screwed down his courage. He knelt beside the crypt, and brought down the machine gun from his shoulder. "Come get some, schvine-hundt," Andrew grunted, using his German grandmother's expression for pig-dog.

ACKNOWLEDGEMENTS

For my mother, Esther, who grew up on a farm and is a priceless source of all things. Her Sunday dinner tales could make horror fans cringe.

Thanks to the usual suspects: Bob Freeman, Peter Welmerink, Chris Fulbright, Angie Hawkes, Cullen Bunn, Nate Kenyon, Mike Oliveri, Cody Goodfellow, John Paul Allen, Jen O (come on Toshi!), and Christine Whitehead.

Special thank you to Tod Clark for everything. I owe you a beer or twelve.

Thanks always to Brian Keene, Norm Partridge, Joe R. Lansdale, John Skipp, and James A. Moore. Your words, guidance and examples are so much help.

Thanks always to my sons John and Aaron.

Shrews
Rural Central Illinois

DEDICATION

For:

"Mick" Huxtable
He was a great guy, and his namesake appears herein.
Mick was a terrific person, and thought it a riot
A character in a horror novel was named after him.
He was nothing like the Hux in this book.
But he loved the tale.
He died taking care of his family.
Rest easy, big guy.

"Man is an animal which, alone among the animals, refuses to be satisfied by the fulfillment of animal desires."
Alexander Graham Bell

PREFACE

Beast of the field

Iris Diaz laughed at Ricky Bravo's easy gait as she watched him walk up behind the farmer. Though Ricky had started out in a stealthy stance, hunched over and weaving his way through the side buildings and lawn ornaments on the vast farm, he had quickly abandoned this creeping action.

Clearly, with the loud voice coming from the boom box and the even louder squealing of the pigs, Rick could've easily stomped up behind the old man in overalls and not have been heard. The dusty black box, situated on the edge of a circular concrete dais just to the left of the farmer, had seen better days. Like its owner, Iris mulled, the box was dirty, beaten up, and about ready to fall apart. She swept her long black hair back over her shoulder, unsure of the farmer's age. A million if he was a day? She'd heard that phrase before, but guessed him over seventy years at least. The oblivious farmer moved fluidly at times, yet seemed to halt in his motions, as if some inner pain reminded him it was there. His skin was burnt dark, giving him a deeper hue than either Iris or Ricky.

Ricky stopped and winked at Iris. He then glanced across the vast property taking in the three long barns, a corncrib, open pens crowded with pigs, and a massive round barn to their right. Ricky aped the act of sizing up the farmer, who stood a bit taller than the five-foot-ten Bravo. Ricky jumped a little, startled by the voice on the speaker as it spewed out a rant:

"*I am the voice of one crying out in the wilderness!*"

The farmer's withered left hand held a small pig in place on the wooden trough. Tiny legs flailing, the snout parted and it squealed as if on fire. Nothing could stop destiny for this little one. The farmer's right hand swiped, scooping down between the piglet's hind legs. This violent action also made Rick and Iris pause...that and the sight of the farmer dropping the small pair of pig testicles into a large galvanized bucket. Near the clean pail was a tiny pen housing a dozen or so piglets. The other babies saw the balls drop, but rendered no opinion of the castration other than to root in the dust.

Iris's silent laughter stopped and her face froze. The sight of the blood on the straight razor in the farmer's hand and Ricky's frozen manner caused her fear to rise like bile in her throat. Ricky was a hard ass; a calculating and dependable runner for the Latin Kings of Chicago down through central Illinois. Only God, or car trouble, could slow him down in his duty of delivering drugs to small communities in the land of Lincoln. The latter was his bane this day, but the tough kid from Cicero found himself struck dumb at the spectacle. So did his drug mule, Iris.

"Prepare ye the way of the Lord!" the box's voice boomed on, as the farmer wiped the bloody blade on a rag that hung from a fence nail.

Ricky cranked his head, right then left, as if to break himself loose from the sight. Still, he remained focused as Iris took another step. The farmer put the handle of the razor between his teeth, reached over into a pan balanced on the trough, dipped his fingers, and brought out something that glistened like butter. He smeared this between the piglet's legs and grunted in agreement to the words thundering from the boom box. The farmer set the pig free into a small pen away from the others and reached to grab another baby hog kept in the wire holding pen by the bucket. He wiped his brow with his left hand that held the small pig, and then looked up, toward the huge round barn. He then set the new piglet down and wiped his fingers on a bloody black rag. Razor back in hand, the farmer shook his right shoulder as if to limber up for the next round.

Ricky snapped free of his shock, scouted around the vast rural property they'd walked to from their overheated car now squatting by the roadside, and smiled. He reached back and grabbed the handle of the .38 caliber snub nose pistol jammed into his ass crack. Iris' stomach turned, the vile act still fresh in her mind, comprehending that the actions were going to march on fast. Her smile returned, as she saw Ricky prepare to take out the farmer.

"Make his path straight!"

Gun in hand, Ricky turned the barrel away from the farmer and grasped the weapon like a bludgeon.

From the far side of the round barn, a figure emerged that halted Ricky's actions in midair. He saw the individual, a slender black man who may have been a couple centuries old, walk into their sight. The black man wiped his hands on a gray rag stringing from the hip pocket of his brown overalls and said, "Mr. Solow, I believe the calf is gonna come tomorrow...." He saw Ricky; ready to pistol-whip the farmer, and stopped.

Bile rose again in Iris's throat as Ricky's focus switched to the newcomer in the yard. This moment of distraction was all Mr. Solow needed. His eyes followed what the black man saw. With an abrupt swipe, Mr. Solow turned his body and slashed open Ricky's throat. The slash was fast as lightning, but cut a savage blow like an axe. The small blade did its appointed job, again, not distinguishing between pig balls and human flesh.

Iris ran forward, but stopped short of touching Ricky. Blood ruined his Chicago Blackhawks Jersey, adding more color to the feathers of the Indian on it. Guts heaving, she held her stomach and squeezed her thighs together. She had her own treasure to worry about keeping inside. Iris didn't intend to throw her life away after the cocky drug runner their superiors had chosen for that day.

Both old men looked at her for a moment, but they seemed more focused on the wounded trespasser, whose crimson blood now mixed with pig blood in the dry brown dirt.

Ricky stepped back, holding his neck on the left side, blood spurting between his fingers. He coughed, gagged, spitting cherry red liquid out his lips; his askew ball cap fell and rolled upright.

Mr. Solow faced the dying man, his gray eyes focused in hard on Ricky. The old man didn't register anger or confusion. If anything, his half smile betrayed bemusement as Ricky pointed the butt of the revolver at him. Iris figured Ricky's original plan still bubbled in his mind, but there was naught in his will left to carry out the project. Piglet still in hand, Solow stepped toward Ricky as he slipped the razor into the bib-overalls front pocket at his chest and reached out for the gun.

Still, Rick pointed at him with the wrong end of the gun, emphatically, as if he squeezed hard enough the bullets would emerge from the weapon via the handle. Alas, this wasn't to be.

"Woe unto you sinners!"

Iris backed up when Solow took the handgrip of the gun in his hand and easily disarmed Ricky. Jugular vein spewing his life away, Ricky staggered and clutched his neck in repeated padding motions, as if he could hold his soul in. He armed up some of his Blackhawks jersey to absorb the blood, but the crude bandage did no good…save to douse the Johnny Cash T shirt under his jersey with scarlet. Iris felt loopy, her head twisting, waiting to see Ricky's spirit escape in the wound on his neck. She cursed the fact she'd smoked the hash earlier and thought it was out of her system.

Solow tossed the piglet in his hand back into the holding pen and aimed the .38 at Ricky. Suddenly, the farmer didn't appear so feeble to them. Firm in his steps the old man's arm never shook as he leveled the weapon.

"No," Iris muttered, but never drew a look from the farmer, nor the black man who walked up on the scene with measured steps. She couldn't do anything and they understood that.

"Woe unto all of the Earth!"

The shot rang higher in pitch than Iris thought normal, yet still stabbed at the inner parts of her ears. The bullet did its job, no matter what the sound. Ricky's head snapped, blood erupting from the back of his head in a small fount. It squirted fast and red, but it was over that quick. Ricky fell down and never budged again. Iris expected slow motion and a struggle, but this wasn't television.

Then, the two men gaped at Iris. Though his face was craggy and withered, it held power like an old actor she'd seen, right down to the cleft in his chin. Solow frowned, lowered the gun, and shot her in the right ankle. Pain exploded in her body as she stumbled, put weight on the wounded foot and fell to the ground. When she rolled over, Solow stood over her and checked the chambers of the gun. As he did this the black man picked up the ball cap Ricky had lost earlier.

"Stop, no, please, by the Mother of God...." she wailed.

He nodded and aimed again. This time Solow shot her through the left ankle and shook his head when the blood spray kissed his left pants leg. As her agony went white hot and her yowls became screams for help, Solow handed the gun to the black man.

"Bring out the cage, Elias," Solow said to him in a steady voice. "She'll live long enough to be dessert for him."

Elias never flinched as he regarded the round barn with a nod and then pointed at Ricky's dead body. He put the ball cap on his head and asked, "What about the fella, sir?"

Solow glanced at Ricky's prone form and said, "I'll help you take him to Hawg. She ain't goin' anywhere."

"This is murder," Iris gasped, hand on her abdomen. "Murderers!"

Solow's face stayed stoic. "Y'all were gonna way-lay me, so don't gimme crap for doin' the Lord's work. It's been a long day."

Unconcerned with Iris, the two men walked over to Ricky, each took up a leg and started to drag him toward the round barn.

Left alone, Iris tried to crawl away. Her mind was on the car, not a quarter mile down the rural road. Perhaps it would start and perhaps...she could drive with two gun-shot feet? Her eyes squirted tears, thinking of the terror filled ride in the farm-lands. She so hated the places not in the city. The open space and rural lands scared her as if they were about to swallow her up. It was too open, too green and so much dirt nearby.

"Sin is what separated God and Man. The Bible says Adam had walked with God in the cool of the evening, but then horror came into his life."

"God, shut up," she told the box that kept going with the sermon.

The pain ruled her body and she stopped trying to advance.

Iris screamed out again, but there was no one to hear. They were miles from the nearest small town Ricky had called Montrose. Iris never cared about a destination, only her role and the fix afterwards.

"When they fell from grace, God came seeking them in the garden and asking 'Where art thou?' How many of you can guess that he knew exactly where they were?"

Iris aspired after sleep or simple oblivion, to escape the preacher's voice, to get away from it all, though the daggers of agony she felt in her ankles refused to allow slumber to come. She damned her cell phone for being out of roaming area when they broke down. She damned Ricky for his "off the beaten path" route to Montrose. She damned their Lord's connections and all of his men, like that seedy prick Mr. Roberts, for giving this duty to them. Lastly, she damned herself for being weak enough, addict enough, and big enough to be a drug mule. Though she kept fighting it, she really didn't care if the condoms and packets of meth or heroin fell out of her vagina.

The pain increased so that the effects of the blunts she had smoked earlier fled from the ocean of anguish. Iris' sense of time faltered as she nearly blacked out. She heard a deep scraping sound inside the barn...no...was it a roar or a squeal, muffled by the walls? Only the grinding gears of a garbage truck sounded like that...not the roar of any animal. Had they stuck Ricky in a compactor of some sort? There was no pattern to the screeching sound. The idea of Ricky, so handsome and lean, turned into hamburger grindings made her stomach turn again.

In her dreamy state of pain, she heard the farmer's box, still preaching, say, *"Do not lie down with the beast of the field, for it is an abomination in the eyes of God."*

Iris blinked and saw that the rag the farmer wiped his razor on was a well-worn, many times washed Motorhead T-shirt. Where on earth would such a backwater man get an article like that, she wondered as the hurting marched on up her calves.

The two men returned and looked down at her. After they exchanged a glance, Elias asked, "You going to shoot her again, Mr. Solow?"

Solow shook his head and directed Elias to take up her left arm. "Hawg won't want her dead."

Though Iris planned to resist, her arms acted like they were replaced by rubber stems and her actions of protest amounted to nothing. Solow and Elias drug her away to the huge barn with ease, each man handling her as if she were a child. The piglets in the holding pen stared at her as she went. Soon, they returned to sniffing and rooting in the dirt.

"Sin had separated them from him, and they were afraid, because their minds were corrupted by filth. When you have filth in your mind, and filth in your soul, that is all you can produce. Garbage in, garbage out."

Solow held her under the armpits as Elias unlocked a sturdy wooden door. He then unlatched a metal screen door and then unlocked a third door, this one made of bars. Closing the doors behind them, they started down a flight of wooden steps. She labored to say something about the drugs inside of her that they were practically ready to pass through her labia lips and stop at the huge pad she wore, but the words got lost on the way to her mouth. The sight of the inner barn, sunken into the earth a full story, took up her breath.

A few lights glowed, showing her a circular pen that reeked of pig feces and fresh cut hay. Several bales of hay strung around the edges of the circle. A series of bales appeared by their boxy construction and placement, built into a children's fort. Between these long lines of bales lay bedding and a filthy pillow.

Iris didn't see Ricky at first, for she was far too distracted by the oppressive stench. She then spotted him strung up about the same time as she saw Elias pull a grimy blanket off a shiny steel fixture. Ricky hung from heavy chains on the ceiling, not far from the rectangular steel case Elias wiped off after he folded the blanket. Ricky's hands gripped a pair of rusty hooks, as if he really had life enough to hold on. It was all wrong; she saw him die. No tears came for Ricky, as she didn't love him, nor like him much. But her eyes grew bleary for her fate loomed.

The question as to why she was alive boiled in her brain, and the answer glistened before her. The rectangular object reminded her of a tiny dog run made of stainless steel bars.

Nevertheless, some sloppy substance clung to the short gates of the steel fixture, mostly at the front and rear.

Iris struggled with the farmer stronger than before, but he was too sturdy to break. Her ears heard the scrape of metal as Elias opened the nearest gate of the metal rectangle. While Solow pushed her down and into the opening Elias made, she heard the slobbering sounds of an animal. Her mind panicked as she thought of some brute they kept in here. Her fears were quickly confirmed as they slid her into the chamber and cuffed her in place on all fours. Eyes bugging, she saw the animal. She saw the thing the farmer had called Hawg moments before...at Ricky's calves.

The pain in her wrists and ankles from the steel restraints never blocked out the horror she witnessed. Certain the packets of drugs in her vaginal canal had torn and she was really in a drug hallucination, she started to giggle. Be it the dope escaping or her mind refusing to deal with reality, she laughed loud as Hawg turned to face her, chewing on a portion of Ricky's calf muscle.

The fluorescent lights cast a halo around Hawg as he crouched. At first glance, Hawg may have been taken for a huge man in a bad Halloween boar's costume. When he planted his feet...*God*, she thought...*hooves*...and stood up, he was easily seven feet tall. His frame reminded her of a professional wrestler, huge, thick, defined in places, but not ripped like a body builder. Naked, fleshy in color, Hawg seemed not embarrassed by his curled penis nor his excrement tainted thighs. Aside from the curly penis and a series of abdominal muscles that multiplied into an impossible array of pectoral formations, Hawg almost would pass for an ugly man...save for the face.

Bald and sleek, she expected to see folded over ears on Hawg. Either he had none, had been clipped, or they lay close to his head. His jaw slung low, Iris beheld teeth, glistening red, and couldn't make sense of where his curled tusks originated...or why they seemed by their glint to be made of steel. These objects seemed to retract in a bit, then curl out more as he worked his maw.

Though his back legs sported hooves, or feet split to appear that way, his long arms sported fingers...hands not to be mistaken for claws. Sharp and dangerous, Hawg flexed these digits and they cracked, popping like farts in the bizarre acoustics of the round barn.

Hawg snorted as he reached down and tore loose Rick's leg at the shin. He snapped the joint like rotten wood and pulled the muscle from bone as easily as meat at a rib restaurant. His nose was big and wide, but not as swinish as she'd assumed. His eyes, though, glowed red in a pinkish background, hooded by a heavy brow like a primitive man she's seen depicted at the Chicago Field Museum. Hawg munched the muscle from Rick's leg, sniffed the raw end he bit into, and then sucked at the shards of bone protruding from the piece. Marrow ran down his chin and dribbled between his pectorals.

Still, she laughed. It was insane and her screeching increased as hands clasped firm on her pants, fumbling with the snaps and zippers. She never fought them as the two men pulled her pants off her rump and yanked them to her knees.

When her panties fell, Elias said, "She's raggin' it, Mr. Solow. See the big pad?"

A matter of fact voice responded, "You know Hawg don't care none 'bout that. I think he likes it better that way."

She heard sloppy steps trod on the floor as the men backed away from the securement chamber. Elias said, "I don't see her bleedin', sir, but her snatch looks too big."

Solow coughed and then added, "It don't have to be pretty, Elias. She'll bleed like Niagara Falls when ol' boy gets done with her."

On cue, Hawg dropped the gristly piece of Ricky and danced on two legs, nearer to them. Hawg dropped to his all fours and made a few strides. In a moment, he was behind her, gripping the sides of the chamber that held Iris fast.

Hawg made a whining sound. It was mournful in a way.

Elias' voice said gently, "I'm on the way, Hawg."

Iris felt a human hand brush her thigh as Hawg's curled penis slapped her on either side of her buttocks. Elias grabbed the creature's penis and guided him to her labia lips. The hand drew away and a corkscrew inserted inside her, extended deep and started ramming like mad.

She heard Solow laugh as Hawg went wild. "Happy birthday, son," Solow said. Suddenly, the two men started to sing happy birthday, barely able to restrain their laughter as the beast grabbed her and forced himself inside her, over and over. His shouts of joy and snarls of anger were one in the same. Hawg gripped the bars on the side of the chamber at first. The nails on Hawg's hands sank into the muscles of her upper back, and slowly slit her open down to her buttocks. Still, he rode her hard, screaming, squealing more like a rusty gear creaking than a pig in the fits of orgasm. Spit flew from his mouth and rained over her back and hair.

Then, it all went wrong.

Hawg started to tremble. Iris's air was nearly gone, unable to draw in a fresh breath from the assault, she gasped with vigor as Hawg ceased in his thrusts. His big body shaking like old leaves in the wind, Hawg started to grunt in short intervals. Iris assumed he would cum and kill her.

"What is it, boy?" Elias asked just before Hawg drew out and held up his arms. A stream of semen flew over her back and into her hair like a jet of water, but she also felt the packets of drugs once stuffed deep start to vomit out of her vagina. They spilled, but not in their containers. Hawg's curled member broke all of them, she guessed, as the ooze of mucky dope and powders leaked from her snatch. A condom fell from her and hit the ground. She'd felt that before, but not with a half human pig beast shooting cum over her body like a kid with a super soaker.

The beast was away from her and running around the perimeter of the round barn. His screams rang frantic and the two men's voices held concern. Round and around he went until Hawg impacted on the inner steel door. With a loud howl, he pulled it free.

"Christ, the locks!" Solow shouted.

From her position, Iris' bleary eyes saw Hawg tear loose the screen door like it was tinfoil. He then stabbed at the wooden door near the handle, lowering his head and using his steel tusks. The tusks sank in the wood abruptly and Hawg yanked back, splintering the door around the lock. His squeal shrilled in glee as the door was open and the fading light of day spilled in.

Once outside, Hawg paused, raised his arms, and beat down on the earth before running away on his all fours.

"My God, Mr. Solow," Elias said, stepping into Iris' view and watching Hawg go. "What happened? Hawg done went feral!"

Solow's voice sounded calm to Iris, even in her groggy state. "See here, Elias. This rotten bitch had dope stored in her pussy."

The old black man stepped behind her and said, "Damn, sure enough. One of them there mules we heard tell of. What a damned world this is getting to be."

Iris heard the rustle of denim and then felt the sensation of a flat cold steel object on her neck. Solow's voice was very close as he said to her, "At least we know no one will ever miss them."

CHAPTER ONE

Feral

Andrew White was visiting the crypt of his great grandparents when he heard the distant scream across the countryside. The sound echoed in the fading daylight, but drew his attention due to its strangeness. Andrew stood from his task in the crypt, stretching his six-foot-five frame. He held open the metal doors to the family crypt and listened again, certain the scream came from the Solow farm not three miles from his house and two miles from the graveyard. He'd hunted and field dressed everything legal and Andrew had never heard such a cry.

"Roasting a pig alive at this hour?" Andrew laughed to himself and stepped inside the small stone building. He eyeballed the two long granite sarcophagi and frowned when another scream resonated in the evening. "All my forty years, never heard anything like that," he said to no one as he grabbed the edge of the stone coffin on his left. He turned a small key on a clasp underneath, returned the key to his pocket and took a breath. "Hello, Gramma," Andrew grunted as he slid the cover away; the stone felt cold to his hands. His skin, so rough from years of hard labor, gleaned relief on the cool surface. He reached inside the box and pulled out a Colt .45 revolver. "What folks won't pay for a genuine relic of the West. Minh, I gotta like your money, though." He then reached back into the box and pulled out a small hand grenade. Andrew thumbed the ridges of the deadly pineapple and smirked. These items went into the pockets of his leather jacket. Andrew closed the lid on this coffin and opened the other coffin in a similar fashion. Again, in the distance, he heard a bizarre wail. These sounds never concerned him as he produced a box of shells and a quarter stick of dynamite.

Once outside the crypt, he locked the iron door, glanced at the crypt next to his family's and adjusted his biker jacket. Hand stroking down his beard once, Andrew walked to his Harley and swung his right leg over it. Hands on the grips, he listened again for the sound. Andrew heard nothing. His Harley roared to life and the straight pipes bellowed.

He had business to do. A late-night pig slaughter or a critter getting after Solow's hogs wasn't his concern. Andrew hated to sell one of his collected guns to Minh in IT at work, but it was better than that perfumed prick Dinsdale from Customer Service. Tim Dinsdale worked at the same factory as Andrew and was a wannabe gun nut. Minh, though, was an earnest collector of historical items. He wanted the gun, had the cash and the ability to keep his trap shut. Andrew owned the guns he had hidden from a recent ATF raid and needed cash, nothing too religious about it. As he guided his Harley on the paved road outside the cemetery, he glanced at his father's grave and nodded. The tiny American flag Andrew's son Jordan often replaced there still flew proud.

Over the straight pipes, Andrew couldn't hear the screams.

Tim Dinsdale could hear them, though. In his hyper euphoric state, he ignored the weird cries at first. Sweat beaded on his brow, nearly making the mousse in his hair congeal. It was easy to block out the world with one's cock in a woman's mouth. Seat reclined in his BMW, the second in command of the Customer Service Department at Ambrose Brother's Printing enjoyed the abilities of the skinny girl from the bookbindery section of the factory. Sure, Andrea was fifteen years younger than him, had no discernable morals and rotten front teeth from crystal meth abuse, but she sure knew how to give head...much better than Tim's eclectic wife. Andrea would even swallow for him, unlike his overweight spouse. *Fat bitch ate everything but cum,* he thought with a smile. He fondled Andrea's firm tits as she bobbed on his cock, breathing through her nose, humming ever so often. Andrea's breasts were so solid that he doubted they were real. Had she sucked enough dick to earn a new pair of titties from some sugar daddy? It didn't matter, all in all. This evening, she was his and that was all that was important. They shared a love for weed and sex, so that was enough to have in common. Though a typical girl of her generation – pallid, low rise pants, tattoo on the pit of her back, and dull witted – she had a few talents.

When the howls outside the car on the gravel road started, Tim barely noticed. They became louder, closer, and he still blew it off, thinking it a crow or a coyote. He was safe and the heat in his balls grew. The cries ceased and he concentrated on his fantasy, of this scab of a crack-whore dressed in lingerie, her normally flat hair poofed up like 1980's porn stars on parade, offering him her ass at last, begging for it that way.

There was no cry or howl when the passenger side window shattered. Glass rained on them and the only sound was a grunt so deep it sounded like an elephant fart underwater. Tim's eyes opened in time to see long claws grab Andrea by the back of her head and the seat of her pants and yank. The deed was crude, executed with great force, enough to make her clamp down and bite through Tim's penis before the claws pulled her away. Her spine snapped as the intruder ripped her through the opening and out into the grassy ditch.

Tim heard her scream, gag, and cough a few times, but then the great cries of a thing he couldn't identify rang out. He had bigger troubles than her health, though. Tim gawked down and saw his penis entirely gone, savagely removed by the sudden action. Warm blood spurted with each heartbeat and his scrotum ran scarlet. His blood covered his new tan pants and the leather steering wheel, but soon, the gushes grew slower and his head fogged. Andrea made no sounds and only the rumble of the beast that busted her in half thudded in his ears. His screams and grunts were regular until punctuated by a torrid scream. Then, it was quiet.

Tim stared over as the thing stood up. One huge claw on the windshield, the monstrosity's tongue slathered its lips and the metallic horns near its mouth. Hastily, the creature twisted and dropped to all fours, scampering away into the fields.

Tim's mind couldn't focus as the darkness weaved in about him. He didn't know what he'd tell his wife, anyway.

"Jordan, come in here," came the voice from the big white house.

"On the way, Ma," Jordan called out, but he knelt by a mound of dirt behind the garage. In the back part of a disused pony pen, Jordan White said a prayer for his dead dog.

"I know you don't have a soul, Buddy," Jordan said to the ground, eyes on the cross made of two branches. "But I miss you anyway."

Though tears were close, Jordan suddenly grimaced. The stench in the air made him almost gag. "Mr. Solow spreading poop already this year?" the nine-year-old boy wondered aloud. He looked in the general direction of the Solow place, heard his mother call again and decided to get up.

He walked around the garage and beheld his mother in the doorway. Busted at the dog's grave again, Jordan hung his head.

"It's all right," she said, sweeping her long auburn hair back. "Just don't let your daddy catch you back there too much."

Jordan nodded. "I miss him, Mom," he confessed and walked to her. "I don't want another dog. You know Mr. Ellington bought a pit bull when Cassidy's puppy got run over. I don't want anything like that."

She gave him a hug, tussled his brown hair, frowned and said, "Cassidy's dog, Genesis, is a menace. Don't you ever get close to them things. They are killers and would make a cheeseburger of your little brother."

He said, "I know it's not like when we went hunting and skinned the rabbits. I know Buddy has no soul, like gramma said." Eyes suddenly alight, Jordan said, "The snapping turtle thing when we went hunting was cool!"

She rolled her eyes to heaven. "Your father and his biker pals shouldn't have nailed that turtle to the tree and gutted it in front of you."

Jordan seemed excited by the memory. "I thought it was like in cartoons, but the turtle was stuck to his shell!"

Her face grew dark. "You step in something?"

He conferred his tennis shoes with a grimace and shrugged. "I think it's from Solow's place. Bad for sure."

She gazed off up the road North toward the Ellington place and then said, "I can hear the straight pipes of your father's bike. I can tell by how his cylinder misses. He'll be home soon. Genesis up the way is barking her fool head off."

"All right." He thought about his grandpa, and how much he missed him as well. He had a soul and Jordan thought of visiting his grave after school. He liked going to the graveyard. It was near the closed-up mine where grandpa used to tell him stories and serve him sandwiches. Grampa was a funny guy and used to tell him so many yarns of the war and how to fight. "Mom, don't tell dad about me back there, ok?"

"Do your reading homework and we have a deal."

Jordan smiled. "Deal."

The Ellingtons went out for pizza that evening and had left their enormous pit bull Genesis to roam the fenced-in back yard. When Hawg passed by, he sniffed the meaty scraps left for Genesis. Like most dogs of her ilk, she went to the fences and barked at Hawg. A piece of muscled anger, the dog growled and slobbered, ready to fight fast to the death.

Both hands on the top of the chain link fence, Hawg stabbed her in the neck with his tusks and drew back, flinging the huge dog over the fence and into the empty field. Genesis rolled, howling in agony, but Hawg was quick to get down on all fours and charge. Tusks delving deep into the dog's side, Hawg grabbed its bloody neck in one hand and her right hindquarter in the other. He stood erect and broke Genesis' back over his head. He tore her open with his tusks and feasted on the slippery guts, rooting in her warm insides. Hawg needed something to cleanse his mouth. The skinny girl on the country road had a peculiar chest, for her breasts had burst at the grazing of his tusks. They never bled, but spewed a salty fluid. Hawg rooted deep, bursting the heart and lungs of the pit bull, determined to get the taste of bad tits out of his mouth.

Andrew passed two people he knew while riding on his Harley. One was his brother, Sheriff Doug White. The cop even flashed his cherries at him as he drove on north. His brother's shifts changed every so often, so Andrew assumed Doug was at work or heading home. Doug didn't seem in any hurry.

"Good day, Sheriff," Andrew said. "Still not smoking?" Though his brother couldn't hear him, Andrew needled his sibling, as all brothers do. He was glad he never started smoking like Doug, so he'd never had to wrestle with quitting, like Doug.

The other man he passed was another biker and Ambrose Brother's Printing employee Randy Huxtable. Hux was a bulky fucker, riding a full dresser with straight pipes, who never saw a snatch he didn't like. An example of this taste sat astride behind him on the big bike. They exchanged a wave in passing. Andrew wagered Hux was out for some back-road loving in the rising moonlight, probably off to get high as well with the gal. Randy, a husky dude with an attitude a mile wide, was a guy whom Andrew got along with, but he hated his lame biker gang attitude and obvious drug connections. His mouth tightened when he thought of the promotions Hux received at work. Not a man of great skills, but Andrew was certain Hux's drug supplies greased his ascension from the bindery floor to hoist driver and then, assistant head of the loading docks. He cursed him in his mind, knowing it was un-Christian to do so, but he did it anyway. The rage in his mind for Jack Sullivan, plant manager and all-around asshole came to the surface, but he let it slide off. Sullivan was unfair and arrogant, in love with his big beige Buick, and forgot where he came from. Since he was now Mayor of Montrose as well, Sullivan's ego was out of control. Andrew decided to forget him instead of going to kick the ass of the man who could fire him.

Andrew passed the Ellington residence and expected to see Genesis in the pen flipping out on him. The yard light didn't show the whereabouts of the big pit bull and Andrew blew this off. He and Ellington went back years, but Andrew still wanted to shoot that fool dog. He hated living so close to such a beast with little kids around.

What he wished he could do was banish the scent of the

pig-shit from the Solow place. Well, it was inconsistent, like the scent was closer at times and then fleeting. Though the Solow place was distant, he could see a few of the barns and the trailers out of the edges of his field where Elias lived, and the old blind lady Luella Goodkind. He pondered going to see Solow the next day, and perhaps dropping off some Braille books Jordan had bought for Luella last weekend.

Hawg heard the loud things on the road pass each other. He hated the roar of these beasts of steel. The vibration in his huge chest made him uneasy. The awful feeling inside he was experiencing after covering the brood sow in the stall made him feel worse. Gilt, bah, she was a long way from puberty, that one.

The machines that roared sounded alike, as if they were kindred. The one carrying two people had a ripple to the sound, something odd about it. Hawg couldn't understand that, but it made him look after that vehicle longer.

Hawg couldn't stop running and trying to satisfy his burning hunger. He was so thirsty and wanted fresh gilt, in the worst way. Anger bubbled in his mind at the one Elias and father had strapped in for him at the round barn. That was no gilt, nor a sow proper, but she did something bad to him. Ever since he entered her, Hawg's heart raced and his mind was afire.

When the wind shifted, Hawg stopped, pivoted, and raised his snout. Red eyes on the paved road, the other gurgling steel beast turned down a farmer's path between the fields. Though at a great distance, Hawg smelled something better than fresh gilt on that machine.

He smelled gilt with blood on it.

"Mr. Solow?" Elias said as he opened the screen door of the main house. His fingers drummed on the door as he waited.

"Come on in, Elias," the old man answered. Solow's voice sounded tired and from a long way away.

"God is asking America, 'Where art thou?' A land founded by people fleeing religious persecution has found itself saturated in hate, clothed in racist language, painted by paganism, and obsessed with personal idolatry."

Elias wiped his feet and removed his straw hat, but never walked in farther than the end of the back porch. He stared across the linoleum floor of the vast kitchen and into the dimly lit living room. Solow put his arm down from handling the remote to the stereo. Elias said, "All my work is done for the evening."

"Good, but you don't need to tell me that. You lose the ball cap?"

"It just wasn't me, sir."

Solow sat across the room from the kitchen in a recliner, legs out. Clad in clean clothes and smoking a cigar, the old man's face gained illumination by the shifting glow of a television screen. On the wall behind him hung matted pictures Elias knew to be Solow's mother and father.

Elias said, "I know that, sir, but, well, what about Hawg?"

Calmly, Solow took a drag off the cigar, tapped it on a glass ashtray and said, "It was bound to happen, Elias. There's nothing we could do in the end."

"But...."

"No use cryin' over it. He'll come home in time. If not, well, that's his destiny to be free."

Hand scratching the back of his graying hair, Elias protested, "But sir...."

Solow's voice grew stronger as he cut him off, saying, "You took care of the sinners and their awful car?"

"Yes sir. It was out of transmission fluid. Easy enough to fix and get rid of."

Solow bestowed a nod and his voice returned to a gentle state. "There's nothing to worry about, Elias."

"I wish I could share that feeling, sir." Elias then backed up and came near to knocking a picture off the wall behind him. As he righted the photo, he blinked at the pictures he'd seen countless times before of Mr. Solow and his shipmates in World War Two taken in Philadelphia.

With a wave of his left hand, Solow said, "Help yourself to a bottle on the porch, Elias. You do good work."

Unsure if the bottle of homemade wine would produce a balm for his nerves, Elias took it and exited the house. He walked in the night, not afraid of Hawg, for he'd known him since he was a baby. Elias feared discovery and imprisonment. He was too old for that kind of life. Several acres passed before he reached his trailer on the edges of this side of Solow's property.

Before he entered the trailer, he paused and looked over at Luella Goodkind's trailer, situated on a lot an acre from his home. He sat the bottle on the step and walked over to her place.

Elias stood on her wooden deck, heard the television inside and called out, "Luella? You need anything for the night?"

The sound of the television stopped and the inner door opened. Through the screen door, Elias saw the gigantic woman sitting on a loveseat. It took a loveseat to hold the enormous girth of Luella Goodkind. Truly a candidate for the fat lady in the circus, the woman giggled and waved at him, eyes closed. The violets on her dress seemed to be a field that never ended. A large German shepherd eyed Elias, but never growled.

"I'm fine, sweetheart."

"Good night, dear," Elias told her.

"Oh, sweetie?" she called out as Elias turned. "Make sure you tell Mr. Solow thanks for the satellite hook-up again. I so adore hearing all the religious channels and shows from the seventies."

"I will."

"God bless," Luella said sweetly and closed the door.

Elias stepped off the deck, but the moonlight made a revelation that stopped him cold. On her bottom step was a splatter of excrement, recently deposited. Elias scouted around the edge of Luella's white trailer and saw a smear on the edge of the white metal skirting. For something to have made that mark, Elias thought, the man or beast would've had to be at least seven feet tall.

Hux cast down a black Harley Davidson beach towel on the dead grasses right before he threw one in Micki Wingler. Sure, she'd been ragging it, but that never stopped Hux before, especially once he'd got cranked up. She was a cute girl, a preacher's daughter, around twenty, a trifle old for the biker in his mid-thirties, but he went with it. He hated them much older and able to enter the taverns to spy on him. He never liked them too thick in the middle, either, but Micki was willing and soon to be a regular buyer of Hux's supply. She didn't perform oral worth a damn, and had little tits, but he migrated on to the main course fast. He wanted to get a nut quick as he had a few deals to make later on. The drug mule from Cicero hadn't arrived yet and Hux wondered what was up with that. Still, his glee went untamed as he concentrated on her slippery snatch.

"Oh God," she kept saying, over and over, chewing on his long hair as it matted her face.

Not caring for her dialogue, but hot in the moment, Hux went to work, grabbing her buttocks and driving his point home, repeatedly. He grinned, wondering what else would Reverend Wingler's daughter say?

The rising stench of fecal matter made his face contort, but never did he slow in his motions. Hux by no means even stopped when Hawg leapt from the field and slammed into his body, mounting his back, embracing the two of them tight. Claws in the ground, Hawg's twisted manhood drove forward and pierced Hux's backside. The biker screamed loud as he was defiled. Hawg penetrated him awkwardly, but several times. The monster's penis corkscrewed into the biker and Hux howled, then screeched at the sudden agony in his frame. Hawg pumped on him numerous times and then withdrew. A single powerful wipe from a claw knocked Hux away, sending him cart wheeling into the ditch. He rolled, pants around his ankles, trying to get up. When he did rise up, the spectacle of Hawg raping Micki was one he didn't want to behold. Blood flew everywhere, easily visible in the moonlight. Hux didn't think it was all-natural from Micki, either.

The beast spasmed on Micki, thrusting deep and she screamed in pain, or at least Hux hoped it hurt. Micki was a slut and, in a way, he almost thought she enjoyed it until the beast roared in orgasm and drove his tusks into her collarbones. Hawg stood up and those tiny bones appeared to snap. Micki plopped back to the wet towel and Hawg took a step back. Hawg then dropped his head and proceeded to root in her bloody hole with his snout.

Head spinning from the blow from Hawg, ass on fire from the assault from the monster, Hux felt his lucidity wane. For the first time in years, he thanked God for something.

Unconsciousness.

Andrew put his bike in the garage and slid the long wooden door shut. The paint on the door chaffed and Andrew lamented that a duty this summer would be to repaint the shed. He surveyed the property north to where the grass terminated at the pine tree windbreak. "Gonna have to get the mowers all ready soon," he said. "Damn time Jordan learned the manly art of lawn mowing."

A distant cry echoed in the night; more than one. These sounds made Andrew pause. Brows lowered, Andrew faced the sounds, still unsure what he heard.

His wife stood at the door, smiling. "Hey."

"Hey, Lynne," he returned her word, still staring off. "Sorry I was late. Had to get some stuff for a collector."

"You boys and your games," she sighed, hand on her hip. "What is it?"

"Weird sounds tonight. Dunno if the coyotes got a pig cornered or what. Ya hear that?"

Lynne cocked her head and she said, "What is that?"

"Not sure," Andrew confessed. He walked to the porch and kissed her on the cheek. He pulled out the Colt .45, never pointed it at her and said, "Reach for the sky."

"Maybe later," she teased.

He hoped so.

CHAPTER TWO

Aftermath

Hawg followed the waterway that snaked through the barren field. Dead grasses and reeds that the hay balers missed still littered the long waterway. Many of the fibrous shoots snapped under his hooves and hands. Hawg paused when he sensed a movement in the grasses. The field mouse he disturbed never had a chance to flee more than a yard when Hawg snatched it up, slammed it to his maw and chewed down. Gristle in moments, the mouse was forgotten with a swallow. Hawg carried on.

When he stopped, he took a few breaths, red eyes glaring at the farmhouse a few acres distant. The property line cut out a large rectangle of pale greenery in the spring field. His instincts flared, but Hawg saw no barn, nor corncrib where more tiny morsels would hide. No machinery or implements infected the grounds, so Hawg recognized this was not a farmer proper.

He ran at a steady pace, seeking cover under the long line of pine trees to the north of the property. The cool wind touched Hawg as he lowered himself by the grasses the plows missed and this landowner's lawn mower couldn't touch. He hid in the dense growth. It served him well for cover as well as it performed its intended duty—that of a wind break. He passed water and looked on. Hawg nearly jumped as he heard a thump near the trees. Something struck a metal object and then he heard liquid. Was someone urinating out here? Snout flexing, he smelled a chemical, not piss. In another moment fire shot up between the trees. Hawg flattened out as the tall man came into

view, lean, towering, bearded and dirty blonde haired. Hawg
ground his steel tusks into the dirt.

Death is on him; Hawg could smell it. He's a killer. He'd
kill me if he saw me, not run like a scared runt. Hawg sensed
danger, but never feared the man until he saw the long knife
on the tall man's belt. Hawg reckoned he could use it. The man
burned something in a rusty barrel, smelling putrid like feces,
and then inspected his surroundings. In his hand he sloshed
fluid in a plastic container. Hawg's red eyes were on him as the
man's nose wrinkled.

"Dad?" a voice called out from the two-story farmhouse.

He gave the field a distasteful expression and backed away
from the burning barrel. "Yeah, Jordan, I'm right here."

The youthful voice called out again, this time with some
humor to it. "Dad, aren't you afraid of the bogey man?"

Still not turning his back on the tree line, the man replied,
"Son, yer daddy is the bogey man." The man walked to the
house and Hawg could hear him say, "Back when I was a kid,
when my Pa farmed this place, I used to be scared going out at
night. It's true."

Hawg heard the boy laugh and say, "Carrying that dirty
diaper, I couldn't be scared of no monster."

The man said lightly, "Yeah, that'd show him, huh? Even
the bogey man wouldn't want your brother's shit pants in his
face." They shared a laugh and the man paused by the door. His
face still in the direction of the burning barrel, Hawg could still
pick up the conversation. "Back when I was your age it was the
Bicentennial in America. They brought out all the Revolutionary
War stuff for us to learn, but they had this ad for Legend of
Sleepy Hollow stamps and movies. Well, every time I heard a
horse in the distance out here, I about crapped my pants."

"Huh. You were scared of the headless horseman?"

"Sure. It's natural to be afraid when yer a kid."

"Are you still scared of him?"

"Naw. When you get older, you'll see that there are worse
things than monsters to deal with. After ya get yer heart broke
a few times, you'll be happy to get a chance to beat the snot out
of some headless guy on a horse. C'mon. Let's get in."

Hawg ripped himself from the damp field and loped down the northern tree line. He paused and started south as the lines ended. He considered the land, wondered if the crumbling stone silo would fall any time soon, then proceeded south. Hawg loped on, traveled half the length of the property before his senses tweaked. A few random trees and high grasses made up the border to this properties' western side. A small garage obscured the large grassy area. Hawg noted a fence post in the far corner of the land and figured it was a pen of some kind, ages ago. No one needed to tell Hawg what the empty lot was used for now. Since the season hadn't greened up all the grasses yet, large spots thrust forth a heavy area of grass. There was a pattern. Hawg stood in a graveyard. By the size of the spots, it was a graveyard for animals.

The scent that drew him in wouldn't have been apparent to any human. The odor that teased him came from under a fresh spot, where loose dirt still covered a recent interment. A small wooden cross stood in the dirt. Hawg slapped this aside and rooted in the looser covering. His keen senses were correct and he started to rut and dig.

Whoever dug the grave understood his craft, Hawg thought, for the animal was down several feet. Any wild dog would never go through the trouble Hawg experienced. After four feet of dirt, it became a personal challenge and Hawg had to have the rotten animal. He struck a layer of lime, fairly fine in its encrustment of the dog's corpse. Still, it soured his ravenous appetite for a bit. Hawg pulled the dog free of the grave and pondered it for a few moments. The lime, dirt and dampness of the earth had turned a gray animal into a grimy black one. Frustrated at the lime, Hawg ripped the animal's head free of the carcass and used his steel tusks to slice open the skin on its back. Almost with delicate motions, Hawg skinned the animal as creatures housed inside it fell free. The fur delivered him little trouble and he peeled it back. Ripping a leg loose, he chewed off a bit of the dog's thigh. The meat was rough, and putrid, but the worms and grubs didn't bother Hawg.

When he ate Jordan White's pet, wiggling beasties and all, it felt like home.

Hux lowered himself into the bathtub and swore at the hot water. The soapy water misted with red blood from his backside and he reached for the toilet paper roll again. Oddly enough, the intrusion of the beast into his body hadn't torn him open. Though it had felt like he was skewered with a forge poker, there didn't seem to be that much damage when he felt around himself. He shuddered at the memory of the violation, how the twisted organ of the creature skewed into his backside, twisting around and driving deep. Hux never understood what even happened until the monster flung him off Micki. Sure, he was embarrassed that he had the cock of a vicious, possibly alien, creature in his ass. Shame coated him heavily that he'd emptied his bowels all over his jeans and boots. To chuck the jeans and soak his boots was one thing, but he couldn't get rid of the memory so easily.

Again, Hux buckled down his will and got under the water. At first, he feared the thing had perforated his bowels beyond the reach of his searching finger. The assault was fast and uneven, but still he bled unevenly. Not a rush of crimson, Hux felt secure that it was only a surface wound, though the one to his mind cut deeper. Certainly, a man's man, the humiliation of being defiled was one thing. The fact that he came when the beast entered him really disturbed Hux. That was one idea he didn't want to focus on.

Over and over, he washed his body and attempted to rationalize it all. It was a monster, he thought, no other word for it. It reeked of pig-shit, but they weren't far from the Solow property. That was one reason many chose that spot to go park and fornicate, few would go near the Solow area if the wind changed. Hux knew the level spots, ones where long grasses made good bedding. He hated bringing a woman to his house or even letting them know where he lived. They came back like cockroaches, he pondered, and he didn't need any sort of pest like that.

Hux burned inside, not just from his ass, but also in his guts. His stomach wouldn't rest and his heart flared with anger. Whatever that thing was, it had to die. As he shampooed his long hair and started to rinse it, he could see many ways for the beast to die. Some were silly, but he had to think of its death. That made him feel stronger.

His cell phone went off, a downloaded ring tone of the band Judas Priest. He gave the phone a doubtful look and reached for it, wincing as he did so. He saw the number and flipped it open.

"Yeah, this is Hux."

"Have you heard from Ricky?" The voice rang cold and distant.

Hux understood the call and said, "I ain't heard from Rick at all. He wasn't at the drop off house when he was supposed to be and no one has heard dick from him."

"He doesn't answer his phone," the voice said coldly. "I'd be loath to lose him or a good mule like Iris."

"Iris? Huh, woulda like to see her, but no, ain't seen 'em." Hux recalled that Iris possessed an enormous piece of womanhood, one even a proud man like himself wouldn't try to best. However, she was an oral and anal specialist; the latter idea suddenly caused Hux to pause. He winced again and said, "What's up?"

"That is precisely what I would like to know." The voice held no humor. "The hour is late and they were due back in Chicago by now."

Tightening his ass, Hux experienced needles of pain in his rectum. He calmed his ass down and said, "I can rattle a few trees and see if anything falls out."

"Oh yes, rattle away," the voice replied. "I would hate to think I have lost someone dear to me."

The line went dead and Hux closed the phone.

"Fucking scumbag," he muttered and returned to washing his disgrace from himself.

Mr. Solow was a light sleeper. He awoke nearly every hour on the hour, but that was his way. He often went to the fridge, took a sip of iced tea, and returned to bed. Once at 3AM he made a baloney sandwich and ate it with a 7UP.

This night he caught himself looking across the yard to his barns and the field beyond. Nothing stirred and it was deathly quiet. The moonlight brought only a peaceful scene, one that made his heart rest easy.

Solow wandered into his front room, flipped on the light, and stared into his curio cabinets. Mementos of the Second World War, and countless arrowheads he'd found in the fields and on hikes were displayed on a velvet cloth. In another cabinet were several bones found at construction sites by his brother, Billy. He missed Billy. Cancer had killed Billy a decade ago. He liked it when Billy visited from down south. Solow sighed, letting go of the lament. He'd never see his brother this side of the grave again.

He poured himself a small glass of homemade wine and sipped it as he walked into his living room. He raised the glass at the old picture from the war, of his shipmates and himself. Mr. Solow's body shivered as he said, "To the *USS Eldridge*."

Solow lit a smoke and again thought of his other brothers and his family, though not so much on the latter. Aside from Billy, he was glad they were dead. Not a man to be burdened by sentiment, he stubbed out the smoke and went back to bed.

But he didn't sleep much.

Hawg felt spent for the most part. He zigzagged across a piece of well cultivated land. This grass wasn't like the lawns of the farmers. This small plot possessed grass already mowed and tended to perfection. Hawg heard tales of men who carried lawn clippings away in bags, unlike Elias who just ran the mower over the grass. Who had time for such tidy behavior? Hawg couldn't understand being so obsessed with the grass.

He leaned himself on an above ground swimming pool and took several breaths. The tarp that covered the pool felt coarse to his claws, but he never ripped it. Whatever tainted his system from the breeder gilt was ebbing away, but still his senses felt edgy. The substance in his body made his nose run and he wiped it on the back of his claw many times.

Red eyes scanning the territory away from the ranch style house, he saw the streetlights of the small town nearby. Hawg had no desire to go there and walked through the side yard by the home's garage. Still, he studied the land toward town and noticed something on his right tusk. He reached up with the nails of his right claw and pulled the red loop off himself. It was a dog collar made of a synthetic red material. On the metal tag was a name, but Hawg couldn't read. He dropped this and took another step.

Not attending where he trod, Hawg took a step on a paved drive and doubled over on the hood of a long car. Hawg slammed down on the hood and his body convulsed. Suddenly nauseous, Hawg vomited on the hood of the shiny beige Buick. After he steadied himself, he vented his bowels and proceeded away from the property and the town.

He ran for a few miles and saw a highway. Beyond this two-lane road was a bigger road, an Interstate perhaps. Hawg loped until he spied a graveyard. He leapt over the trimmed bushes at the out of the way spot and stayed on all fours, searching for a way through the maze of stones and crypts. He stopped and stood, seeing two crypts away from the rest. Something about them drew Hawg in. He approached them and took several breaths. He was so tired. Hands on the metal gate of one, he gazed up at the neighboring crypt and the word etched on it. Those letters were familiar.

Hawg pulled back and snapped the lock and the extra chain that held the gate in place. Inside the crypt were two stone coffins, close enough together to remind him of his nestling spot in the round barn. Hawg stepped in and lay down between the coffins. The fit was not too tight, but perfect for his body.

He slept and never dreamed.

Andrew hated the day shift, eight to four, but it allowed him to spend more time with his family. The operators at the plant ran bitchy and, usually, so did the bosses. When he worked the other shifts at the print factory, his time with the boys and his wife suffered. Sure, on second and third shifts he had more time to ride his Harley and go shooting with his buddies, but he'd also lost his focus on life. He contemplated this as he sent Jordan off to the bus.

The other day Andrew saw Jordan visiting the grave of his dead dog. As Andrew walked the property, looking into the barren fields, he knew Jordan would take a bit before he accepted the animal was truly gone. Andrew liked to think he wasn't as much of a hard ass as his mother and father when it came to animals dying. They'd drilled into him fast how an animal had no soul and to stop crying. That hurt, but in time, it rolled off, like most things. He buried Buddy out behind the garage so that the grave wasn't in plain sight. The boy would always know the dog was there, but the constant reminder every time they left the house wasn't necessary.

Morning routines died hard and Andrew arose earlier than he should. He often blamed the habit on Marine training, but like his late father, he was an early riser. Out to get the papers, he regularly burned some garbage and walked the perimeter of his land.

When Andrew walked behind his car and popped the trunk with his key chain, he glanced at the dog's grave, visible from that angle. His head snapped that direction in full as he saw the displaced dirt. He pocketed the key-chain and walked to the edge of the old pony pasture. Sure enough, the grave was disturbed.

"Goddamn coyotes," Andrew muttered and headed to the garage. He pulled open the sliding door of the shed. Then he grabbed a spade and a shovel.

Once at Buddy's grave, he saw whatever dug him up went deep enough to finish the job. He swallowed hard at the grim sight of the dog's paws and head, discarded on the dirt. Though in possession of a strong stomach, Andrew wavered for a moment, but found his balls fast.

"Damn you, Buddy," Andrew said and screwed down his guts. "Couldn't train ya to do squat. Now, you're a pain in the ass beyond the grave." He let out a sigh and said to the dead parts, "Well, better get ya back in place before Jordan gets home."

Never bothering to get gloves, Andrew picked up the bits of the dog left over, three paws and the head, plus a few grisly bits he assumed were intestines. Again, he struggled with his gag reflex.

"Skinned lots of animals in my life, Buddy, but you take the cake," Andrew mumbled as he swept what pieces he could find into the deep hole. "Ya smell like a pig." As he jabbed the spade into the hole, forcing the pieces in farther, he pondered how true that was. It did smell like pig-shit at the grave.

Andrew glowered in the direction of Solow's hog farm. The wind hadn't shifted and Andrew felt perplexed. Eyes fixed on the lower sections of the disturbed grave, Andrew perceived deep ruts. "No coyote digs with paws like that," he said to the ground. "I haven't seen a wolf in these parts for a coon's age."

He filled the grave again and stomped on the dirt. The disturbed soil was level with the ground, so he stepped into the field and scooped up some dirt. He deposited this on the grave, then returned to get three more scoops. With the spade and using his boot, Andrew returned the mound to normal.

When he walked away from the scene, he crushed the wooden cross Jordan had fashioned from two sticks.

Jack Sullivan was the Mayor of Montrose, Illinois. The position was not a difficult one, overseeing the various boards and police functions. Jack also managed Ambrose Brothers Printing as the Mayor slot paid little. A sturdy man from simple beginnings, he'd come a long way from his days as a brawler, and fixing errant machines in a metal shop. As he put on his pale pink shirt and cream-colored pants, he didn't regret those he'd brushed aside to get where he was, nor the neck's he'd stepped on. His grim satisfaction over them carried him onward and he frequently couldn't suppress a smile. He combed his dark hair, and then brushed some dye into his mustache before declaring himself perfect for the day.

When Jack stepped from his home and saw the hood of his prized Buick Park Avenue covered in vomit and blood, his smile faded. When he looked down and saw he'd trod in feces, his manner grew darker.

"Oh, those resentful little pricks," he shouted, cutting loose on a diatribe of curses.

His wife Betty opened the porch door and said, "Jack? What is it?"

Holding up his soiled leather right shoe, he grimaced and then said, "I have to change my shoes."

"I see," she said, her brown eyes fluttering

"Those little fuckers, they think they're so smart," Jack snarled. "Who?"

"Oh, the pukes we fire in the back end of the plant who can't keep a job, them and the shit for brains morons we have to hold down to run the place. They think they are so tough and smart. Look what they did to my car. If they think the overtime is bad now, they don't know anything yet."

Jack struggled to get out of his shoes and then stumbled, stepping in more excrement with his socks.

Betty tried to repress a laugh but failed.

Jack's cell phone rang and he nearly hurled his briefcase in anger before reaching to his belt to answer it.

"Yes, this is not a good time."

"Not even for a good pal like me?"

Jack's manner cooled, but his bile still was high. "What is it you want, Hux?"

"Some friends of ours are sorta miffed. You know anything about some business last night that never got done?"

"No," Jack said flatly. "I have my own troubles right now."

"Well, I'll do my best to see that this doesn't become one of your troubles."

Jack closed the phone and figured this was the start of a really shitty day.

Jordan waited for the school bus and peered back at the disused pony lot on their place. From where he stood, Jordan couldn't see Buddy's grave in the mock pet cemetery. He put his head down as the bus grumbled in the distance. He liked it better when his dad took him to school, but his mother wanted him to use the system like the other kids. Jordan hated most of the other kids, but he liked the girl up the road, Cassidy. When he walked onto the bus, he looked for her like every other day. Not spotting her, he sat down and asked the driver, "Where's Cassidy?"

"Her daddy said she was too upset to come to school," the hefty lady at the wheel told him. "Something about her dog dying. That's hard on a kid."

Jordan blinked and pondered that. Genesis was dead? That

was odd, for the dog was a monster. Jordan's mom Lynne had forbidden him to go near Cassidy's home when the Ellington's bought her. If that dog was so mean, Jordan wondered how it died. Probably hit by a grain truck on the way to the elevator up the way, he figured.

While the bus traveled, he saw flashing lights a mile or so away, down a farmer's road.

Lynne White looked to the south as the bus left and she spotted the flashing lights as well. In a hurry to get the two-year-old boy, Kenny, in gear for day care, Lynne called to Andrew at the kitchen table. "Andy? The police are down south here."

Though he glanced at the newspaper and sipped his coffee, Andy held Kenny on his left knee. He nodded to her words and said, "Wonder why? Accident on the road?"

"It appears to be down in the waterway or by a side road past the Solow place."

Disinterested, Andrew sipped his coffee and said, "Huh. Will have to ask Doug later if he heard anything."

"I have to take Kenny to the daycare then have a school board meeting after classes. If you work over this evening, my mother will have to get the boys."

"I know," Andrew said and rubbernecked up at her. "Ya look great for a lady in her thirties."

Her conservative suit and over the knee skirt shined immaculately in the morning light, as did her wry smile. "Down boy. I have a million things to do today. Do you think you'll have to work over?"

He held Kenny with both hands as Lynne put the boy's shoes on him. "I don't know. I work for assholes, hon."

"Andrew, mouth!" she admonished him.

Andrew looked down at the boy before saying, "Yeah, yeah, I'll try to behave. But, ya know how it is. It changes from day to day."

"I can't believe they would work you over out of pure meanness."

Kenny slipped off his lap and Andrew said, "Ya would be surprised."

Lynne bent down, kissed his cheek fast and said, "Love you."

"Love you, hon," Andrew replied as the two headed out the back door.

He checked his watch and started to put his lunch together. Out the south porch door, he saw the flashing lights.

Hands on his knees, Douglas White gazed through the broken passenger side window of Tim Dinsdale's car. Eyes scanning the interior again, he thought the expression on Tim's plump face a mixture of confusion and humor. He chewed a toothpick in the corner of his mouth and shook his head.

"Alex, this guy, Tim, always had a smirk on his face," Doug said quietly to one of the other county sheriff's deputies. The younger officer's face flushed and he rubbed his eyes.

"Say what, Sheriff?" Alex said to the husky man staring into the car.

Doug spit out the toothpick, gave a nod and glanced at the bloody mass between Tim's legs. "Yeah, Dinsdale was a mover and shaker at the printing plant. A real backstabbing jackass I hear tell, always had a smile on his face." Doug stood up, towering over the other cop and sighed, eyes on the girl in the ditch. "I'd say their smiling days are over."

A blonde officer named Matt Crouch knelt by the body of the woman, a long cotton swab to her lips. "I think I found Dinsdale's weenie."

Alex turned fast, grabbed the hood of the car, and vomited near the tire. Doug allowed him his privacy, but did face his direction. Alex didn't share Matt's strong stomach or dubious lothario reputation. Doug needed the former this day, for certain.

It was then that the morning light showed an impression on the passenger side window. If not for the sun, he might have missed it. Doug squinted at the print and said, "We need to get a copy of this."

"What is it, fingerprint? Hand print?" asked Matt, taking a step closer from his position.

Doug's eyes traced the huge impression on the windshield

and said, "Not sure what it is, but by the looks of her, well, hell, I don't know."

"Hope the M.E. gets here fast," Matt said as he turned back to the woman, stabbed at her chest with the swab. "Look, Doug, she had fake boobies. Whatever ripped her up popped them open, proper."

As the cop next to Doug threw up again, he said, "Wonder what would do that to a person?"

The ruts gouged in the young woman from her throat to her vagina didn't tell them a thing, other than they didn't want to see what had made the marks.

"Some nut ball," Matt declared, taking off his hat for a moment to wipe his brow with the back of his hand. "Has to be it, Sheriff. See how the line of these ruts run? No animal did this. They are like machetes or tiny train tracks."

"A mystery for the M.E., Mr. Loring," Doug glanced at Tim again and thought of the man's wife. "He didn't have any kids. I suppose that's one less headache."

Alex recovered somewhat and confessed, "I'd never want to have to tell a woman that her husband is dead."

Doug ruminated; *I ought to let my brother, Andrew, tell her. Tim Dinsdale fucked him out of two promotions and confined him to the bookbindery. He may do it as a singing telegram.*

He pondered the hatred Andrew sported for Dinsdale, but banished any thoughts of his brothers' anger reaching such a level as this crime. Andrew was a hunter and a mouthy biker, but this…was beyond him.

Elias arose before sunlight, did a number of feedings, and returned to his trailer for breakfast as the sun bathed the fields. His father before him taught him to get the tedious work of the day through first and then start with coffee and a meal. As he scrambled some eggs, he looked across the way at Luella's trailer. Her working dog, Duke, appeared via the dog door to perform his morning necessities.

When he ate, Elias couldn't share Mr. Solow's optimism that everything would be fine and Hawg would come home, no harm to anyone. His stomach burned with dread. Elias turned on the radio and listened to the local station. Content that there was no news concerning anything unusual, he finished his breakfast.

The dull growl from Duke outside made him put down his fork and wipe his mouth. Elias got up and peered out his door.

Duke stared into an empty planter, normally used for flowers in the summer. Though Luella couldn't see them, she liked their fine scent when reading her Braille books in the afternoon warmth. Duke growled into the oblong box, angry at whatever was there.

Elias exited his house and waited at the edge of his deck. Duke peeped up at him, but then returned his gaze to the planter. The old man stepped across the small distance, curiosity growing as he walked.

He peered down into the planter and the dog backed away from it. Inside lay a pile of pulpy guts, a liver, and a portion of a heart. Elias squatted down and touched the bits.

"Half assed warm," he sighed and shook his head. "Dammit, Hawg, this ain't good."

"Look, Mr. Sullivan," Doug said as he regarded the smear of shit on the driveway. "I have bigger issues this morning than your vandalism."

"That's Mayor Sullivan to you, officer," Jack snapped, chin up high. "I want these fools caught. I have my pride. I want a complete investigation of this area."

Hiding his disdain for people wasn't his strong suit but Doug soldiered on. "Look, Mayor," he said with a stern voice, eyes fixed on the Mayor. "A farmer on his way for coffee at the grain elevator found two dead bodies not two miles from here." He hoped Sullivan's expression would soften at these words but he came up snake eyes.

"Yes? Who are they?"

"It's a very unusual crime. I believe both of them worked for you at the printing plant."

Jack frowned but said nothing more.

Doug reached to his breast pocket for a fresh toothpick and said, "That deal and Reverend Wingler's daughter never came home last night. You ought to have a minister and his wife raving at you on the phone."

Jack's eyes narrowed, but his anger still boiled. "Sorting out dead bodies or where a slut preacher's daughter passed out isn't my concern. I have a business to run."

Betty appeared from the house, smiling. She had dressed for the day in a smart lime green suit and applied too much make up. Betty was almost ready to leave for her job in the county recorder of deeds office when she pointed at the grass near the edge of the drive. "Sheriff White, I think this is a clue."

The burly cop turned around and took a few steps toward where she pointed. Down to his haunches, Doug reached down.

Hands in the air, Jack raged, "No rubber gloves or anything? You'll never catch these men!"

Doug's voice was steady as he replied, "This isn't television and this is just a dog collar." He picked up the object and held it up in the morning light. "No prints will be had on such fabric, but there is blood on it." Doug opened a small case on his belt and drew out a tiny baggie. Depositing the collar in the bag, he said, "Probably the same as the stuff on your hood, but we'll have to see. As I said, the guys will be busy today with the two bodies. I'm sure the team will be over as soon as they can, Mr. Mayor." Sarcasm dripped from Doug's words as he towered again, leering at Jack.

Though he didn't appear any more consoled, Jack put his hands to his hips and said, "How did they die, these two people?"

Hands to his lower spine, Doug stretched and said, "One bled to death, the other was ripped open, maybe by a wolf or something."

Eyes narrowing, Jack wondered, "Or something?"

With a shrug, Doug let his hands dangle and said, "It's kind of a mystery, but that doesn't make her any deader. We need to get next of kin notified before this gets out of control."

Jack's expression darkened. "What do you mean? This wasn't some gang land execution murder, was it?"

Now it was Doug's turn to be confused and wonder what was in Sullivan's head. "It's a weird gang, if that's the case. I'll keep you informed, Mayor. We'll get to this car business as soon as we can."

When Doug started to walk back to his cruiser, Jack exclaimed, "What about my Buick? How am I supposed to get to work?"

Doug gestured at Sullivan's wife, starting to get into an older model Nissan. "Car pool it, Mayor. I can't think of everything."

Once back in the car with Alex, the younger officer rubbed an eye and said, "What a dickhead, Sheriff."

"That he is," Doug affirmed as he took off his hat. "I pity those who work for him."

Doug pitied a third of Montrose, Illinois.

Hawg was awakened in the crypt and he didn't like what he heard.

"Yeah, this place is out of the way, but kind of like hiding in plain sight. We can blow off morning class at least."

"Old Route 66 is right there and people drive on by. Cool."

"Yeah."

"This weed is killer, Bruce."

"Potent trip weed, Paul. Scored it from the promised land."

"Columbia?"

"No, Woodford County."

Hawg started to dislodge himself from between the stone coffins as the laughter of the male voices skipped across his mind. He could smell their flesh and the acrid odor they brought with them.

"Check it out, Bruce, these are graves from before the Civil War."

"When was that anyways?"

"No wonder you suck in history class."

"Get bent, Paul. See, this gal died before 1861. Aw man, look at that! At the end of this grave it just says BABY. Eerie man."

Coughs echoed in Hawg's ears as he slipped out of the crypt the rest of the way, just out of their sight. He stared up at the neighboring crypt that bore no door, but several bars. The letters etched on it were familiar to him.

"Wonder if it was stillborn? Reckon lots of kids were back then."

"Shitty hospitals and all. Hey, Paul, you ever see the Witch's Chair?"

"Heard of it for years. The grave where if you sit in it, you die?"

"Some drunk kids sat in it and wrecked years ago, my older brother said, but yeah, that's the story."

"One of them there Urban Legends, Bruce?"

"We aren't too urban. There it is."

Hawg kept low to the ground and behind the shrubs, watching the two skinny teens stare at a large brown tombstone. Indeed, it resembled a seat with a high back on it. Hawg looked up through the greenery and saw the outstretched arms of a stone figure. He'd seen this persona above him before. It was God.

"Paul, I heard there is an inscription on the chair, something about 'he would sits here will disappear' or something like that."

"Back here, Bruce. See, it's all faded and washed out. I think it says something about a chair being empty so you'll be missed."

"Check it out! A pentagram! Stars, man!"

Hawg passed water in the grass and his tongue ran over his teeth. These fools stank. One was blonde, the other darker haired, but that one was very plump. His partner was lean, powerful, slender legs. Hawg's tusks thrust out farther, saliva dripping from them.

"What reeks around here, man?"

"Waitaminute. This is a guy in the grave. See? His name is Dana Wellman, but he was a General, not a witch. Dana can be a girl's name. What a load of bullshit."

Hawg rose up on his hind legs.

"So, if I sit here, like so, I ain't gonna die?"

Lynne White was ready for class to begin when her cell phone rang. Normally, she turned it off before the start of the day, but duties had kept her from this action. "Yes, Andrew, what is it?"

"Hey there, love the caller ID. Thought I'd tell ya this quick, hon. Talked to the Ellingtons up the way?"

"Yes?"

"This is gonna break yer heart. Genesis is dead."

"Cry me a river," Lynne replied with scant emotion, eyes skimming the papers in front of her. "Hope they aren't fool enough to get another one."

"Figured that'd make you tear up."

"She get hit by a car? That elephant would wreck someone badly."

"Naw, Lucas said Genesis was mangled up like by a pack of wolves. Weird."

"Wolves? Interesting. Well, I have to run. Thanks for the heart-warming news."

"My pleasure."

"Love you."

"Love you, hon."

Lynne turned the phone off and thought she felt better with wolves in the neighborhood than a pit bull.

Mr. Solow was mixing batter in the sink when Elias stepped into the back door.

"Morning, sir."

"Good morning, Elias." Still turning the batter, Solow let a few moments pass before he said, "No, Hawg never came back."

"He was near Luella Goodkind, sir. He left some meats for her in the potter. I don't think it was from no animal."

Solow nodded and said, "Fetch me the Tupperware container from the bottom of the fridge. I'm looking forward to a good lunch today from what we took yesterday."

Elias took out the green container and felt the contents roll around some. He didn't feel very hungry as he contemplated the pig's balls.

CHAPTER THREE

Deepening

Micki Wingler woke up several yards from the road where Hawg assaulted her. The pain from her crotch sliced so intense she cried out as soon as lucidity gripped her. The agony emanated from the wound in an unending stab, not in waves like she'd read about in books. Tears flowed over her grubby face, marred by mascara, sweat, and dried tears. Her left hand reached down to feel of herself and pulled back fast. The pain increased and she decided it didn't matter what damage was done. The hurt was all she understood.

The wind blew a bit and the icy pains made Micki think the edges of her hipbones were exposed to the air. She felt like she had to urinate and couldn't stop the action. Micki wept again as she couldn't stop the water from running from her, adding to the burn and pain down below.

She cried out for Hux, but the words muffled. Her throat full of mucus, nothing but a bubbly wail escaped her lips. Micki actuated her head and a geyser of pain rippled across his shoulders and flowed down her spine. Micki experienced portions of her body she never recognized were there before. Never would she have believed one's earlobes, little toes or clitoris could hurt so bad. She felt like her clit was shoved up to her bellybutton. Micki reached down and could no longer feel the stud in her tummy.

The brutal sensations felt like a dozen bones all over her broke in the attack. Still, she could move, though her pelvis felt in worse pain than the rest of her. Micki aimed to shut it out, to ignore anything below her waist, but the constant pain refused to allow this. She cried out again but heard no one nearby.

Attack? In all of her hurting, that word seemed rather light. Violated, raped, ripped open afterwards and left for dead, she couldn't put a word on it. She thought of demons or monsters her father preached about in fiery sermons meant to scare people out of Hell. This was no fairy tale destined to tempt the bladders of preschoolers and her body was ruined.

Long since fallen from the graces of her father's faith, Micki did something she hadn't done in earnest for years.

She prayed. She prayed to die. After so much blood loss and being exposed to the elements, Micki couldn't understand how she lived. If the loss of blood didn't get her soon, she assumed the pneumonia would. Her nose clogged with snot and her lungs rasped shallow. Pain gouged her shoulders at her collarbones.

The sound of a crow cackled in the distance.

Her torture carried on until Micki turned herself over. Terrible fires of pain ravaged her again and she flipped back onto her buttocks. Crazed with pain, she kept pushing herself, shoving her body into the tall grasses away from the dirt road. The dead weeds formed a thin wall, but it felt good, almost cloaking. She liked it.

Overwhelmed, she passed out again.

Douglas White closed his notepad and stepped out of the empty field near the Ellington's place. He flipped open his cell phone and pressed a button.

"Yeah, Billy? After you are done taking pictures of Dinsdale and the girl, head on up the road a piece. You know the Ellington's that live past my brother? Yeah, well their dog was killed last night. Pretty damned bad. Yeah, I know they have a pit bull. Whatever killed it, didn't seem to mind."

Lucas Ellington stared at Doug with steely gray eyes. His complexion was pale from years of working third shift at Ambrose Brothers Printing. Though not terribly upset, he lowered his voice and said, "Let me get this straight, Doug. Something like this happened not far from here?"

Doug turned to Lucas and confessed, "Yeah. No need to

make a major case of it, Lucas. A couple were killed not a mile or two down the way, out parking, you see?"

Eyes widening, Lucas said, "Maybe you should warn everyone, Doug. No man did that to Genesis. A pack of wolves, maybe, but the ground in the field here is soft and I see no series of prints."

Matt squatted on his haunches, eyes scanning the spot where the chain link fence ended and the muddy field began. "Look, here sir."

Doug walked over to his fellow officer and Lucas followed him. Both men inspected the spot where Matt pointed. "That's no wolf print, sir, but what would you call it?"

He blinked and then rubbed his chin. "All right, Mr. Ellington. Looks like Satan killed your dog." He then stared into Ellington's face and asked, "What's it seem like to you? Still think I should tell everyone about this?"

Lucas saw what they all beheld: A set of prints, deep in the damp dirt, each track split. "Cloven hooves?"

Doug sighed at Lucas's pronouncement. "There has to be a more rational explanation, of course. I'm still searching, though."

Matt stood, shook his head, and said, "Maybe a mean assed wild boar?"

Still near the ground, Doug extended his hand and touched the print on the left. "Awful big for a danged boar, fellows. It does look like a pig's split hoof though, not like that of a bull."

Alex giggled, half in shock, saying, "We better go ask Mr. Solow if his pigs have gone hog wild."

Matt half laughed but the other two men didn't. Doug stood, exhaled loud and said, "We better visit everyone around here. If there is something wild around, then it may have scarfed a few piggies at the Solow place."

As Matt took a call on his phone, Alex said, "Wow. You think it's Bigfoot? You recall when Bigfoot was spotted down by Mahomet in the eighties?"

Doug waved at the tracks. "I remember that. No. Not with prints like that I don't think it's any such thing. As I said, there's a rational explanation someplace to all this. That's what we get the big money for, right?"

They walked back to the cruisers in Lucas's yard. When they reached the police cars, Matt closed his phone and said, "That's dispatch. They say Reverend Wingler is still missing his daughter. He wanted us to know, again."

Doug shook his head, eyes to the heavens. "You tell him his daughter is a crack-whore and will put out her ass for a fix?"

"Nope."

"Good, but she still could be anywhere. I reckon she stays out plenty of nights. Wonder why that Holy Roller is so upset this time?"

Matt rolled his eyes heavenward and then said out of the corner of his mouth to the sheriff, "I bet the old blowhard knows where she is, probably wants us to do his job for him."

Doug looked to the sky once and said, "You'd know about gals who stay out all night, Matthew."

Matt wore a devilish grin and walked around the car. "Not guilty this time, sir."

Lucas stiffened as the police started to get back into their cars. He asked Doug, "Do you have kids?"

Doug said, "Lucas, you know I have two."

Pressing his point, Lucas said, "I don't care how old they are or how worthless, will you stop worrying about them?"

Lucas turned, not waiting for an answer.

Doug closed the door to the car, not giving one.

Hux arrived late at work, but that was all right. Jack Sullivan never reprimanded him as hoist drivers were a more fluid lot in their duties and Hux gave the orders to a degree on the docks. Bindery foreman Debra Johnson could blow all she wanted about his practices and hours. She wasn't his superior, no matter if Debra walked like she sported a bigger cock than him. He loved thwarting the "crypt keeper" as some called Debra behind her back. The withered old woman, ever full of piss and vinegar, loathed Hux and still bashed into him at times, no matter what his loyalties.

His habits didn't make everyone so happy. Certainly, this made many angry and plant gossips like Mary Ann Statler whisper at what secret Hux must have over Sullivan. He never missed a chance to wave this talebearer, for Mary Ann couldn't keep a secret if her sixties Bouffant hair-do depended on it.

Many joked about Hux having dirty pictures or some damning knowledge of the boss, but most knew the score. Hux knew that even the older ladies in the plant like Lena Alsdorf understood Hux was a drug connection. Though near to sixty-five, Lena comprehended that if the scum of the plant went to Hux for a fix or a dime bag, then the boss just may know that as well. She stared down her nose through thick glasses on the other hoist drivers like Brian Miller and Jimmy Mans who looked the other way at Hux's activities.

After a spin around the bindery floor on his hoist, past the perfect binders and saddle stitchers yielded up no info about the delivery from Cicero, Hux headed to the pressroom. He stopped by the end of the presses where gigantic rolls of paper fed spinning rolls, advancing the material to plates and ink. The roll tenders and joggers that were part of his inner circle also knew nothing.

Earl Gamblin, forty years in the plant and head pressman down the line, sent Hux a distasteful glance, but never told him to leave the line.

He talked to Gopher, an aging man with buckteeth.

"No word on the street, Goph?" Hux asked him, waving at Tonya Harmon, noted herpy girl of the pressroom.

Bloodshot eyes stared back at Hux as Gopher replied, "Not a scratch, Hux. I'll tell you if I hear something juicy."

Flummoxed, Hux waved off Tonya, who was probably on the way to ask him for a toot. He returned to roving the bindery floor, noting the panty lines of the new girls trained by Paula Grimes on the perfect binder. Paula was another of the aging gals, had been married a few times and lost a few husbands to cancer or booze. Hux thought she was married to a cop but wasn't sure.

He heard Mary Ann Statler walk up to Paula and say, "I heard that Andrea Ennis never showed up for work again."

Paula replied, "That a wonder, Mary Ann?"

"Well, with the company she keeps, no."

A greasy headed man named David Blakely eyed Paula's

trainee as Hux passed by. David struggled to keep the dip in his lip in place, spitting some into a soda bottle. When he saw Hux, David put his head down. Hux never stopped to make fun of the socially inept man. There would be plenty of other days for that.

Hux's chin rose at big Andrew White who worked the end of the binder. The green eyed, surly farm boy nodded back, but said nothing to Hux. They'd had a run-in years ago, but Andrew was not afraid of Hux, his biker pals, or anyone else. This didn't stem from White's brother being the Sheriff. Hux understood one didn't mess with a man like White, who'd survived a raid from the ATF unscathed, hunted with Ted Nugent, and served in the first Gulf War. Andrew knew the score and never bothered him. He was a good guy, but creepy all the same. He carried a ton of bitterness about a demotion years ago, but Hux stayed out of plant politics like that.

"Hey man," Hux said to Andrew. "You have a spare nitrix for my projectile knife launcher?"

Andrew nodded. "Yeah. I'll get one out of my locker at break."

"Cool. That thing works like a beauty."

Eyes on his work, Andrew said, "Thanks."

"Pretty amazing the way ya rigged it up under the headlight on my ride."

Andrew was quiet for a bit and said, "It isn't too tough to do."

Hux left him alone. He didn't know if White brooded or not, but he certainly wore the face of a man who did.

When he stepped outside for a smoke, he nodded at Kenny Snow, the man who ran the docks, who stood in deep conversation with Annette Moyer, a computer analyst from up front. He figured there must be trouble with the main network as he saw Minh from IT scrambling around earlier. Hux watched Moyer's tear drop shaped ass as she walked away and wondered how they were lucky enough to get an egghead like Minh in their midst. The small man never spoke to Hux, but his eyes told a tale of disgust when he did make contact.

The signal for his cell phone kicked in. After a drag on the smoke, he flipped open his phone.

"Yessir," he said, reading the caller I.D. "Cannot find out a damned thing about things just yet."

The voice on the other end couldn't hide its feelings. "Really, Mr. Huxtable, that's not what I wanted to hear."

Cold and mean, Hux felt spiders run down his back at the voice. "Do you know for sure they left Chicago?"

After a brief silence, the voice replied, "They left yesterday afternoon just before rush hour. There's always radio silence on a delivery. Talking with you is highly abnormal, but we need to know what happened."

"From what I see, they never got here," Hux said earnestly, waving at Scott Grady, the personal assistant to the head of the pre-press department. Scott regularly bought speed from Hux. "Scanner and internet in the hoist driver's office is on the fritz, but earlier it had no reports on a bust or any such thing hereabouts. Maybe they headed off on you."

"Unlikely," the voice said icily. "Rick doesn't have the balls for that."

"Well, maybe they'll turn up."

"Maybe I need to send two new operatives to check for myself."

Hux' jaw tightened at this, knowing that two goons from Cicero would make sure they harassed him bad before leaving. Not wanting to endure that, he was not about to take it…and that meant killing whoever they sent down to town. Hux didn't fear that action, not after what happened to him last night, but he figured a ball would start rolling he never wanted to get in the path of.

"Free country, sir. I can't make them appear outta thin air."

"They have a global positioning device in the car unknown to them," the voice informed him. "I know they are in Livingston County, but the exact locale is muddy. My operatives will be there after noon and have a check around. You may not even know they are there. I'll be sending Mr. Roberts, though, and he adores you."

The line went dead and Hux felt like smashing his phone to pieces. Roberts. Great. Hux met him once on a trip to Cicero with the gang. Roberts was worse than a killer. The time he'd done wasn't for murder or suffocations, but for pedophilia. Hux would rather never see him again.

On the way into the plant he overheard Wilma Rynning, a funny middle-aged lady, say, "And they say Reverend Wingler is going ballistic over his daughter."

A tall, thick woman with bleach blonde hair and sagging breasts named Alice Sanka replied, "Now he's concerned? He should've been worried about the company she kept for years."

Soon, the rattle of the machines drowned out their words, but never calmed Hux's nerves. He figured the creature killed Micki and only worried over his own self. He eyed the big breasts of Della Rodgers as she walked by. Though a bigger gal than he liked, he would've taken the op if it came his way. But Hux heard she was knocked up and unsure of the father. He was glad it wasn't his.

Hux smirked at the banners along the high walls of the plant. Black and white hands clasped together promoting diversity and teamwork. The letters were so big, he often thought of a movie where the trigger words in ads really said OBEY and CONFORM. If this was true in the factory, so far, it wasn't working so well. Everyone looked out for themselves and had a difficult time swallowing the teamwork pill due to the blatant favoritism and hypocrisy of management.

Deep inside, he felt the pain from the beast. The uneasy feeling never left him, nor did the personal shame of what happened to him…or the ultimate in his mind…that he came as the monster thrashed into him.

Andrew White never carried a cell phone, as he said it was about like having a tag in his ear. However, a message came down at break to call his brother Doug from the office in the bindery.

"Yeah, Doug?" Andrew said into the black-corded phone in the small office area. "What's up?" After Doug relayed information about Dinsdale, Andrea, and Genesis, Andrew frowned. "Figures. Dinsdale died that way, huh? Funny as hell, really. Ah well. Forget that."

Doug asked him, "Anything happen by your place last night?"

"No, I…." Andrew's voice trailed off. "Crap. Ya know, it did. I never told the boy or Lynne, but something dug up Buddy's grave and chewed up the body. I covered it back up. I figured it was coyotes or a wolf."

"Huh," Doug said and fell silent for a few moments. "Well, I see we have a pattern. Better keep the kids and yourself indoors, brother. I don't know what is going on just yet. Keep your ears open."

"Will do."

"And get a damn cell phone."

Andrew laughed as he hung up.

The stout woman in the office pulled the phone back and snapped, "Personal calls to the office are getting tiresome, Andrew."

Andrew glared at Carol Brant, short, homely, and rude, and found it not so hard to believe her hubby was an alcoholic. "Doesn't bother y'all to order pizza on the line." He exited the office and shook his head.

A few of the dayshift women passed him by. Paula Grimes stopped and playfully slapped Andrew on the left arm. "The little troll woman givin' you some trouble?"

Andrew watched Mary Ann Statler walk past and made sure the gossip didn't hear him as he whispered to Paula, "Carol is in there still pissed she got passed over as an extra in LORD OF THE RINGS. I hear they press her face in dough up at the bakery to make Orc cookies for Halloween."

Paula burst out laughing, winked, and bustled on toward the smoke shed near the lunchroom.

Andrew beheld the high wall by the upper office, toward Jack Sullivan's office. Under his windows hung the banners promoting diversity, teamwork, and safety. Down the aisle, far above their heads were a series of American flags installed after 9/11. Typical of Ambrose Brothers Fuck Up A Wet Dream Teamwork, they were displayed the wrong direction until the veterans of the plant objected. He made his share of mistakes in life and in the plant, but the idiots at the top took the cake.

Eyes staring at the long path that led from the office down past the stitchers to the back door, Andrew wished he could walk out and keep going.

Doug, Matt, and Alex stood near the back door of Mr. Solow's house. Doug glanced at the curling driveway as he fished into his belt pocket. Alex rapped on the screen door and Doug pulled out the plastic bag he had deposited in his pocket at Sullivan's house. The name on the tag was BUDDY. His frown deepened and he ventured to find an answer in his swirling mind.

When Solow came to the door, Doug replaced the article on his belt.

"C'mon in, boys," the old farmer said with a smile. "Just frying up some goodies for lunch."

Matt looked at his watch. "It's barely after ten, sir."

Solow laughed and eyed Doug. "I get up before dawn. Come in and sit a spell, boys."

They all had met Mr. Solow, worked on his farm as young men and accepted his hospitality before.

"Been a while since I seen you, Matthew," Solow said to the blonde officer. "Been ten years since your daddy and I busted up that VFW brawl."

Matt took off his hat and nodded. "Yes sir. Always meant to thank you proper for letting us walk the beans back then. So many of the kids are employed by the seed companies to detassle corn, it's hard to get private work anymore."

Solow patted Matt on the arm as the young cop sat at the table. "Your pop and I go way back. I paid for a mass for him just last month."

Matt nodded, visibly moved at Mr. Solow's words.

Mr. Solow stared at Alex as he sat down and said, "You look a might peeked, boy. You need something to eat. I got just the thing to give you all a lift." He went to the stove and turned a metallic pan over. "Y'all like deep fried hog balls?"

While Alex was swift to excuse himself and exit the house, Matt let go a chuckle and faced Doug. "Okay if I have some, sir?"

"Doesn't matter to me. They smell damn good." As he sat to the left of Matt, Mr. Solow scooped up a generous helping of the fried hog balls. After he poured them ice teas, Doug explained why they were there.

Solow sat down and speared himself some food. As he

munched and the cops did likewise, he said, "Hmm. I haven't heard nothing, but the property is enormous. We pull the hogs in at night. I'll ask Elias and see what he knows. I'm sure he has walked the back lots today."

"Mind if we ask him?" Doug wondered as he chewed.

Solow shrugged. "Be my guest. Saw him earlier and he never mentioned anything. He still looks after Miss Goodkind out on the back forty, don't ya know?"

Aware of how Solow paid for the aged blind woman to reside on his land, Doug nodded and said, "It's routine, sir, and all for the safety of all. I'd hate to have Luella or Elias hurt by wild dogs or whatever it is doing this to things."

Mr. Solow's eyes narrowed. "Oh? What do ya mean by that?"

Matt swallowed and said. "This is great stuff, sir. Well, it's like this. We saw some funny tracks, not from a wolf. It may be nothing. Like a wild boar...but that is all speculation."

Solow smiled. "If I see any, I'll shoot 'em in the ass and ask questions later."

Doug smiled and gave a nod. "That's all I can ask."

Matt knifed at his plate, saying, "These are from baby pigs, right? These here are kinda bigger."

Mr. Solow gazed at his plate and said, "Sometimes a hog can be blessed. Eat up. You fellows need some Sweet Potato pie?"

Matt ate up the two larger offerings on his plate and said, "You've been too kind and we better take off, sir."

"I'll keep my eyes peeled, fellows. Anything you need, just drop me a line."

Doug and Matt drank their iced tea, then stood up. Doug said, "Appreciate it, sir. You don't mind if we walk the property lines?"

Solow shrugged. "Not at all. Go right ahead."

They stepped outside and saw Alex near the cruiser. He appeared a shade of green.

"That boy needs to grow up some," Solow commented in a low voice.

With a wink to Mr. Solow, Doug whispered, "They don't make 'em like they used to."

They split up at first, Alex and Matt going wide, taking the edges around the long barns, while Doug walked through the center of the land. He walked past a circular stone cover that denoted a cistern near the hog trough. Several babies ran amok and he reckoned the snack they just had came from them. He'd seen Solow castrate pigs years before. A couple rags hung there by the trough. Doug half smiled, wondering why the old man used a Johnny Cash T shirt to clean his tools after such grisly work. From everything he knew of Mr. Gilmore, the old boy didn't strike Doug as very sentimental.

The three policemen walked the acreage of the Solow property and found nothing suspicious. They even ran into Elias who showed them a few of the hog barns. As the two younger men went with Elias, Doug walked up to Luella Goodkind's trailer. The Seeing Eye dog, Duke, stared at him, but never growled. The hefty woman sat on a large swing outside, working a crochet, creating an afghan all the same color.

"Ma'am," Doug said afar off as not to startle her. "Doug White from the Sheriffs' office."

"Morning, Douglas," she said with a giddy voice. "What brings you out here?"

"Oh, this and that. Getting along all right, ma'am?"

Her smile radiant, the heavy woman said, "Oh yes, as good as I can."

"Have you heard any coyotes in the night, Ma'am? We've had a few strange incidents lately. Found the body of one down by Injun Creek only last week."

The blind woman's countenance was quizzical. "Why no, nothing like that."

"Make sure you tell Elias or Mr. Solow if you do."

"Of course, dear."

"That'll be all, ma'am."

"Don't be a stranger, young man."

Jordan White was pleased to see Cassidy Ellington at lunch. His gleeful smile faded as he read her face, cleaned up, but still red and tearful.

He sat across from her and waited a few moments before he spoke. "What did you get from the Accelerated Reader list?"

Jordan asked her, and looked back down at his food.

Cassidy made no motion, other than to nibble on her bottom lip a bit. "Those books are lame."

"I like my comics better," Jordan confessed and she made no action to eat her lunch. "The superhero ones are better than the Bible ones Mom gets me."

"Yeah."

"Sorry about your dog," Jordan said, right thumb trapping the edge of his tray.

She never touched her food, but fiddled with the straw on her milk. "They made me come to school. Mommy says I have to get over it."

Jordan surveyed his tray, remained indifferent about the pizza rolls, and said, "My gramma was like that when Buddy got ran over." He swallowed, emotion welling up in his throat, but Jordan's voice came out fine. "She said animals have no souls, so we can't mourn them forever."

"How does she know that?"

Jordan shrugged, glanced at a banner strung over the lunch line that promoted drinking milk and said, "She grew up on a farm. I guess she knows. Dad said it was in the Bible, but never said where."

A single tear ran down her face. Jordan always thought she had steel gray eyes like her father, Lucas. Cassidy admitted, "I hated her, Genesis. She was big and mean. Now she's dead, too." More tears came and she rubbed them away with the back of her hand.

"My grandpa died two years ago. I didn't want him to go. I still visit his grave and put a flower on it."

Cassidy took a few breaths and asked, "Why?"

Jordan blinked. "That's what you do for dead people. I put one on Buddy's grave, too."

"But why?" she persisted.

He didn't thought very long before saying, "It shows you care, I guess. I'll never forget my grandpa or Buddy. Well, Buddy was just a dog, though."

"It's worse when people die, I suppose," Cassidy said in a quiet voice.

Eyes again on the walls, Jordan ignored the posters that endorsed character, diversity, and togetherness. Jordan said, "Yeah. Since people have souls, it's different."

"What if people didn't have souls?"

"They do, though," Jordan answered. "Buddy was all right, but it wasn't the same as grandpa. He told me things, like fighting in the war against the Japanese. He was a person. I was thinking about going to his grave after school."

"Why?"

"Why not? I ride there sometimes. It makes me feel better."

Cassidy appeared listless and asked, "Mind if I come along?"

"That'd be okay. It's just across the way by Route 66. We can make it on bikes and be home by supper. I can show you the entry way to the old mine as well. It's right by the highway but no one sees it."

Cassidy said no more and stared at her tray.

Jack Sullivan read invoices on his desk, and saw that scheduling left the weekend open. His thumbs squeezed the pages as if he tried to get something to squirt from the edges. He also saw by the ads sold and page numbers that the overtime would be lighter this week.

"What a week," he said to no one.

He then read an offer from the plant in Macomb to take some of their volume to let them have a weekend off. That plant did oversized work on a thicker grade of paper. The operators on the floor would balk for sure as they hated such replacement work. He couldn't suppress a grin when he made the calls, locked in the extra paper rolls to run the pressroom this weekend and thus, force the bindery into more overtime.

Positive that one of his employees had defaced his beautiful beige Buick, Jack was only starting to calculate his revenge.

"Let them call in or burn vacation days," he said, a grin stuck to his face. "Time is mine in the end."

When noontime approached, he closed the shutters of his office and retrieved what aped a huge class ring from his brief case. Twisting the stone, Jack let the ring open up and reveal the powdery substance inside. He placed this to his right nostril and inhaled fast.

Mind tingling, he peeked through the blinds of his office. He looked across the expanse of the plant, the edge of the press-room and on into the bindery and smiled.

Hawg's sleep was fitful. He wasn't used to that. Back in the round barn at home, the world was close and his nights felt restful. Though he seldom saw the sunshine like on this day, it always granted him a feeling of glee. He slid from the stone chamber again. Hawg felt cold and alone. Elias wasn't there to feed him or tell him stories. The only ones near to him were dead.

As he stretched his body, the shivers from the night before returned to Hawg's flesh. The feeling from the ruined gilt burned in his mind, but he told himself it was from hunger. Though he had eaten well in the round barn, and since then, Hawg felt famished all the time. Hand across his stomach, Hawg only understood hunger and that he must quell it. He glanced at his fingers, saw that dry blood crusted on the joints and nails, and remembered his morning meal.

Red eyes on the remains of the two teens, propped up on stones, ogling him with dead eyes, Hawg moved forward. Having fed at their throats and bellies earlier, Hawg started on the fatter one's right leg. Earlier, Hawg tore through this one's belly only to see the inner workings of the chubby kid's waist. Nothing to eat there, he'd progressed on. Though the skinnier one fed him well enough, the fatter youth's leg looked appeal-ing. Hawg easily tore through the denim covering and sank his teeth into the cold flesh.

As he filled his gut, Hawg felt his body calm down and the day lighten.

CHAPTER FOUR

Visitations

Micki awoke in motion. She didn't know how long she'd been crawling in her sleep, nor where she was at the moment. Again, in her bleary mind so saturated with agony, Micki heard a sound that was familiar, one that had probably roused her to action in the first place. Unsure of her motivations, she followed the wail of the train. Micki smiled, recalling childhood trips on the train. This smile made her hurt, too. The trestle that passed the old mine entrance wasn't far from where she and Hux had parked the night before. A mile? Perhaps a bit more? She lived in Montrose at the parsonage and her sense of space wasn't as good as the farm boys she'd blow for eight balls.

Tears ran down her bloody face as she recalled how the rural kids and the "town" kids hated each other in many ways. It was immature and silly, but she wasn't feeling very superior any more as she crawled across the field, sometimes adhering to a waterway path in the high grasses. The main field areas felt rugged as if freshly disked for the spring planting. Cover provided by the waterways felt better to Micki. The weeds and dry reeds made her feel safe as if the monster couldn't find her again.

Micki thought of the creature. In the middle of the sex, suddenly there was this gigantic thing crushing her. Hux was bigger than an average man, certainly more filled out and stronger than the skinny boys she'd hung out with and relinquished her virginity to. This man, this thing that got on her and in her, was far bigger than Randy Huxtable. Hux sported a small beer gut that often bounced or rested on her stomach as he thrashed into Micki's self. Micki thought the new arrival was just a big man, one with no fat to him, but a great deal of bulk. Her hands had gone flat to his chest several times as he thrusted on her. Aside from seeing his red eyes, and the strange metal objects on its face, Micki recalled that his chest was different, as if his pecs were too many to count.

Her insides convulsed and she stopped for a moment. Inside her, the beast was different as well. The organ wasn't like Hux or any other man. It was sharper, twisted, hit her in ways no man did unless they changed positions many times. Micki thought the thing inside her changed sizes many times, but the memory made her body scream.

A couple of times, she blacked out from the agony in her pelvis. Not knowing how much time had passed, Micki awoke and started her task anew, still making her way toward where she thought the train line ran.

The train that ran north and south wasn't far, she told herself. From where they were, she thought the trestle ran in a more open area, next to old Route 66 and past a cemetery. Surely, someone would be around to see her from the road.

At two in the afternoon when Andrew saw he was on the overtime list, he shook his head from side to side with great violence. "Fucking pricks," was the nicest thing he said. The rest of the crew on dayshift were equally angered as the board numbers hadn't indicated any OT was in the offing. After a few folks bitched in the office, they were told the workload had shifted and they had to stay.

Gopher leaned over the yellow railing that separated the pressroom from the bindery aisle. "Screw you guys again, Andy?"

"Yup, Gopher, and no kiss, either," Andrew said, not hiding his distain.

Thumb over his shoulder, Gopher said, "Ol' man Gamblin said we are down for the weekend already."

"Peachy," Andrew muttered, thinking how he was supposed to take Jordan to the premiere of a new movie on Sunday after church. Down the line of paper rolls by the end of the press line, Earl Gamblin shook his head and wore a sheepish look.

"They don't give a flying fuck about us," Mary Ann Statler spat, purse clutched to her side like it held gold as several women walked outside to use their cell phones. "Why, back when I started here...."

Perspiring from the heat of the press ovens, Gopher leaned over closer to Andrew and whispered, "When that bitch started here, we engraved plates for press on stone tablets."

Andrew was past carping about that. This behavior from management was old news. He thought of making plans for who was to get Jordan later and walked across the bindery floor. He thought of how Gopher smelled of booze. Gopher drank so much, he sweated it out all day, Andrew reasoned and he waved at Minh. The small man kept to the aisle and made a motion to his back pocket. He obviously had Andrew's money for the gun and bullets, but would pay him later.

"Hey," Minh shouted. "I hear that Tim Dinsdale never showed up for work today."

"So?" Andrew shot back, a sour expression on his face.

With a grin, Minh replied, "I hear his wife is going bonkers. He never came home last night."

"Great. Tell you a secret? My brother told me he's dead."

Minh laughed, knowing how Dinsdale had helped boot Andrew from the prep department at work. "You're joshing me! Dead?" Minh gave no sadness to this news. "I knew that would break your heart. What's going on in this town?"

Andrew eyed him and asked, "You writing a book?"

Minh mocked a serious look and said, "Kiss my ass, cracker assed cracker, and we'll call it a love story."

As he walked away, Andrew glanced up and over his shoulder. Andrew spotted Jack Sullivan up in his office, beaming down over his kingdom.

"Wonder if he has pants on," Andrew said as Alice passed him by and made no secret of pointing up at the office.

Alice laughed and Andrew saw Jack's grin fade. He knew full well Sullivan realized the joke aimed at him stung. Still, Andrew couldn't hide his frustration. Minh followed Andrew's gaze up to the office and ducked his head, trying to hide from the daggers Jack spat from his eyes.

He borrowed his buddy Don's phone to call Lynne. She couldn't pick up and he had to leave a message. Andrew then called her Grandmother who usually picked up Jordan from school when Andrew worked odd hours. He left a message with her, but she'd been visiting a sick lady from church, so she never got the word. Andrew also called the school and told the secretary to tell Jordan not to get on the bus and to wait for his gramma…but she was busy, and in the early stages of Alzheimer's, and forgot to relay the message.

That is why Jordan climbed on the bus at three when school let out, got home to an empty house at 4:15, and took a bike ride for the cemetery with Cassidy soon afterward.

While even the hoist drivers received word of OT for the evening, Hux donned his jacket at four and bid the main dock boss farewell.

Angry hoist driver Brian Miller said to Kenny Snow, who ran the dock, "You going to let that bastard get away with that?"

Kenny was hesitant, but called the bindery office. They never got ahold of Hux as he left, so Kenny pressed the issue to Jack Sullivan's office. He fired back an angry message that he was in a meeting with other department heads and he'd get back to him.

He never did.

Hux felt alive when on his bike, but his ass still ached from the night before. He wondered if he'd ever be able to put that behind him. The troubles at work didn't concern him. He had other worries and plans for the evening.

When Hux saw the car in the driveway of his small house, his heart sank. The parking sticker for a Chicago locale betrayed its origin. Still, his Harley rumbled on in beside it. He took off his glasses and eyed the men inside.

Both figures were dressed casually in jeans, knit shirts, and tennis shoes. One wore a hooded polo shirt from the University of Illinois at Chicago, the other a dark windbreaker. Each man appeared well groomed and had hair sheared short, but their eyes set them off. The man in the driver's seat never blinked. His hollow eyes ran deeper than the pockets on a billiards table. The other man seemed to have eyes half shut, almost stoned in a way, but they opened wider as he spoke to Hux.

"Nick Roberts, Mr. Huxtable. Here to find what was lost."

"Good for you," Hux replied, trying not to flinch. He never got off his bike. His skin crawled at the snakish Roberts. Hux thought the guy even looked like a pedophile.

The voice out of Roberts was slithering, cloying as he said, "The signal in Rick's car is in this community, outside to the south. Would you care to follow us there?"

Hux trembled, needing a fix, but his nerves were on fire enough to carry him on.

"Sure," he said.

They pulled out of his drive and Hux followed them, having every intention of killing the two freaks from Chicago and dumping them in the stone quarry once they were out of town.

Jordan and Cassidy pedaled fast for the first mile on the black-top road. Several farmers in trucks passed them by, and waved. Since it stayed light longer in the spring, Jordan gauged they'd have plenty of time to make the stop at the cemetery and head back before his parents came home.

"Why wasn't your dad home?" Cassidy asked Jordan as they went downhill, no longer pumping their legs.

"He must've had to stay over at the plant," Jordan replied, enjoying the glide on his blue bike. "My dad works a lot."

Cassidy nodded, pulling on the drawstrings of her hooded polo shirt. "My dad, too."

Since her mother worked evenings at the WAL MART and her dad overslept due to his coming night shift, no one stopped Cassidy as she left with Jordan.

The two exchanged few words on the trip. Jordan decided talking about Genesis was a bad idea. He never wanted to talk about Buddy much after the dog died. Though Cassidy said she hated Genesis, it was one more bad thing for her to experience. Jordan heard his dad and uncles' talk of letting a woman "be" when they were angry. He tried to let Cassidy "be" even if she was still a girl.

They rested a few times before reaching the passageway under the train tracks. The slots were big enough for them to ride through. Jordan pointed to an area near the southern base of the trestle beams.

"See there where the boards are rotted away and the concrete blocks are gone?"

Cassidy made a sour face. "Coal mine entrance, yeah, I remember."

"My Grampa used to sit with me here and tell me stories about the old days of Montrose. Ever been in there?"

Her face turned ashen gray. "No. You?"

"Dad and I checked in there once. He said he used to get in there when he was in high school, but they boarded up the entrance better and bricked it up. It's fallen apart now, and I slipped in to look around the mouth of the mine. Dad was too big."

"God, that'd be creepy."

Jordan shivered a little at the recollection. "It looks like a cave and nothing was there but some rotten railroad ties and metal wheels from carts."

They climbed off their bikes and pulled them up the shallow ditch beside old Route 66. Cars traveled on it still, but it was vacant at the moment. They passed over it to the entrance of the Galen Memorial Park. Cassidy endeavored to ride her bike, but kept hitting rough spots on 66. Jordan didn't try and pushed his bike around the black patches on the gray road.

Jordan stopped at the next ditch and grabbed up a few wild flowers with yellow petals.

Cassidy guessed his intent and said, "Weeds from the ditch for your grandpa?"

Jordan answered, "He was country. I dunno. Country flowers for a country boy."

"Anyone live there?" Cassidy asked, pointing to the old house to the north of the cemetery.

"Doubt it. An old couple used to, dad said, but they are in the cemetery now."

Both rode a little farther, then coasted down the gravel entry-way through the open iron gates. Cassidy eyed the concrete pillars that held the gates, but Jordan whizzed on in.

"What is it?"

Cassidy stared back at the trestle and said, "I thought I heard a voice."

"Probably a rain crow. That's what gramma calls them. They sound like a baby crying, holding its nose."

"That's weird."

"It's true," Jordan assured her.

Micki awoke, up on her knees, reaching out of the tall weeds toward the train trestle. She heard voices, high pitched, but was certain she never imagined them. Desperate, Micki yelled out for deliverance, trying to plead for help.

When she pleaded to God or anything to help her, the words of one of her father's sermons rebounded in her head.

"Let me remind all of you, dear hearts, that there is no Mother Earth. A great many environmentalists are out to save the planet, for the Earth is their god. The worship of the Earth is nothing more than the worship of Baal, for which God commanded the strict penalty of death. Their reverence is misguided, misinformed, and brings the judgment of God, not once in a while, but every time!"

She stayed in that position for a few moments before falling back to the prickly grasses. Micki wasn't about to pray to Baal, but she wished God would hurry up. She tackled the task to store up strength for another shout, but the blackness closed in around her.

A slight bit of terror crept into her mind as her bloody nose caught something on the wind…something ghastly and rotten….

Lucas Ellington woke up, went to the bathroom, and thought the house strangely quiet. He couldn't find his daughter. Not worried at first, he made several phone calls. After going outside and finding the garage door open a crack and her bike missing, he grew more afraid.

He received no answer from the White's next door and decided to call Andrew's brother. Though Doug would be off duty, the Sheriff didn't live terribly far away. He was a good egg and would…well, what would he do?

"Calm down, man," Lucas told himself. However, his body refused to comply. Fear struck him and he couldn't make it stop. Was he getting old or did the fear make him want to piss again so soon?

Jordan said, "Check it out, someone is here."

Cassidy climbed off her bike as she followed Jordan up to a small car parked on the side of a hedge away from the road. The beat-up Chevy sat there. It was missing two hubcaps and most of its trim. A pack of smokes lay on the dashboard and a half full bottle of soda was in the divider consol.

Jordan pulled his head from the car and said, "It smells in there, like bad smokes and beer."

"I don't see anyone," Cassidy said quietly. "We better go." Her little nose wrinkled. "This place stinks."

Jordan nodded once. "Maybe this guy drove through something. Sure smells like it." He glanced at the vast graveyard full of odd sized stones, above-ground crypts, shade trees and a couple statues. "My grandpa's grave is over here."

Cassidy followed him, still looking around for someone.

As he stopped by a large gray tombstone, Jordan pointed at a small gray building near the rear of the cemetery. "See the place over there that says 'White' on it?"

"Yeah, by the big Solow crypt?"

"My great grandparents are in there. Tell ya a secret."

Her eyes looking down at the marker at their feet, she took her toes away from the veteran's flat stone and said, "What?"

"Dad says his great grandparents are really buried in the back of our property not far from Buddy. That was how they did it in the olden days."

Cassidy blinked. "Then what's in that crypt?"

"Well, let me tell ya…." Jordan started to say, but his expression changed. "The doors look open."

"Huh?"

"On the crypt, see? The bars are usually locked, but they're open."

Jordan placed the flowers across the base of his grandfather's stone. He then took a few steps away from the grave and stopped. "That's goofy."

Cassidy glanced at the car and said, "We better get out of here, Jordan White. Maybe whoever is in that car is a grave robber."

That idea made Jordan scared and he hid it as best he could. "Yeah, we oughtta go then." Still, he hesitated, fascinated by the crypt. As he turned, something caught his eye and he didn't follow her. Jordan walked over behind a row of stones and said, "Jesus."

Halfway to her bike, Cassidy stopped and called out, "Jordan?" She then lowered her voice and hissed his name again.

He wasn't budging from the spot where he stood and she soon joined him.

Cassidy was speechless as she too saw the two bodies, one on the grass, one partially on a tombstone.

The body on the ground separated at the midsection. Not even his spine connected his ruined upper torso to his waist. A stunned expression was frozen on the youth's face. Even if very muddy and painted in blood, the two kids could make out his expression of shock. His ribcage exposed, Jordan couldn't name the organs or pieces of his innards that lay spread out and crushed. The lower section of this young man's leg was gone, savagely shorn to the knee.

The other body was still sitting on the tombstone that resembled a chair. His head remained attached to his body, but hung on just barely by what Jordan guessed was a spinal cord. Most of the neck had been ripped loose. Jordan then saw a large portion of this young man's right thigh gouged from his jeans. But the teen still sat there as if he'd passed out and would soon rise again.

Neither nine-year-old said anything, so stationary at the sight. Jordan raised his head toward the crypt, and saw that something appeared lodged between the two stone caskets. He swallowed, eyes on the hind legs he thought were of a man, but were cleft like pig's feet. Big pig's feet.

Slow in his motions, he reached out and took Cassidy's hand. She never objected as Jordan started to back away from the spot. Though they were not moving fast in their exit of the area, Jordan kept looking back.

Just before they passed by the car and the crypt would vanish from his sight, he saw the feet in the crypt stir.

When they stopped to pick up their bikes, they heard a shrill screech in the graveyard. Cassidy stared at Jordan, who could only motion for her to follow him out of the entrance. Always a talkative boy, Jordan had no more words to say.

The shrill scream was as loud as a plane overhead and rattled around in both of their chests.

Hawg awoke, ready to feed again. He pulled himself from the crypt and stretched his long body out. Nostrils flaring, he returned to the two he'd made a meal of earlier. Their bodies were colder and stiffening up on him badly. Still, he started to rip open the other thigh of the youth in the stone chair.

He stopped in his motions, sensing something amiss. He let the teen go and dropped to all fours. Snout to the grass, he rooted all around and caught the scent of others. Boy and gilt, unbled, he smelt them deep. Their scents hung faint so Hawg understood them to be small, perhaps unworthy of his time. After all, he had meat and would find proper gilt as the night wore on.

Then he heard voices, yes, children. He tilted his head, letting his ears pick up their words. Terror filled their throats, breaths popped in and out fast. In no hurry, Hawg trotted across the graveyard upright, trailing their scent. He passed the youth's car and stopped once he reached the entrance to the cemetery.

Hawg saw the two children, hardly bigger than runts in his red eyes. They appeared comical to him, scrambling across the highway, down a ditch and toward an opening in the train trestle.

They spotted him as well. The girl screamed and the boy did his best not to, though his terror was clear in his eyes. Hawg never relocated, he only stood up tall on his hind legs, staring back at them. The boy was a runt, not worth eating. More meat awaited him back near the crypt. The other wasn't yet gilt and wouldn't be worth his time.

Would they tell others of seeing him? Hawg reasoned they would. From tales old Elias spun him about the world and how many feared what was different, he couldn't see older ones believing them...until they found the bodies Hawg left behind. Would slaying them only prolong the inevitable? He didn't want to go back to the barn, at least not yet. Though the outside world was fearsome, he wanted to live and explore. He would just move on and these little ones would have a story to tell.

Just as he was about to turn and go back to the crypt, Hawg caught a scent, a smell that drove him wild. Blood time. It was wafting on the winds from the trestle. Could the little one be gilt already? Surely not, but his loins burned at the odor and he wanted it more than food. His desire burning, Hawg dropped down and leapt through the entrance to the cemetery.

"It's coming after us," Jordan yelled and stopped under the trestle. "Cassidy! C'mon!" He dropped his bike and bolted south along the trestle path.

She screamed again, yet mimicked his actions. She ran after him and they stopped at the opening of the mine they'd seen earlier.

Jordan pulled down a board that lay over the upper entrance, revealing a small slot of darkness. He grabbed her by the wrist and strove to boost her up, saying, "Ya gotta get in. It's only a yard or so of a drop."

Cassidy was up the opening and saw nothing but blackness. "I can't go in there!"

When they heard the beast howl, her own scream stopped in her neck as Jordan pushed her legs. Cassidy slipped through the gap fast. Jordan grabbed the edges and pulled himself up. He swung a leg through the opening as he saw the creature step into view. Jordan froze; not dropping in the mine. The red eyes of the monster scanned the area, steel tusks shining in the afternoon sunlight. Cassidy pulled on his legs and Jordan fell into the mine opening.

They had only seconds to breathe before the beast ripped

at the sealed entrance. It pulled away several more boards, and even a few bricks, casting more light into the spot where Jordan and Cassidy held each other. The monster was like a digging machine, determined to get them. Dust rained on them and the howl of the beast popped their ears.

Jordan eyed the dismal tunnel behind them and prepared to run into it.

Suddenly, the beast stopped. Eyes on them, nostrils sucking wind fast, a look of confusion registered in its face. It stepped away from the opening a few feet, head tilted. It kept breathing, smelling. Then, back to them, it roared in the air.

Cassidy whispered, "What is it?"

Jordan shook his head fast, still holding her tight. "Dunno. God, I don't know. Look! It smells something."

Micki worked up her courage and cried out again, but the only response was a recollection…a reminder of the time her pain came to her. In her blind agony, she thought she heard the beast again. No, it couldn't be….

But the strong odor of fecal matter returned and the deep grunts filled her ears. Micki felt the sharp claws swipe at her, knocking her backside to the weeds.

Over her stood Hawg, his organ swinging, tongue on his tusks.

Then, her nightmare started all over again.

CHAPTER FIVE

Going Home

Hux killed his Harley as Nick Roberts stepped out of the small car. The other man with him, a quiet man of possible Mexican descent, also exited. He contemplated Hux, then stared off to where Nick stared. Roberts looked down at the device in his hand and then back to Hux. The only sound in their ears was that of the lapping water in the belly of the vast stone quarry.

"Well," Hux said, never getting off his Harley. "Looks like yer shit outta luck, pal."

Roberts frowned and stared back at the object in his hand. "No doubt about it, this is where the tracker is. Very strange."

Hux folded his arms across his chest as they all stared across the vast expanse of water before them. The piles of sand, rock and gouged out bluffs hemmed in the artificial lake. The area appeared more in tune with a canyon in the southwest, for the cold, lifeless arms of the rocks embraced the waters.

"Quarries are mighty deep," Hux told them in a matter of fact voice. "Good luck in getting your tracker back now."

Roberts dropped his hand and turned to face Hux. As he did this motion, the other man reached behind his back. Before a gun could appear, Hux had a small derringer from the sleeve of his leather jacket in his hand, aimed at the Mexican's face. The man froze, gun in his hand, but aiming at the ground.

"Y'all don't wanna do that now." Hux said with a calm voice, eyes wide, but showing no fear. "Don't be pinning this on me. I had nothing to do with it."

Rage boiled through Roberts' serpentine face. "Who else

could've double crossed us, fool?" Eyes to his partner, Roberts snapped, "He couldn't hit anything with that little thing. Kill him, Rico."

True enough, derringers were very inaccurate. Hux never pulled the trigger as Rico went into motion, eyes focused on the small gun in Hux's hand. The biker's left hand rested on the gas tank of his Harley and he drummed his fingers once. From under the cams of the bike something hissed, the air split and Rico jerked in his motion, never able to boost the gun. He gawked down, seeing the black taped handle of a blade protruding from his belly. The rest of the weapon was buried inside of him, probably knicking his spine, for he suddenly couldn't move.

"Dumbasses," Hux said as he climbed off the Harley like it was a steed. "Bring a gun to a knife fight." A few strides brought him close to Rico. Derringer to the man's temple, Hux pulled the trigger. The bullet made a pop as it left the chamber and a similar echo when it entered Rico's skull. The man, screamed, twisting backward before flipping over the edge of the quarry. The splash was great and the sloshing sound soon ebbed away to nothing.

Roberts' face flushed. "I didn't think you'd have the stones to kill someone."

Hux shrugged. "After the first one or two of you dope heads, it's easy. But I never killed the mule on the way down. Ya gotta believe me, I never crossed y'all up. I know nada about it all."

Roberts broke a sweat at last, his destiny apparent. "Wonderful trick with the projectile knife under the bike. How did you do that?"

"I built the block to the Harley myself. Talent is there and when the will follows, one never knows what can be made to spec." Hux squared himself to Roberts. "Now, what to do with you."

Roberts sneered, "You kill me, your life won't be worth spit here."

"If I don't kill you, you dance back to Cicero and I wake up dead some morning anyways. I can't see that as a good thing, sparky."

Right eyebrow rising, Roberts said, "Perhaps we can compromise."

"I'm listening."

Though the first thing both men heard was a distant howl echo across the territory.

Jordan and Cassidy couldn't see what Hawg did beyond the ditch. They heard the creature's repeated short grunts and the pained screams of a woman. Still, they clutched each other and said at the same time, "What is it?"

Jordan spoke up and said, "It looks like a pig and a man had a baby."

"That's impossible," Cassidy said quietly, her bottom jaw shaking so much her teeth chattered.

Jordan trembled and said, "Yeah, I know it is. It looks like one, though. The metal stuff on its face might be a mask."

"Where did it come from?"

Jordan said nothing, trying to understand it all. The cries of a female voice, gurgling and coughing as Hawg howled, stabbed in his ears so hard he wanted to plug them up.

"Will he come back for us?"

Jordan was quiet for a while and then said, "I don't know. He can't get in. Did you see how mad he got when he couldn't break the beams and bricks?"

Cassidy's tears erupting from her eyes, she cried, "What if he can when he gets back?"

Jordan said, "Then we have to run farther into the mine. Maybe he'll leave."

They heard the screams for another minute, though it sounded like longer. The human shouts stopped long before Hawg's howls calmed.

The beast stepped back into their range of vision. His manhood swinging, slick and bloody, his eyes focusing on their bikes under the trestle. At last, Hawg stared at the mine entrance. Chest pumping, the creature sucked air until its breaths evened out. There seemed no hurry to its actions. With rapid steps, Hawg trotted to the mine entrance. Claws on the beam, he peered into the opening and at the faces of the kids.

Again, he took deep breaths, but slower this time.

"Go away," Jordan said in a halted voice. "Get!" his voice rose in power and he ordered Hawg, "Get on home now! *Get*, you hear?"

Red eyes glimmering, Hawg looked at the little girl. Her bottom lip quivered along with the rest of her body and her nose started to run.

They could smell him. His breath was fetid and ghastly, but slowing down its pace as he stared at them. A droplet of blood fell from his left steel tusk and struck the beam that prevented his entry. Not one drop of sweat beaded on the beast, though.

"Go home!" Jordan ordered. "Get now, hog!"

The beast turned from them and paused. They gaped at his curled tail, then held their breath and he dropped to all fours. After a few moments of stillness, the beast trotted away. Cassidy put her hand on her mouth when Hawg started to defecate running at full speed. In another moment, he was gone from their line of sight.

They stared for a long time before Jordan said, "God, we gotta get out of here."

Cassidy gripped him tighter. "Not yet. I can't move."

Hand on her long hair, Jordan nodded. "I'll stay with you."

Hungry from covering the ruined gilt, Hawg departed. The little ones weren't worth his labors to get to them.

Hawg traveled along the long grasses of the waterway. In his mind, there was a slight bit of trepidation. Hawg comprehended that his actions would draw attention. The safety of the barn called to him, true, but his freedom brought new tastes, adventures, and also fear. Still, he didn't want to go home. He never wanted to be shut up in the barn again, no matter how much he missed the feeling of safety there. No, this was much better. Even if the men found a way to get rid of him or cage him, this freedom was worth it. It was so much better than confinement. He hated a pen. He hated a fence. Hawg hated walls. When he inspected the space where the children hid, he felt the confinement loom. The place where he slept the night before was secure, but it wasn't quite home.

His gait steady and consistent, he heard cars on occasion and flattened out to avoid detection. Eyes were everywhere in the outside world. That meant danger. Hawg neared his home, the olden place where he lived for ages. He couldn't recall for how long. In his head, there was no concept of time, but he was glad the open spaces near the Gilmore farm allowed him liberty to progress, unmolested.

Hawg spotted the trailer of Elias, the old man who fed him and cared for him all of his days. He missed Elias. The man was good to him. Hawg felt no anger for him or the farmer. Eyes keen on the other trailer nearby, Hawg slowly inched closer to this place. Nostrils extending, Hawg neared the porch holding the corpulent woman, covered in a half-finished afghan.

Her head tilted, eyes closed. Her dog's head rose up, ears back. However, the dog never barked, but a low whine held in its throat.

"Easy Duke. Hello? Are you there?" she said.

Hawg drew close to the deck, but never set a claw nail on it.

"I know you are there, honey. Are you being good?"

Hawg breathed deep, but uttered no sound. His tusks drew in a bit.

Luella said, "I hope you are not being too naughty, honey. Those men are around and looking for something to blame for bad things. You be good, you hear me, Hawg?"

With a glance under her deck, Hawg thought only to rest. His stomach was full, but the run over to Luella's had burnt off some of that. The joints in his body ached. The exercise made him feel incredible. He was not used to being so free and able to explore his abilities. He glanced to the farmhouse of the Solow place. His head snapped back, focused on what he saw.

"What is it, boy?" Luella asked, concern on her face.

Hawg lowered to the earth and couldn't take his eyes off the house and the round barn.

"Take a rest, honey," she told Hawg. "You must be tired. They all came by earlier. They won't bother me none again for some time."

Luella reached under her afghan in progress and pulled

out a red blanket that covered her legs and midsection. "Here, baby, you go sleep for a spell."

Hawg rose up, stood on his hind legs, and faced her. He took the blanket and lowered down. Hawg crawled under the deck and spread out the blanket. Down low, he flopped over on his side and was asleep in a minute.

Luella humming a tune lulled him to sleep. Soon, Duke was out as well.

When Lynne White returned home after the school board meeting, it didn't take her long to add up the errors of the day. She checked messages, and called her grandmother. Each message was a new building block in horror as she realized Jordan wasn't home...and by the calls from the Ellington's, neither was Cassidy.

She called the bindery office, unconcerned with the snippy lady Carol Brandt who worked there. Lynne flatly told her what an emergency it was and to get her husband from the production floor.

The first thing Andrew did was tell Lynne what a load of crap it was they kept him over, as the work they wanted never had trickled in yet. When she explained the mistakes that led to Jordan being misplaced, or being gone, Andrew dropped the phone and told the office woman, "I have to go. My son is missing."

Still snide, Carol said, "That'll be a full occurrence, Mr. White."

Rage boiling, Andrew shot back, "Like I give a shit about that. My son comes first."

He stomped from the office and out onto production floor. Andrew never retrieved his lunch box or coat. He almost collided with pre-press assistant Scott Grady. The bulbous neck of Grady flexed as Andrew nearly bowled him over. Andrew made no apologies and headed to his truck, never answering inquiries from various folk as to where he was going...save for Wilma Rynning. The portly woman was the brains on day shift, held the only copy of the employee handbook and would do anything for a pal.

"Can I have your cell phone?" Andrew asked and then told her of his plight.

Wilma fished in her purse and said, "Only if you wear those package friendly pants your wife doesn't like to you to wear." She smiled and gave him the phone. "When are you going to show me that big thing?"

Desperate, Andrew smiled, "The day they walk me out of here."

Wilma handed him the phone. "There should be a half hour on it. I have minutes left and that is the back-up I took from my daughter."

He thanked her and hurried away. Andrew hated leaving work, but it was as if none of it mattered. All he wanted was his son. The image of him crying the moment of his birth ran through Andrew's mind as a dull fear permeated his flesh. Jordan screaming at his birth, him shitting coal black in the pan while they cleaned him up...him asking questions during the children's sermon at church...him being scared of the Green Goblin at the movies...him saying "I love you, Daddy."

Once out of the plant he called his brother, Doug, who was already aware of the disappearance of Cassidy Ellington.

Doug said, "Be a might odd if both kids were gone and not together, being neighbors and all."

Andrew shifted the truck, his voice far more full of concern than his brother's. "Maybe they're just out playing in the water-ways. Maybe we're just overreacting."

"Lucas and Lynne say the kid's bikes are gone."

He thought fast. "Well, they couldn't go far."

Doug agreed. "Sure. We've already went down the main roads just now. I have everyone out, Drew."

"I'll swing down old Sixty-six and come up that way, all right? I'll hit the dirt roads as well."

"Calm down, Andrew. I'm sure it's all right."

Andrew's free hand gripped the steering wheel until his hand felt wet. He took a few breaths and said, "You ever find out what tore up Genesis or Andrea?"

"No."

"Then I can't calm down, for Christ's sake. Of all days for

them kids to be out wandering, Jesus God."

"I'm calling everyone off dayshift to come out to hunt, Andrew. I'm sure this will turn out okay. Matt is calling local farmers to see if they saw them."

Andrew closed the phone and took another breath.

"I promised Jordan I'd always be there for him," Andrew said to the cab of his truck. "Ain't I a piss poor father?" When he turned onto Route 66, he caught a glimpse of Ambrose Brother's plant behind him. He flipped the building off and drove on.

The interior of his truck felt stifling. He reached over, picked up a napkin leftover from a fast food joint, and wiped his nose. Andrew rolled the window down and thought of putting on music or the radio. Nothing sounded right.

"Wish I'd taken the Harley today," he said, pondering how he hadn't due to the cycle needing an oil change. "Wish that were my biggest worry now."

With no one to talk to but God, Andrew said nothing more.

"No, I haven't seen the children," Mr. Solow said into the receiver, his voice softening as he spoke. "But I will go out and have a look around." Earnest concern filled his tone as he said, "Yes, I'll talk to Elias as well. God bless, and I hope you find them safe." When he hung up the receiver, Solow stared across the room at his hired hand. Elias sat on a small bench at the end of the kitchen, looking into the living room. "What are you thinking, Elias?"

The old man peered into his glass of lemonade and said, "Lots of things, sir. I'm thinkin' I need something a might stronger than this, sir."

Solow rocked in his chair a few times and then slowly stood. "Silly children. Darn shame it is, you know? I hope they haven't wandered into trouble."

"Oh, Mr. Solow, stop it," Elias said, voice cracking, hand shaking so much the ice cubes in his drink rattled. He gripped the glass with his other hand to stop the action. "You know, if Hawg got 'em...."

"We don't know that."

Anger in his voice, Elias fired back, "But what if he did?"

Solow's eyes aimed out the kitchen windows. "Then he did. It's the way of the world, Elias. We are all sinners come short of the glory of God. Just because they are cute doesn't make those kids any less guilty of original sin."

Elias got up fast, spilled a bit of his drink, and said, "Some of our sins are worse than others, sir."

Solow's brows dropped. "I've paid a long penance for my sins, Elias."

"What 'bout them little ones? They interest on your bad sins, huh?"

Indignant, Solow replied, "What would you have me do, Elias? Call the police and confess to what? They'd think me mad."

Elias shook his head. "I don't know what to do, sir. They tie Hawg to us, we all go down."

Solow relaxed and said, "Everyone has to die, Elias. Perhaps this is our time. Maybe this is God's will to make me clean at last."

With a grunt, Elias said, "I'm going out for a look around for the kids and then for a drink, sir. G'Night."

Solow watched him step out into the fading daylight. He peered across the property, but saw no children.

After the sunlight started to fade, Jordan decided to climb out of the mine entrance. "We better go, Cassidy. We can't be in here all night."

Cassidy barely let him go as Jordan started to get out of the mine's opening. He hung out of the entrance, pulling her up after him. In a few seconds, they were free, but never left the opening. Ready to scramble back in at a moment's notice, they held their ground.

Jordan sniffed and said, "It's gone."

"I hope so," Cassidy said, hardly above a whisper, still afraid to shift until Jordan pulled her.

Their steps were slow as they checked the area under the trestle. With caution, they picked up their bikes and climbed on them. They never left, still afraid of what could be nearby.

"I heard someone out here with it," Cassidy said, scanning the ditches. "I don't see anyone."

Also looking around, Jordan said, "We better get home. God knows what time it is. My Mom will kill me."

Just as they were about to head east, they stopped, hearing the approach of a vehicle. The screech of tires was deafening and both children nearly screamed. Soon after, the shout from a man was nearly as frightening as the howl of the beast.

"Jordan!" came the voice.

Both children felt relief as they saw it was Mr. White. When he ran over and embraced them, they couldn't understand why he was crying.

He hadn't seen the monster.

CHAPTER SIX

Discoveries

Mr. Solow poured himself a glass of homemade wine in a glass shaped like a barrel. The wine's color was bright red and in tune with the beets & potato mash Elias used to create it. The taste strong, Solow never winced at the flavor. It flowed down over his chest and he walked over to his tape cases, trying to decide on a topic. He drank more and enjoyed the feeling inside.

When his phone rang, he took another step, a sip of wine and furrowed his brows at the caller ID slot.

"God bless technology," Solow muttered as he picked up the phone. "Hello there. Solow residence."

"Evening, Mr. Solow," came the sweet voice on the line.

"To what do I owe this pleasure? Do you have enough supper tonight?"

"Oh, plenty, dear, but was wanting to share a little nugget with you."

"Naughty girl. You always were a tale bearer."

"Can you guess who is sleeping under my deck?"

Brows elevated, Solow swallowed and thought for a moment before he replied, "Huh. Elias just went out to poke around and drink…."

The woman on the line laughed until she snorted and said, "Silly man. Old Hawg is sleeping deep, Mr. Solow. I fear he's been a bad boy."

Solow nodded to no one, index finger running around the mouth of his glass of wine. "I reckon he has. It's his nature. He's a pig."

"Too bad you couldn't get him back to his home tonight, sweetie."

Solow thought of that, but it seemed like an unlikely enterprise. Too bad he didn't take a tranquilizer gun, shoot Hawg, and use the end loader to scoop him up and lock him in the round barn again. Unfortunately, he didn't have a tranquilizer gun and the end loader was low on fuel until Friday's delivery to the tank.

"Thank you for the call, Luella."

"Trying to look out for the boy, Mr. Solow."

"You done well, hon. I reckon Hawg will come home when he wants, though. No brow beatin' is gonna make it happen sooner."

"Night, Mr. Solow."

"G'night and God bless, Luella."

Solow hung up the phone, took a drink and selected a sermon called the WRATH OF GOD. After he placed the tape in the stereo he sat down in his rocker/recliner and drank some more.

"I'm sure we've all heard messages about the grace of God and the love of God, but how many sermons have we really made concerning the wrath of God? While not a comfortable topic, let me assure you, my dear friends, that his wrath is as real as his love, mercy and charity."

Solow refilled his glass and rocked to the voice of the preacher man.

"Jesus asked, what will it profit a man if he gained the whole world and lost his own soul? He was not looking for an answer, though, for He knows the answer. He IS the answer! He knows where all of the wealth of the world is, every diamond, nugget of gold, and pool of oil. But he knows something you don't! He knows how long eternity is and how dark it will be without him. Your mind cannot comprehend a million years, nor imagine fifty billion years. The man who would trade his soul for the wealth of this world is a fool!"

"Consider the value of your soul. Your one little soul was the reason Jesus came to Earth, incarnated as a lowly human being, where He died for you. Your soul was the reason the Son of the Almighty God allowed Herod's men to spit on Him, whip Him and mock Him when

they said, 'Hail! King of the Jews!' It was the reason Jesus was taken to the top of Calvary, where the created drove nails through the hands of their Creator. It made him separate from his Father in that moment when he became the ultimate sacrifice for sin and exclaimed, 'MY GOD, MY GOD, WHY HAVE YOU FORSAKEN ME?' He bled, suffered, and died alone for the redemption of each of your little souls!"

Lynne cried one moment and was full of anger the next at Jordan for his absence. Both Andrew and Lynne couldn't let him go though, same as the Ellington family with their daughter.

The reunion took place at the cemetery's edge, though the kids refused to go back inside. In front of Douglas White and his officers, the kids told the tale of seeing a giant pig-man. They then told what he did to the mine entrance. Alex reported to them that something had been there all right and Matt found more tracks in the muddy areas of the ditch by the trestle.

"Pig man?" Doug questioned and listened to their tale thoughtfully. Alex and Matt went into the cemetery and returned fast. Doug dismissed the kids to their homes with their families. Andrew stayed near his brother. He walked with the police past the teen's car.

"Ever hear such a thing?" Andrew said, his voice full of wonder and relief.

Doug took the toothpick from his mouth and snapped it in half as he shook his head. "That's kids for you. My son tells me of an army of trolls under the bridge down the way he sees all the time. Kids."

"It's the steel tusks that makes it all crazy," Andrew said. "What are they...seeing...?" His words fell off a cliff as he saw the ruined bodies near the crypt illuminated by flashlights from Alex and Matt.

After he pulled out a flashlight of his own, Doug gave the bodies a once over and called on his radio. Still in plain clothes, Alex stayed away from the scene, looking ready to vomit again. He placed his hand on the statue of Jesus by the shrubs and used it to balance himself and his guts.

Doug told him, "Run along home, Alex. Rest up. Tomorrow will be a long day."

Face flushed, he nodded and left the cemetery.

"Jesus Christ," Andrew said, staring at the ruined bodies. "A giant pig man did this, huh? Cute."

Matt frowned and said, "Looks like it anyways. See, how there is a furrowed rut down the bodies, just like Andrea?"

Doug grimaced, his light following the path of the slashes, then stopping on the spot where pieces of meat hung off thigh-bones. "Slots for the steel tusks? Mighty hard to accept, boys. More likely some tool or weapon of a killer. I'd rather hunt a wild boar than a serial killer. Pig man...."

Andrew half laughed. "That's all crazy talk, no matter how fucked up these bodies appear."

Matt pointed at a few of the stones, light dancing over brown splashes on the granite effigies. "Sure looks like pig-shit around here, smells like it as well. Isn't pig shit supposed to be mostly water? I recall hearing that somewhere."

With a rub to his right temple, Doug said, "Still hoping for wild boar, though. I know what the kids said." He made a weak laugh and said, "Christ, fellows, I don't know what to make of it for real. It has to be a crazy guy of some kind, Andrew. Better thank God Jordan remembered Pa's old tale about the mine-shaft entrance. Fast thinking for certain."

Andrew glared at the family crypt where his weapons lay, and at the broken gate. He stepped inside and observed the cof-fins. These objects didn't appear disturbed. "Yeah, thank God." He knelt, noting smudges of feces and blood on the lower sec-tions of the coffins.

Alex grabbed for the bottle of whiskey under the front seat of his police cruiser. The car edged out of the cemetery as he opened the bottle. Once on Old 66, he upended the best thing Tennessee had to offer. It burned going down and he didn't stop, all of the images crowding in on him. Worse than the broken body of Andrea and the torn-up pit bull, that punk kid Bruce had been gnawed on. The bones were even missing in spots. Whatever ate his flesh had chewed and pulverized bone as well. What serial killer or human could do that? A quarter mile away, he stopped and puked all over the patched pavement on the highway.

He called a few Montrose city cops, alerting them to the crisis at hand. Alex drank again, cherries on top of his car to provide a wide berth. He then called a few friends to let it all out. Tears streamed down his face as Alex even talked to his mother for a few minutes, but never confessed to his greater fears or weakness.

He drove and drank, not knowing what to think of it all. None of the other police, his friends or even his mother could provide solace for him. His courage wasn't as strong as the other men, but he liked being a cop. It was regular, safe work in these parts. Montrose had its share of minor scuffles, but it was nothing a former football player like Alex couldn't handle. He enjoyed being a county deputy and it beat working as a guard at the prison or a grunt in the printing plant. He met his ticket quota and enjoyed the rides better than working in that damned plant, which Alex had done in summers after high school. That was enough to convince him a greener pasture existed elsewhere. Never would he have dreamed this would happen.

Alex saw death on the highways and kids mangled after a country-drinking binge ended badly. These things twisted his guts. This thing that was happening was beyond that.

Of course, it was all-insane to think of a pig/man/creature like the kids swore to. He kept telling himself that they were just kids, but in the back of his mind something nagged. His grandmother and her relatives had the second sight, or intuition. Alex's mother still had prophetic dreams. None of the family thought much of their premonitions since their Apostolic Christian faith looked down on such things. Alex never was much of a seer, but he had strange feelings, and ever since they found Dinsdale and Andrea, his stomach wasn't right. With the revelation of the children, it seemed to fit in his mind with what was wrong. Now, he couldn't deal with that truth.

Alex crossed the countryside a few times and then caught a whiff of the Solow place. He slammed on the brakes, nearly losing his handle on the bottle.

Suddenly, he knew what to think of it all.

Hux rode to the Green Parrot tavern that most biker types

frequented in town. A loop of the original route of Old 66 had once snaked past this business at the edge of Montrose. In the seventies, just before the interstate came in, the route adjusted. The section of town where the biker bar resided was home to a recycling center and a junkyard, a metal garage converted to a Pentecostal church and the VFW hall shielding a louse-ridden trailer park. It was a spot few went to who didn't belong there. Hux parked his Harley in line next to the other motorbikes. Across the front of this line was a hitching post like in the old western movies. The original owner of the business, Larry Myers, installed that as a gag. Now, after years of weathering, the wood appeared more authentic than Larry ever planned.

He sat on the bike for a bit, contemplating if he had made the correct choice regarding Roberts and the dealers or not. "I'd hate to move on and start over somewhere else," Hux said quietly to the unpopulated lot. Although riding out and disappearing in Idaho appealed to him, this was his home. His choice to accord Roberts what he wanted, a scapegoat for the drug dealer overlords, was not easy, either. Roberts liked the idea of a body to blame instead of dissolving the dope line to the area from Cicero. Hux was a known commodity. Besides, this furnished Hux the chance to rid himself of the competition from the south.

The main serving area of the bar was a squared set-up brooded over by a looming bald man. Bottles lined the shelves behind him and many sat drinking around this bar. The bartender, Dola Davies, levered his head at the new arrival and started to get Hux his beer of choice.

"Double D," Hux said in greeting to the bartender, glancing around the watering hole.

"How's tricks, Hux?" Double D asked, but appeared unconcerned.

Hux smiled, thinking of the irony of Dola's nickname. His upper body denoted the label Double D, and there was a picture from Mardi Gras week over the bar to prove it. Double D still kept the beads he earned wearing the huge brassier.

Overall, it appeared a normal night at the Green Parrot, or Dirty Bird as some called it. Younger bikers Johnny Atlas and Cody Greenwell sat, arm wrestling and swearing, trading shots in the shoulder. Kimmi Jo Patrick showed her tits for shots of Jim Beam. Tyler Bellot was bragging about the size of his penis, that it even bested that of famed county cop Matt Crouch, who was a legend. Tyler never mentioned he was a one-ball man, a fact he had confessed in a drunken stupor to Hux once. Hux wagered one was all one needed.

In the back corner of the dim bar sat Big Ed Nelson, machinist at a local shop, most feared biker in the county, connection for the largest cash crop in southern Illinois to Montrose. Hux's Chi-town bosses dealt in higher grades of crack, smack, and meth, so Big Ed and his pot business was small time to them, and antiquated. However, Big Ed hated Hux, even if they got along in public. Big Ed was old school, nearing fifty, and cut from a cloth unfamiliar to "kiddie" bikers of a younger generation.

A dozen bikers called out Hux's name as he walked in and he waved, motioning for a beer to the bartender. Double D drafted Hux a brew and sat it on the bar as Hux endowed Big Ed a mock salute.

Ed leaned forward, stubbing out his smoke. He took a shot of whiskey before chasing it with a sip of his long-necked bottle. Big Ed stroked a long beard of reddish hair peppered with gray. His bloodshot eyes focused on Hux as he said, "Well, look who's still alive. Merry fucking Christmas."

A smile aimed at his scapegoat, Hux said, "Still doin' time in this flesh, buddy."

Big Ed gave him a look as if to say, *I ain't yer buddy*, but the words never popped out. "Sit your ass down, Hux and tell me dirty stories. The news on the radio and tube is makin' my ass hurt."

His rectum still stinging, Hux walked over to the table near to Big Ed and sat down. He shifted on the wooden surface and said, "That's what I had in mind."

The jukebox changed a song and silence reigned for a few moments...just as old Elias stepped into the smoky room. Elias half tottered as he approached the bar. All eyes riveted to him as he grabbed the bar, then sat on a stool. The old man placed a five on the polished counter and asked for a drink.

The bartender focused on Big Ed. The burly biker smoothed

his long hair back and nodded. When Double D served Elias, the bald man's face appeared like he drank lemon juice.

As the music picked up, as well as Kimmi Jo's top, Hux said, "Damn, time was, his kind wasn't allowed in here."

Ed shrugged. "They ain't, but never know when the piggies are watching or in the neighborhood. It may be fun, so leave him alone. What is it you wanted, Hux?" Ed's gaze narrowed at him. "Something wrong with you?"

"Just looking at the world with different eyes, man. When I was a kid, even the crap on the walls in here impressed me. The napkins signed by Jim Dandy of Black Oak Arkansas or the pictures of Dan Hampton of the Bears with ol' Larry and his son kinda have lost their luster to me."

"What are ya smokin'?" Ed chided him and took another swig of beer. "If I wanted to eat humble pie, I'd have let the kitchen stay open."

Tyler offered Hux a cigarette. "Relax, man."

Hux declined the smoke and Tyler shrugged before putting the cigarette behind his ear.

Double D cut the sound on the jukebox and turned up his scanner. "Hey boys, listen to this shit!"

Though anger bubbled in the bar at first, they all listened as the voice of Alex filled the bar. They heard his frayed voice telling a few of his buddies, on the open police band, about the dead teens in the graveyard. They heard him talk of the butchered dog, of Andrea and Dinsdale, and of the kid's tale of a giant pig man.

When the scanner went dead, a strange silence reigned in the bar. Hux gazed at the wall filled with mirrors containing confederate battle flags and southern rock band logos. Though it was dank and warm in the bar, Hux felt so cold.

"Ain't that the shits," Big Ed said, leaning back. "I heard some folks died last night and a young thang was missing."

Drunken bikers started swearing, angered at the idea the cops kept secrets from them. Wild tales started to flow about a monster on the loose and how impossible that was. More anger came as many shot down the ideas and called them crazy.

Big Ed eyed Hux, who fell silent and stared down. "You

know something, don't you, Randy?"

Hux snapped his head up, but his face couldn't hide his guilt. He said, "Aww, c'mon, it's all…."

"All what?" Ed leaned in and transferred a grim look. "Fess up, man."

"I saw it, last night," Hux confessed and the bar grew quiet, eyes staring at him. "I saw it out on the frontage road near to the Solow's place."

"What was it?" Kimmi Jo asked, mesmerized, tying her greasy hair back, and adjusting her sports bra under her shirt.

Hux swallowed and felt his rectum pulsing. "Just what they said. It looked like a giant guy crossed up with a damned pig. I know that ain't possible, but it was true. That's what I saw. The moon is damn near to full, so I saw his tusks. They shined like they was steel."

Ed asked, "What were you doing out there? Acid?"

Laughter rippled in the bar. "That isn't important. What is, well…" he regarded Elias, who was swaying on his bar stool. "… wonder where something like that comes from?"

They all knew who Elias was and where he worked. The man caused no trouble, but the stripe that hung out in the Green Parrot had no use for him or his race.

As if on cue, Double D served up Elias another beer and said to him, "You don't raise no pig men out on the Solow place, now do you?"

"Not every pig one sees is on four legs," Elias said, words heavy with drunkenness. "It's hard to be a good man and not a pig, sir."

"That story on the band is scaring folks bad," the bartender said gently, the entire tavern listening to the exchange.

"Change is bad," Elias answered, words pulpy and wet. "I knew it was bad from the beginning. We never shoulda kept ol' Hawg, but he was tame like, you know? Never no trouble. In fact, he got rid of troubles. He was a good boy, gentle even. Now, them accursed drugs got in his self and he done went feral. If he kilt them young folks, that's a shame."

Suddenly, he snapped to alertness, understanding his long tongue. Elias slipped off the bar stool and looked at the room.

Everyone stared at him, mouths agape. Elias faced the door and walked to it with more grace than he had entered with.

"That fucker," Cody Greenwell raged, his oily pony tail waving. "He knows about this monster! You all heard him."

Big Ed said to this biker, "Easy kid...." His words weren't condemning, though.

Many grunts and cries agreed. Another biker said, "We need to call the cops."

Ed eyed the muscle-bound biker who had spoken and said, "Ease up, Atlas."

Tyler ran a hand through his blonde hair and said, "We oughtta string that bastard up!"

Soon, a dozen men were on their feet, full of fury. They started to file out of the bar and Hux looked at Big Ed.

"You gonna stop them?"

Ed shrugged and lit another smoke. "They're fulla crap. Mob mentality. Once the cool air hits them, they'll sober up."

They saw Elias' truck lights leave the parking lot, soon followed by a half dozen bikers.

Ed sighed and stood. "Then again, I may be wrong."

"And God will judge them all, sheep on one side, goats on the other. Unto those found faithful, he shall give a crown of life and life everlasting in Heaven. To all of those unworthy, he shall cast them from his sight. These that are unclean will be cast into the lake of fire and be tormented forever and ever."

"C'mon out, you old prick! I know what you done!"

Mr. Solow got out of his chair fast, then slowed down. True, the voice yelling outside startled him, but his ire faded fast. The wine in his system caused a rush to his head, but this soon bottomed out. He rubbed his chin, fingered the cleft there and then sighed. Teeth tight, his mind focused well on the danger at hand. He shut off the tape and headed across the kitchen. He put the glass down on the dryer and took a breath. Like any farmer in such a situation, he reached for the shotgun behind the door. Once on the porch, he reached into the pocket of his winter coat that hung there, pulled out two shells. He never loaded them into the chambers of the pump shotgun as he kept it at the ready at all times.

From his side porch, he could see the police cruiser in his back yard via the outside lights. At first, his fear returned and a feeling of resignation sank in. However, when he saw the man shouting wore plain clothes and held an empty whiskey bottle, his mood lightened.

"Damned fool, so young," Solow sighed, gun lowered.

"You bred a killer, didn't you? Come out and tell me you didn't make him!"

Solow stepped onto the back porch and opened the screen door. The gun in his hands pointed down and Solow handled it gingerly as if to show he had no intention of using it. "What is it you are shouting about, young man? Who is that out there?"

"You know!" Alex said, charging up to him, but stopping short of contact after his eyes focused on the shotgun. "I heard tell from the kids about the pig man thing out hereabouts."

Solow blinked. "What? Do tell, son."

"I'm not your son, old man. God, tell me all about it!"

"You are Alex Brown, aren't you? Wilbur and Kristen's boy? Your mom still have a good rhubarb crop?"

"Shut up about all that!" Alex's head shook violently and spit flew from his lips. "I saw what he can do. I saw his prints. I know, it's gotta be from you!"

Solow frowned. "Young man, that's craziness. I think you've had too much to drink."

"What craziness? That there's a pig-man about butchering folks or that you raised it?"

Solow said, "Both of them things, son."

Alex's face tightened as he sneered, "I am not your son."

With a nod, Solow said, his voice turning cold, "Don't I know it. My son would be taller."

Alex gave him a sideways look as the odor of fecal matter increased. Solow saw the expression of the cop as he sensed the smell, but tried to focus on his next line of threat. Solow figured Alex even heard the foot falls in the yard just before the cop reached out and grabbed the farmer's shirt.

When Hawg's right claw closed around Alex's wrist...the one he had near Solow... time stopped. For a moment, all froze.

The shock of the added presence of the huge beast, towering over both of them, stopped time.

Red eyes burned at Alex, so feral and angry, they were all too human.

Hawg snapped Alex's wrist like a dry branch with his right claw and swiped at the cop's neck with his other hand. Blood spattered on the milk can standing by the back door, but the slice didn't cut open the cop's neck all the way. Alex twisted, gagging, stumbling toward his car.

Hawg bellowed and rammed him in the back, tusks driving through Alex's upper back under his shoulder blades. The creature's charging momentum lifted the cop and propelled them both forward. Alex's body took the brunt of the fall on the top of the car. The windows all smashed out at once. Alex's neck and spine broke under Hawg's weight. Tusks out and head in the air, Hawg licked the blood on his teeth. A-straddle of him, Hawg howled and brought up his right hand. He dropped it fast, pulping Alex's head on the top of the ruined police cruiser, shattering the line of lights. The cop's head deflated like a ball, pieces of his skull poking out on gray smattered edges amongst the ruined lights. The ejecta from Alex's head shot forward, adding a stripe to the top of the brown county cruiser.

Hawg stood on the hood of the car, hooves denting in deep. He licked the brains from his fingers and long nails, but turned his head to spit out hair. Hawg then climbed off the vehicle, staring at the body dividing the glass that spidered away from the impact point.

Hawg turned his head. He eyed Solow and took a breath.

The farmer put the gun against the inner wall of the porch and took a sip of wine. He stared at Hawg. Their eyes met and there were no words.

That's when they heard the straight pipes of Harleys out on the back of the property. Both turned to look in the direction of the sound. Hawg then faced Solow again.

Jack Sullivan cursed the distant sound of the Harleys as they echoed in the night. He walked up his drive, let off by a friend from the pub on the south side of town. Before he walked into his house, Jack relieved himself by the Chinese bushes Betty was always on him to trim before it was time. The resonance of the bikers annoyed him, but it also triggered a few memories of his youth. He once undertook hanging out at the Green Parrot tavern with that one bad assed biker, what was his name? Big Edward? Ed wasn't about a cult of personality and hated wanna-bes. Jack moved on with his life and made something of himself.

He said to no one, "I hear tell you are still around, Ed, leading biker troops and organizing Labor Day raffles for Jerry Lewis telethons."

Once, Jack heard Ed bought a cheap Honda and sold hits to it, five dollars a pop. Harley riders from all over the county and farther away came in to hit the strung-up bike with a sledge to gather money for Jerry's kids.

His mind still buzzed from the call he received from Douglas White. Even though Jack had tied one on, the story about the kids and the monster came through clearly. He wasn't drunk enough to buy it, but Doug White sounded disturbed, even if he kept his head about him.

"Stupid rednecks," he muttered, shaking off. He gaped at his pants and saw a few dried spots. He swore again, angry that he must've dribbled earlier in the night. He hated the idea of being seen like that in public.

"Here, here," a voice said from the shadows of his home.

Startled, Jack was near to pissing on his pants again when he snapped, "Who's there? Show yourself, fucking punk!"

"Calm yourself, Mr. Sullivan," the coy voice drawled as the figure stepped into the porch light. "I'm not one of your subordinates to talk down to."

"Then who the fuck are you?" Jack said, his voice bordering on a growl.

"You can call me Roberts," the name said calmly. "I'm from Cicero."

Jack's face drained of color and he fell silent. The eyes of the man in his yard seemed striped like a reptile. Jack blinked, writing this off to the effect of the tequila shooters.

Roberts said, "Mr. Huxtable and I are trying to hash out an arrangement for a lost shipment of goods. I didn't want to disturb you with a phone call so I decided to do it in person."

"What's any of that to do with me?"

"Please don't insult me, Mr. Sullivan. Your hands are far from clean in the distribution phase of these operations. I am here to remind you of your duty and to make sure Hux follows through with his promise."

"What did he promise you?"

Roberts grinned. His teeth shone bleach white in the moonlight and glow from the carport. "That is something you may ask him, something about a scapegoat. However, you will make sure he delivers so I can face my superior with a smile."

Jack swallowed and said in a balanced tone, "I'll see it works out."

"Good." Roberts turned to the shadows again. "I'd hate for anything bad to befall your family."

"Me, too."

"Your daughter?"

Jack's mind was ablaze; fear for his teenaged girl burst in his thoughts. His anger rose, blood pounding in his temples at the idea of this swine threatening his daughter. His hands flexed, for they grew hungry for the puke's throat. All of his years behind a desk hadn't dulled his abilities so much that he couldn't take out a skinny drug courier.

"Yeah? What of her?"

Robert's said, "Forget her, Mr. Sullivan. It's your son I will rape if this fails. You copy, good buddy?"

The mocking tone of the man from Cicero echoed in his ears longer than the sound of the Harleys. At least the noise from the bikers faded at last.

Jack Sullivan's world twisted and he cursed himself for ever getting involved with these people. "So easy at first," he said to no one, thinking of how his desire to control everything led to his actions dominating the drug dealers in the town. It took a little bit of thought to dictate to these little fools and the rewards were good. His retirement home, condo timeshare in Florida and other vacations were lavish due to this bit of control. Never did he plan on any of it coming back to him.

He vowed not to let them make a fool of him and that Hux...he'd make sure it all worked out.

CHAPTER SEVEN

Executions

Hux fell in line behind Big Ed as the biker convoy followed Elias. As usual on his ride, Hux felt stronger. He wasn't certain how his plans would be affected by this silly action, but he felt staying near to Ed would be best. Certain that the other bikers were armed, be it a knife, gun, or some other implement, he felt safe behind this small army out to do terror.

The old man Elias drove well enough, and never once tried to shake the gaggle of bikers that trailed him. Elias went out on Route 66 then cut across country. His slow, fixed tempo aped a man followed by the police. On occasion, he veered over the striped line, but made the correction fast. The bikers carried on, never slackening in their slow pursuit.

Hux could imagine what a few of the men had in mind for Elias, but wagered Big Ed would stop them before things got out of hand. He wondered why Ed let the stupid pursuit carry on. Perhaps Ed wanted to see what the exercise would yield. Hux needed Ed, for a bit…but needed his scapegoat bad.

Even in the cool night air, Hux fought to suppress the nervous tremors in his pelvis. Ever since the attack by the creature, he couldn't sit right. The pain throbbed, but usually faded. His own macho bravado refused to let the violation go. The smoke helped but no matter how much he dulled the pain to his ass, the pain inside his head couldn't be so easily doused. Hux had to have revenge on the beast somehow, but his mind focused on matters at hand. Sure, the drug dealers would kill him in time, no matter how much he sacrificed to their ego. Hux kept after his plan to sacrifice Big Ed.

When Elias stopped at his trailer on the edge of Solow's property, the dozen bikers lined up and left their lights blazing on the truck. Elias climbed out of the cab and wobbled in his steps. He turned to face the ten men and three women who had dismounted from the bikes in front of Hux and Ed. One of the men held a length of chain in his right hand. One of the women spun a tiny automatic pistol in her right hand. The last two stayed seated, watching.

"Ed," Hux said quietly. "This is pretty dim-witted."

"What is it you know, old man?" Tyler sneered, blonde hair waving as he thrashed his arms. "Tell us about the pig-man."

Kimmi Jo climbed off the back of a Harley and screeched loudly, "Come along, Elias, we know how to get talk outta you. Don't we all?"

Elias vacillated once, then planted his feet and shouted, "I don't know nothing, and you all should get along home." But his gaze toward the big house acres away made them all shout his denial down. They cursed him, cussed his pleas down until the old man dropped his hands to his sides.

One of the more portly bikers grabbed Elias by the right arm, shook him and said, "Yeah? Is that where he is from? Tell us more, old fart."

From out of the saddle bags of a Harley came a round object. The blonde biker, Tyler, held it and exclaimed, "I got it here, fellas! This is something he will understand!"

Hux put a hand to his beard and rubbed down once as he recognized the rope spool. The bikers shoved the old man back and forth, taunting him as Tyler tied a knot. Tyler looked at Big Ed and winked.

Big Ed said nothing. Arms folded across his chest, the big man just watched.

When they put the noose around Elias' neck, the old man fought them. He kicked a bald biker in the crotch. The man, nicknamed Johnny Atlas due to his washboard stomach and huge biceps, went down to the ground. Elias swung his arms, bloodied the nose of another biker, but they were too many. One of the women giggled as she produced a pair of handcuffs and secured Elias' hands behind his back.

Hux commented, "Kinky bitch. I bet those are the ones she used on me."

Ed boomed in with great authority, "Tell us what ya know, Elias, and this stops now."

Tyler tossed the rope over the branch of a silver oak tree as Elias said, "You know better, Ed. I won't betray my family."

"Solow isn't your family," Big Ed reminded him, the sound of his voice cutting the frenzy of the bikers down a bit. "You ain't from around here."

Johnny Atlas, still careening from the shot to his nuts, snapped, "If Solow gave a shit, wouldn't he come down here and help your sorry ass?"

Noose tight around his neck, Elias calmed and replied, "The Lord provides." Then he smiled.

Hux never felt so cold as the feeling that smile awarded him. His body shook and he gripped his brake to stop his hand from shaking so much. His mind thought of his gun, but he never reached for it.

Elias gazed down at them all and said with a smile. "It's too late to stop it now, boys."

There was no cry, no warning, and no way to comprehend what was coming when Hawg struck the first biker. Tusks deep in the kidneys of the man in leathers, Hawg lifted him up fast and thrust the screaming body into one of the women. The twin jets of blood from this dying biker bathed the hands of Kimmi Jo Patrick. She gawked at her crimson hands, perplexed, before her wide eyes took in what happened next.

Two bikers died instantly when Hawg grabbed each by the head and pulped their skulls together. Faster than a man clapping his hands, Hawg was through with them. His expanding claws gray with brains, he howled, his screech so metallic it made Hux's hair stand up. The beast leapt forward, his momentum knocking the bloody handed woman and two other bikers down as he landed before the blonde man, Tyler. Claws on Tyler's biceps, Hawg drove tusks into the man's neck. The beast then wrenched his head back. Tyler's head came free of his neck and geysers of blood spewed up, poking up into the night a few times as his heart gave its last punches at life. Hawg twisted and the head flew from the tusks, bouncing off the front fender of Big Ed, smearing blood and gray matter on his wide white wall tire.

A couple of the bikers moved to mount up, but they ran too close to Hawg's stride. One stumbled, trying to get his leg over the bike. The other fumbled with his saddlebag, but in his panic, dropped the gun stored there. Seizing the left arm of one of these fleeing men, Hawg ripped the limb free and slapped the raw arm into the face of the other man mounting up. The biker who lost his arm screamed, gaping down at the blood spurting from his shoulder. Fingers in the blood, the biker cried out, as if patting the wound would make it better. Though the man Hawg struck with the limb clutched his face, dealing with the pain of a broken jaw, he soon lost all worry as Hawg swiped at his head awkwardly, opening up the back of his cranium. From under his 'do-rag, his brains made their exit, staining the Harley tank top bought in Woodstock, Illinois.

While that biker fell forward and his bike thrashed over to his left side, Big Ed and Hux fired up their Harleys. Ed pulled his gun, but the pandemonium of running people didn't provide him with a clear shot. A few of the men pulled knives, but faltered at the moment of truth and paid the price.

They started to pull away as Johnny Atlas made it to his bike. When a woman tried to get on the back, Johnny pushed her off and into the arms of Hawg. Screaming and crazed, the woman fought Hawg like a cat on fire, clawing, punching, and biting with all she had. Like he handled a beehive, Hawg picked her up in the air, only touching her sparingly, and smashed her to the ground. The slam took her wind out, long enough for Hawg to leap up and pounce on her back with his hind hooves. Her shoulder blades snapped and she gagged, failing in her attempt to rise up and run. Hawg turned, bellowed, and went low enough to the ground in his motion to smell her backside. Atlas roared away from the property after Ed and Hux.

"Go, go!" Big Ed yelled at his men as they followed Hux off the land.

Hawg took a step toward Elias and reached out toward him. He yanked Elias close to him, turned him around. Elias closed his eyes as Hawg gripped his wrists and snapped the cuffs.

Elias pulled off the noose, eyes twinkling at Hawg.

Red eyes flaring, Hawg looked away from him and toward the escaping bikes, now joined by the fourth rider. He started to follow, but one of the bikers he had knocked asunder started to rise up. This man wore brass knuckles on his right hand and swung at Hawg. He struck the creature hard in the solar plexus and Hawg roared in pain. The dire right swung again, but Hawg grabbed the fist with his left claw. He extended the man's arm and bit into his wrist. With a growl, he snapped off the man's hand at the forearm, sending him to his buttocks.

The man screamed, grabbing his ruined wrist. Hawg fell to all fours and charged, tusks digging into the man's thighs. He bit through the man's jeans and into his groin. The deep yell of the man changed in tenor as the gelding was complete. Not done, Hawg rooted, his tusks carrying in further, his teeth grinding into the man's pelvis and lower abdomen. The biker choked and lost his ability to yell as Hawg burrowed on, through his intestines, liver, and under his ribcage. Hawg split his sternum and bit into the man's heart.

Hawg rose up, tusks and face bathed in crimson, eyes on the fleeing bikers.

And he was off, loping after them in long strides.

Betty knew better than to ruffle Jack when he'd been drinking. She entrusted him with space and let him get a shower before she said anything. Content to lie in bed and read, Betty played her cards close.

"The police took everything they could off the Buick today."

"That's good," Jack said as he sat on the bed clad in his bathrobe. He directed his eyes to the floor and seemed lost in thought.

"They sprayed it down as best they could. I had Trish run it through the wash a few hours ago."

He nodded. "Good." He half smiled, knowing Betty did this to quell his anger. "Thanks."

"Though Doug took this, that other cop Matt returned it to me." She held up a plastic baggy with the small dog collar in it.

"He said it wasn't part of the crime scene and was just trash. He said I could throw it away if I wanted to."

His face listless, Jack took the bag and asked, "How's Jack Jr. doing?"

Betty turned under the covers and said, "Fine. Sleeping like an angel."

Jack stared at the collar. "Buddy. Who the fuck is Buddy?"

"Common enough name for a dog."

"I suppose."

Jack then related some of the tales he'd heard that night from the cops and how Andrew White's son was nearly killed by something. It all sounded crazy to him, he told her. He then silently cursed the echoing bikers in the night.

"Jordan White," Betty said and fell deep in thought. "He must be getting big by now. I saw him in the paper a few years back with that show dog Schnauzer of his. It scored well at the 4-H Fair last year."

Jack lay down and said, "What? Jordan's dog? What of it?"

"Just a little irony, honey. I think that dog was named Buddy."

Eyes focused on the ceiling, a smile played on Jack's lips as he said, "You don't say?"

Andrew sat on the edge of Jordan's bed and listened as his son said, "It was weird, dad, but I am not lying."

"I'm just glad you are all right, Jordan. Sorry we got crossed up today."

"Hope you don't get busted for leaving work."

Andrew waved a hand at the SPIDER-MAN wallpaper as if to disregard his workplace. "That place doesn't matter. You do. I'm sorry I wasn't there today."

Jordan peeked past his father, like he could see the monster on his ceiling. "If we weren't so little. That thing would've got us. He couldn't get in the mine. Better you weren't there."

"Yeah. Still, I'd have blown its damned head off for trying to get you."

"Are they hunting it? The cops?"

Andrew nodded. "I think they've issued a call to all the

city, county, and state cops to start a bigger search. In daylight they're going to get the choppers and the crop duster guys out, too."

"It slept in the crypt," Jordan reminded him. "Maybe it'll go back."

"Maybe. I think Doug's guys are watching that place now."

"Good."

"Better get some sleep, son. You don't have to go to school tomorrow."

That idea made Jordan smile as he rolled over. "Night dad."

"Night Jordan. Love you."

"Love you, too."

"Say your prayers, son."

Jordan lowered his voice and said, "Now I lay me down to sleep, I pray the Lord my soul to keep. If I should die before I wake, I pray the Lord my soul to take. God bless Mommy, Daddy, Gramma, Uncle Doug, Aunt Brenda, Jacob, Nathan, Gramma Faulks and Buddy. Amen."

Andrew went to his room and held his wife.

Mr. Solow stood in his yard, looking at the police cruiser and the dead cop on top of it. Alex's sphincter released and excrement ran down his pant legs and onto the hood of the car. Some dribbled in the dents made by Hawg's hooves. He sighed, not concerned about the weak-willed cop. It bothered Solow that Alex, in his drunken rage, had correctly guessed about the origin of Hawg. How long until the Sheriff followed suit? Solow didn't know, but he refused to get upset about it all. He still had a life to lead and responsibilities.

He then gazed across the expanse of his property at the trailer of his hired man. The screams and reports from the Harleys dissipated at last.

With a sigh, Solow took another drink and went into his house. Though he felt like another drink, he resisted the urge. Solow went to the bathroom, drained himself, and washed his hands.

Then, like any good citizen, he called the police.

Hawg didn't know if he could catch the bikes in a flat out run, but he saw their brake lights and scanned the field. He saw where they were bound, to cross the field and head back to the route by the train trestle. Hawg loped on a diagonal path, slicing the distance between them, placing himself ahead of them by far.

The screaming metal machines worried Hawg. He didn't fear them, for avoiding their touch was no problem as their movements proved linear. Nevertheless, if he stood in their way, they could easily outmaneuver him. Rather than try his hand at this fate, Hawg decided on a more instinctive course of action.

Near to where the black top ended as the road forked toward the trestle opening, Hawg saw a large culvert. Though this tube wasn't big enough for him to fit through, the hole gave him the idea for the biker's fate. Their machines ringing in his ears, Hawg slammed into the side of the ditch near the culvert, digging like mad, burrowing for all he was worth. Fistfuls of dirt at his sides, Hawg rooted with his tusks and mouth, more of a machine than those that rumbled toward him.

Hux relaxed some, figuring that they'd outdistanced the beast. His vindication running high, Big Ed would surely be on his side and fall in with his plans. Though he wanted the beast dead, Hux thought of how he sat and watched it rip into the bikers. Never once did he draw his gun and shoot. Never once did he move to fight the creature. No, he ran away. Throat heavy, eyes misty, Hux needed a drink.

Once he waved at Big Ed in a friendly way, seeking reassurance. Ed mouthed "Fuck off" and that was that.

The four survivors blared on down the road, determined to get back to Route 66 and the Green Parrot at the very least. Hux didn't know what Ed would think of for his next course of action, but like the rest, he was sure fleeing and surviving was at the top of his agenda. He glanced back at Ed, Johnny Atlas, and Cody Greenwell. None of them watched the road consistently. All eyes hunted for Hawg.

Hux was the first to spot Hawg as he popped out into the

ditch, as if he'd just come from under the road itself. Terror gripped Hux's heart, but there was little he could do to warn the others. He doubted his senses at first, thinking his mind brought forward the horror that haunted him.

He was also the only bike to make it cleanly over the area before the blacktop started to buckle.

CHAPTER EIGHT

Hawg Wild

Micki opened her eyes when she heard the roar of the motorcycles. The darkness and severe cold duped her into thinking death was there at last. But the horrid sounds forking into her ears and the pain that shot across her rigid frame told her otherwise. The weeds, the pinpricks of agony that raced all over her body, all of these remained and stung worse than before. There was no way to shut it out or keep it away. The pain in her joints felt icy, but the ruined sections of her skin burned at the edges.

Her mind murky, Micki felt drugged and started to lose a sense of herself. Unable to concentrate, only seeking a way to be free of the experience, she again cried out. Immediately, she closed her mouth, afraid that the creature would return yet again, somewhere near to the loud bikes. The reality of the beast was clear enough in her mind, even if she started to forget much about herself.

At first, she thought it all a terrible nightmare, and she would wake up in a bed someplace. Her mind bore down to focus on where that would be. Images of parents and a house bubbled in her mind, but the heat and violence of her last day smashed these roads to freedom away.

Soon, Micki thought that her slayer had returned to rape her once again. No, the pain was too vivid and the smells too potent for it to be hallucination. The comfy bed and smells of her mother's potpourri cooker faded out.

It really happened, she wailed in her mind, *the bastard returned again and used me.* She heard the cries of children and then it all happened again, not as bad as before, for the creature never tried to kill her...only to use her for sex again.

When she heard the roar of the Hawg in the night with the host of Harleys, she could only think of turning invisible.

The rear wheel of Hux's motorcycle dipped as if he had hit a pothole. Panic set in as Hux turned his head and slackened his speed.

Though Big Ed followed him at a close clip, the big man experienced both tires dropping on the sinking pavement. He handled the dipping bike like a bronco and easily rode over the sudden flaw in the road, pulling up and finding level ground again. His balance askew, though, Big Ed hit his brakes and nearly wiped out.

The men behind him didn't fare as well. Johnny Atlas turned his throttle hard, picking the wrong time to increase his speed. The spin of his tires and the abrupt drop of the pavement caused him to twist sideways. He saw Big Ed stop beyond him and turned his forks to avoid him. The bike roared as it dropped and slid sideways, flattening out. It hit the lip of the dropping pavement, exhaust pipes connecting hard. Atlas' Harley flipped over. Johnny stayed with his bike, his left leg breaking as the first skid occurred, then flopping over and smashing on his right side with the bike. His shoulder separated and Johnny's right forearm snapped, still clutching the throttle. His leg pinned under the bike, Atlas' pants and skin ripped off as the momentum of the crash took him farther up the road, past Big Ed.

Johnny's wreck compounded Cody Greenwell's, who wobbled from side to side under the road's change in elevation, but couldn't avoid an impact with Atlas' motorbike once he cleared the depressed area. Cody's front tire smashed into the pipes under the cycle and the rider went airborne, ass over elbows, clearing the wreckage, but moving at a high rate of speed. Cody hit the pavement at over fifty miles an hour, his ass and back taking the impact. Cody skidded for several yards, screaming as he went, his shouts of pain joining the dying engine sound.

Big Ed sped away from the crashed cycles. In the moon-light and from their headlights, he saw the long trail left by the last biker on the pavement. A mixture of denim, leather, and skin coated the road. The cool night air made steam rise from the fresh wounds. Cody's right hand vibrated, reaching for his leg. Hux saw the handle of a weapon there, but the hand never made it to the goal.

Hux revved his throttle, pointed at Hawg with his left hand and shouted, "Fucking thing burrowed under the road! Let's get out of here!"

While Hux started to move away, he hesitated, for Big Ed didn't join him.

Ed reached into his saddle bags as Hawg leapt onto the road. The beast made for Johnny Atlas, helpless under the sputtering Harley. Atlas shouted in pain, crying out and sobbing. Hawg snorted and stalked around him, then reached down to pull the bike off him. Not used to the weight of the machine, Hawg lifted it a few feet with his left claw before it slipped from his grip, crashing on the suffering man again.

Hux shouted at Ed, "What are you doing?"

Hawg looked up from Johnny. He focused in on Hux and Ed.

Ed pulled a chain with enormous links from his saddlebag. He held the chain loose and stared Hawg down.

"C'mon, ya sonofabitch," Ed said loudly, clear in his threat. "Ya think I'm gonna run away and die like a bitch, yer wrong."

Hawg squared his shoulders to Big Ed and roared, taking up the challenge.

Ed swung the chain around once, clearly drawing Hawg's attention. That's when he lifted his other hand, holding a snub-nosed revolver. "You lose, dickhead," Ed said and fired.

The report of the gun was loud enough to make Hawg jump, but the bullet Ed fired struck Hawg's right side. In motion to the left of them, Hawg squealed in reaction to the blow. Again, Ed fired, trying to strike Hawg once more. Unsure if he'd hit him, Ed fired a third shot as the beast dropped into the ditch.

"I winged him," Ed declared, happy with his act, but not celebrating. "Shit fire and save the matches!"

Hawg leapt back on the road, springing into the air high above Ed's bike. Ed fired again, but missed. There was no way to stop Hawg from landing on him, but Ed made a desperate bid for survival. He let the gun go as Hawg hit him, and stretched the chain out. The force of the beast took Ed from his bike and pinned him to the pavement. However, Ed held the chain up, stretching it across the maw of the screaming creature, muzzling it for a moment.

Hux watched as Hawg convulsed on Big Ed, trying to get a better position. However, his back hooves slid on the grim ejecta trail of the last biker to crash. Hux felt the hate for the beast, even if he wanted Big Ed dead, he couldn't hold back any longer. As Ed flailed under the creature, Hux pulled out his derringer and fired at Hawg. Both shots sounded puny and never hit the mark. They did get Hawg's attention and he pulled away from Big Ed and faced Hux.

Though Hux turned his bike, preparing to flee, he never left as the sight on the road riveted him in place. Just as Hawg was going to bound after him, Ed unraveled the chain and swung it like a rope. The chain wrapped Hawg's ankles and the beast tripped, slamming to the pavement with a screech. The steel tusks clanged on the pavement as Hawg's head bounced.

Hawg rolled over and over, nearly slipping in the ditch, kicking, and trying to free himself from the chain.

Ed was on all fours, trying to find the gun he had dropped. Swearing, he picked up his bike instead. He swung a leg over it and hit the starter. Luckily, it fired up fast. Ed rode over to the struggling beast and reached down. Hux was amazed at the grace and luck of the move Ed performed. He grabbed the end of the chain and looped it over the hitch on the back of his full dresser. The tactic was sloppy and Hux figured it would never work, but he read Ed's plans. Ed cranked his throttle and the Harley went forward. The chain extended and Hawg went with him. The beast screamed as if afire in the deepening night as Big Ed dragged the beast after him. Hux was right with them, also fleeing. The feat only lasted about fifty yards as the chain came loose off the hitch, unable to carry the weight of the beast.

They paused, looked back and beheld Hawg rolling in the

road, screaming. Hawg glistened wet in the moonlight. Covered in blood, either from the gunshot or the dragging, Hawg's screams turned to howls of rage.

Ed's fist hit his tank and he said, "Piss on this. Go!"

Both bikes rumbled on and they headed toward Route 66.

Micki put her fingers in her ears. She just wanted it to stop, the noise and her life. The screams, the echoes of the bikes, all of it sounded like chamber music in Hell's waiting room. Would such a place be better than this? She was unsure but longed to be free of this insane state of purgatory.

The sounds separated and the motorbikes seemed to get closer, but the beast still screamed, farther away.

She rolled in the weeds and hid as best she could.

In her ears rang the words of a man, his words full of threats and anger. His tone was meant to instruct, control, and protect. He told her bad things happened when one was bad. If you sowed to the whirlwind, really bad things came back to haunt you.

Eyes shut tight, Micki knew she'd been bad. She didn't hate God for his judgment. Never before had she been so close to the Devil and his kisses, though.

Such pain was alien to Hawg. His right side ached and the skin on his back felt raw, like a host of bugs fed there. Blood ran off his back, down his sore buttocks and from Hawg's side. He held his claw over the gun wound, trying to make the hurt stop. Loud grunts came from his innards and burning pain was all he understood.

Up on his hooves, he noted the wrecked bikes as he tested his limbs. His legs still worked well. Hawg stretched his limbs and thought nothing was broken. Tusks out, he bellowed at his victory over the steel machines. Hawg walked to the scene where he had made the pavement dip low. He noted the last biker, unconscious on the road, then walked over to Johnny Atlas. Still awake, the man glowered at Hawg with tear-soaked eyes.

Left hand out as if to ward him off, Johnny croaked, "God, no...."

Hawg dropped his head down and bit off Johnny's fingers. Chewing fast, the pinkie fell out and struck Atlas' knee.

The pain saturating his body made Hawg feel tired and empty. After he spit out Johnny's wedding ring and chewed some more, Hawg felt ravenous. Johnny still begged and cried.

But not for long.

"It's been a helluva night, Mr. Solow," Doug White told the old man as the floodlight from this cruiser illuminated Alex's dead body.

"Sorry to call you out, but I didn't know what else to do," Solow said, still holding the wine glass in his hand. It was full again.

Doug nodded and eyed the glass. "Got another one of those, sir?"

"I bet you could use a stiff belt right now."

As he shook his head at the sight of his dead officer, Doug said, "Several, but it'll have to wait. Duty calls like a banshee this night, sir."

A second cruiser stopped at the scene, lights ablaze. Matt exited the vehicle and pointed toward the spot where other lights flashed on the edge of the property. "Doug, you won't believe what's over there."

"Try me."

Matt studied the pulverized head of his friend and said, "Uh, well, yeah. More of the same."

Hands on his waist, Doug bit the toothpick in his mouth and faced Solow. "And would you say it was some kind of monster? Are you sure of what it looked like?"

Solow sipped the wine and shrugged. "Douglas, I wouldn't know what to call it. The thing was really big."

"I can't believe I'm asking this. You know your pig flesh. Did it appear like a pig man to you?"

After he imparted a doubtful stare, Solow took a second sip of wine and said, "It's awful dark out here even with the yard lights. It just looked like a really big fella to me. Like a wild man, crazy in its eyes. It 'taint possible to cross breed a hog and a human being, Douglas."

"I know that, but I'm going on what the neighbor kids said."

"Kids," Solow chuckled, and rubbed a tired left eye. "Whoever or whatever it was never spoke a word, so maybe it is some nut case escaped from the Kankakee crazy house."

As he cracked his knuckles, Doug said, "They shut most of that mental home down, Mr. Solow. I think it's all offices now, but I'll follow every lead."

"You do that."

"Going to have to get a detailed statement from you, sir. Probably best to come with me anyway. I don't know how safe it is out here."

"I understand. I'll tell you everything I know. Damn terrible world now, Douglas. It is different from the world I grew up in. Life is cheap to these people."

Doug felt a sermon coming on so he said to Matt. "Elias up there?"

Matt nodded. "Luella is still alive, too. Some of the usual suspects from the Green Parrot didn't fare so well."

"Better take them in for their own safety, at least for tonight."

"Way ahead of ya, but Luella doesn't want to go."

Doug said, "I'll talk to her."

Once on Route 66, the two bikers opened it up. Their speeds cranked over a hundred miles an hour. As usual, when they wanted to find the police, they couldn't.

The trip was fast and terminated at the Green Parrot. At the mock hitching post outside, they saw several more motorcycles.

"Gang's all here," Hux said lightly as they killed their Harleys.

Big Ed leered at him. Rage filled his voice as he said, "You fucking pussy, I oughtta kill you myself. You'd got a hard on if that thing'd a killed me off, huh?"

Hux held his ground. "I tried to shoot it, man. Have you ever seen anything like that before? How'd I know what to do?"

Ed reminded him, "I knew what to do. That's why you're a punk fuckwad wanna-be and I lead." Eyes narrowing at Hux, he added, "Anything to say? Ain't no one here to see it, but I'll still stomp your ass into a mud hole and walk it dry. I should use my pig sticker in on my chair. That would be fitting, huh?"

Hux said nothing. He let Ed go inside first and stayed by the row of bikes. From out of his leather jacket Hux pulled several plastic bags. Though appearing empty, Hux had planted enough residues to be convincing. He then text messaged Mr. Roberts and invited him over to see what Ed held in his saddlebags.

He closed the phone, disgusted with himself. He'd planned to kill Big Ed and plant the evidence so Roberts could say all was kosher with the world. Roberts wanted a sacrifice. He wanted Hux to kill for him. It was all a power play.

On the way into the bar, Hux felt cold, different than before. He didn't know if he would ever be the same again. There he had his chance at revenge. He could've used a bigger gun on Hawg, but he'd hoped the beast would kill Ed for him. Now, all of his pain came back. The violation, the lack of action, he burned inside, for he had failed again in his eyes.

When he entered the bar, Ed stood telling the tale to a half dozen men and Double D. The man behind the bar said, "Calls came over the scanner out at the Solow place."

"Cops are all over it by now, Double D," Ed affirmed, taking a long neck bottle from the bar and swigging it.

Hux asked, "How long until they come here?" The bar seemed stunned at this idea. "They'll see who is dead. They'll find the guys on the road. Elias will talk. We're in deep shit."

Ed gripped the bar with both hands like he meant to rip it from its moorings. Head down, he said, "No, he won't. Elias won't say shit to the cops, not about us personally. The cops will know where the others hang out, though."

"C'mon, man, get real!" Hux said loudly. "They were gonna string him up. They'll put us away for that."

Head still down, Ed said, "He won't talk. I'm not relying on him being a good ol' boy, either. He knows." Ed's head rose up and his eyes drilled into Hux' face. "That old boy knew that creature was nearby. Didn't ya see him? Did ya see it near him? He wasn't scared and asked, what was it? It was too late to stop it now? Yeah, that ol' sumbitch knows the score."

Hux recalled looking back and seeing Hawg free Elias. The creature snapped the cuffs like they were made of paper. The beast knew Elias.

Ed stared at Hux. "Connecting dots like a motherfucker in your head, huh? Good luck with that, ya fuck."

Double D leaned both meaty hands on the bar and said, "The cops will come here, I'd bet on it, no matter what."

Ed folded his arms across his chest. "I suppose we better clear out then. No use going to jail on drug charges filed in overzealous questioning." He cleared his throat and said, "No way the mayor will keep this one under wraps."

One of the bikers picked up a helmet and said, "Someone's here, outside."

Hux expected it to be Roberts but doubted the man would enter such a place.

The figure outside the Green Parrot was too tall to walk in the front door, anyway.

Though Elias sat in the back of a police cruiser, Luella Goodkind refused to leave her trailer. Her corpulent frame stayed on her couch, her dog Duke at her feet.

"I've lived most of my later years here," Luella told Doug, hand on her Bible. "I'll die here if I have to."

"Ma'am," Doug said gently, hands on his gun-belt. "Please be reasonable."

"I am a reasonable lady," she responded evenly. "You can take me to the station if you can lift me."

The police officers exchanged glances, knowing the enormous woman had them dead to rights. Her smile knew and they all shared a small laugh.

"I'll leave Matthew here to guard the place tonight, all right?"

She nodded and smiled, her teeth dim. "Matthew was a good boy, years ago. He weeded my flowerbeds nice, I am told."

Matt tipped his hat, felt stupid for doing that but said, "You'll be safe with me, Luella."

Luella said, "I don't doubt it."

Doug stepped onto the deck with Matt and said quietly, "Any word out of Elias?"

Matt gestured at the dead bodies and said, "He's pretty sure they all slipped on a banana peel."

The sheriff knelt by Tyler's body and shook his head in disgust. He saw a cigarette still stuck behind Tyler's ear and his mouth watered.

"Why I saved you, I don't know," Roberts told Hux as they stood beside the waters of the quarry.

Hux looked down at his hands. Blood still tinged the edges of his fingernails, though he had wiped much of it on his pants. "Glad you let me in your car and didn't leave me to die with the others."

Roberts knelt by the side of the water and reached out. His hands shaking so, he couldn't get a handful of water to his face. After several tries, he succeeded.

"I've seen men die my entire life," Roberts told him. "I saw my uncle strangled when I was five. I saw a grandson of one of Al Capone's enforcers put a body on a meat hook, alive, and then beat him to death with brass knuckles. I've never seen anything like that scene outside the biker tavern."

"I hope they all die, anyhow," Hux said with no emotion, eyes fixed on the water. "I'd hate to have lived like that."

Roberts washed his face, over and over, eyes shut. No matter how hard he squeezed his eyelids, Roberts couldn't banish the scene outside the Green Parrot.

When he had arrived at the Green Parrot, he almost had passed by, thinking something was up outside the watering hole. Well, it was, or rather down...the neon glow of the beer signs and tavern logo had shown on the tall creature by the hitching posts. Roberts had thought it was a drunken redneck, albeit a big one, dithering outside the building, nude. When his car stopped, he had seen the line of boots up on the hitching post. Six pairs of feet lay up on the long post and the tall being went to work. He had reached down with his sharp claws, tearing into the pants and leather chaps the men on the ground wore. Roberts had frozen in his car at the sight, seeing the tall beast tear the balls off each man, systematically castrating each one, then depositing their sacks into a biker helmet.

The gruesome act graded worse by the fact that each man had awakened as he was gelded. The screams rang in Roberts' ears, a loud shout of agony, suddenly turning sharp. Fingers in his ears, wet, he couldn't scrub the noise free.

Then the beast had left them alive, moving on like it was God's work. He hadn't brained one of the bikers. The creature had gone about its business and filled the helmet, then started back toward the tavern door when Hux had burst out a side window and had run toward the car. Roberts had broken from his shock and they drove away.

"Were there any alive in the bar?" Roberts wondered.

Hux said, "Hawg killed the bartender when he forced the door. Splattered ol' Gunner's head."

"I see. Hawg?"

"As good a name for the thing as any."

"I suppose."

"Big Ed..." Hux mumbled, his voice falling away like the wind dying down.

"What?"

"It was him Hawg wanted, well, him and me I guess as we escaped him at the farm. How he tracked us I'll never know."

"Did this Hawg get your scapegoat, Big Ed?"

"I guess. He went after Hawg with a saber from the wall of the bar. He never drew blood on Hawg, though." Hux almost wept as he said, "Gotta hand it to Ed, he was himself unto death. Hawg bit into his knee, took Ed out low. It was a crush of bodies, but next thing I knew, the guys were all knocked out and Hawg had started to drag them outside."

"How was it you survived?"

Tears sprang to Hux' eyes as he admitted, "I played dead, rolled Ed's lifeless body on top of me. When Hawg went out with two guys to the hitching post, I ran in the shitter and hid. When you showed up, I ran. I busted out the kitchen window and jumped."

Roberts nodded. "No glory in dying for that thing."

Hux nodded, but the tears came again. Over and over, the extractions played out in the man's mind. The claw coming up, the spray of blood and clear fluid, the screams so deep, changing pitch....

CHAPTER NINE

Night and Morning

A ndrew took a call from his brother. He sat up on the bed and listened for a long time, never speaking. He turned the phone off and stared off at the darkened wall. Slowly, Andrew got back into bed. He told Lynne what went on at Solow's and in the territory near them that night.

Lynne snuggled close to him and said, "All that around us and we were none the wiser. God, that's terrible."

He stroked her long hair and said, "Angel of death passed us by, couple times today. I thought I heard the bikers out and about."

"Good night. What's going on out there, really, Drew?"

"Sounds like a crazy killer. It's all so nuts. Doug sang the song from DCFS again, that they will want to review the kids tomorrow."

Lynne's voice lowered and her attitude bristled as she said, "Better they are in their own beds than at some strange place."

"Yeah." Andrew thought of how many guns he kept at his home and felt safe against any intruder. The fact that many died so near to them would abolish sleep for the night, though. "That prick of a mayor, Sullivan, will have a load of crap on his desk in the morning. Hope he gags on it."

His mind afire, Andrew thought of how many times he had failed in life, screwed up at better jobs at work that landed him in his position...thus making sure he was nowhere near Jordan when he really needed him. If the boy had died, it'd have been his fault and Andrew couldn't get that out of his mind.

He struggled to force such thoughts away. This was the life he had now, he told himself, and he'd protect his family better than before.

"What is it, Andrew? I mean, what is this thing?"

"Doug seems to want to believe Solow, who saw it, that it is just a big guy, a lunatic or some such thing. That sounds more plausible than a giant pig-man, no matter what the kids say they saw."

Her fingers drummed on his hairy chest. "That's how he must've looked to the children. Terrible."

"Yeah, I guess."

Lynne was quiet for a few minutes and then said, "Mr. Solow is lucky Alex stopped by when he did. Poor old man, that killer would've made fast work of Solow. Him with no family, wife or kids."

"Yeah."

"Some crazy maniac would've done him in."

"He's probably armed, but so was the cop," Andrew mused, eyes staring at the tiles on the ceiling. "Still, whacked about the bikers at Elias's trailer. Sort of lucky all that commotion drew the killer away from Solow."

Again, Lynne was lost in thought for a time. "I wonder why Solow never married."

"Dunno. My Pa used to think he was injured in the war and couldn't have kids or perform, you know?"

She needled Andrew and said, "You need injured."

"Thanks. Dad never knew for sure. Said Solow used to keep company with an old widow, then another one after she passed on. I think they willed part of their cash to Solow, as they had no family or some such thing. It happens. Folks get lonely when they are old."

"Sad he has no kids or family to pass on his property to."

Andrew thought of the specter of losing Jordan again and shivered. "Yeah. I think he does have relatives down south, Arkansas or Louisiana maybe. When I was about twelve, I recall a trailer coming up from down south with some of his kinfolk along. They brought new stock for the farm."

"How can you recall it so exactly?"

"I was in confirmation and that is about the time they caught John Wayne Gacy in Chicago. I remember Pa and Solow talking about executing Gacy themselves as they built on the big round barn."

"I never knew your dad helped build that barn. I saw it on PBS as part of Illinois events once. I thought it was a hundred years old."

"They used parts of a crib and barn razed by a tornado. It's an old practice. Yeah, after they brought in the new stock, Solow, his family, Pa, and my older brothers helped to build it. I generally screwed around on the farm, but I watched, fetched iced tea and nails, the usual."

"New stock all the way from Louisiana? I wonder if he had more calves back then."

He said to Lynne, "Not good to keep breeding the same bloodlines together. You get bad yields in any animal, I guess, if ya do that long enough."

"I'm glad Luella is all right."

"Yeah."

Lynne half laughed. "Gramma told me Luella was the fat lady in the circus years ago and she wasn't from around here. Wonder how she ever landed here?"

"She's been a fixture out there on the Solow place as long as I know," Andrew said. "My older brother Thomas said she went blind as a kid, drinking grain alcohol."

"I never knew that. Wonder what the connection is to Solow, why he lets her live out there?"

His hand rested on her back as he said, "I think he claims Christian charity or some such thing. I dunno. Never asked him."

Lynne raised her head and asked, "Doesn't Luella have a Cajun accent?"

Hawg hated town. It was loud and he felt as if the buildings would collapse on him at any moment. Even though the structures he passed by were small, he worried they would suddenly join as one, form walls and then crush him down. The open spaces were better. Glad he'd found the bikers who escaped at the edge of the small town, Hawg happily returned to the rural fields. When he regarded the stone streets of Montrose, all he saw was Hell. When he turned his head and the country loomed, home wasn't far away.

Something tugged at the edge of his mind, as if the job was not complete, but he buried this idea and went where it felt safe. He kept off the streets and jogged in the gravel by the worn road. Hawg traveled near a huge metal building that housed several trucks and then past a tractor repair business. The orange glow of the parking lot to Ambrose Brothers Printing caught his eyes, but he kept on, searching after the open spaces.

The night deepened and he grew tired. Sleep would come soon, but he had one more duty to perform. Unable to run on all fours because of the load he carried, Hawg jogged along slower than usual. A few times, he went down and ran badly on three limbs. He abandoned this idea and returned to his hind legs.

Pain coursed over his body, burning down his back, worse in his side. Hawg needed rest and a chance to feel better. Still, he persevered.

The flashing lights of the men with guns littered the country night. The moonlight set a glow across the barren fields, but the police drove several of the country roads. On these vehicles long spotlights flashed across the fields, probing the plowed lands for a figure. Hawg comprehended they were out in force, probably with police from neighboring counties, looking for him. Overhead, he spotted a helicopter with a spotlight beam scanning the waterways. This was an easy enough object to avoid. It was slow and far from him. The light beam made it easier to evade.

With his pace steady, legs and side aching, Hawg made his way back toward the Solow farm. His body hurt so from the gun wound, but the bleeding had ceased. Hawg touched the tender area around the place where the big biker had shot him. Pain reared up again as his claw neared the spot. He wondered if the bullet had passed through him or left a fragment in there. Hawg stopped, rested a few minutes to let the new pain he caused himself subside, and then kept on, his velocity never slackening.

His wound brought a different emotion to Hawg: fear. His anger and energy had suppressed the feeling for the most part. He couldn't deny the sensation and only wanted to be closer to home the nearer to the forefront of his mind the emotion came.

But when he slowed close to Elias' trailer, he saw police cars and ambulances still working the scene.

Over at Luella's, a policeman sat on her deck, watching the scene at Elias' home. The area by Elias' trailer was cleared out for the most part, so Hawg stayed in the distant waterway and waited. He held the biker helmet and watched the helicopter in the distance.

Though weary in his body, Hawg faced in the direction of where he had slept the night before. The helicopter hovered in that area of the country, shooting its beam down on the railroad tracks near the graveyard. Frustrated, Hawg stuck to a long tree line that divided the fields. Certain he was covered, Hawg watched Luella's house and waited.

After a while, he decided to cross-country again, toward where he had slept before.

Micki heard distant rumbles and dived for the deep ditch by Route 66. Her thoughts of Hawg boiled in her brain as she discovered the open culvert. She wished the edge of old 66 would open up and swallow her, anything to hide her from the monster. The culvert would have to do. Micki's mind snapped into lucidity every so often, but her waking moments still clogged with bleary visions of a distorted world. Nothing showed right and sharp to her hazy eyes. The moonlight glowed green and fuzzy. The highway tilted and threatened to discharge her off the planet. She wondered how cars would drive on a diagonal path. Afraid of the beast returning for her, she hid. Once down in the culvert in the deep ditch beside the road, she turned over on the cold stone tunnel and the pain increased.

She felt worse sensations than stabbing pains from her ruined sex. Tiny taps, like children poking her, that's what it was—no, she felt the sensations like rivulets of fluid, but they had smaller paths. A swipe of her right hand sent some of this feeling away, and brought the realization that a host of bugs infested her crotch. Grubs, ladybugs, and a few things she couldn't identify in her weary state tormented her further as she let out a deep sob. Too afraid to cry out, she suffered and hid from the distant rumbles. The pain from the cold surface was too much so she crawled outside again. The weeds felt better on her, but the pain was still there. Micki felt exposed and afraid, though. She could feel the monster.

Never would she experience that again…she had to hide.

Again, she prayed. Prayed very hard.

As if in response, a beam of light struck the ground near her. At last, her mind burned, *deliverance!*

But this elation was short lived. The beam of light from the heavens moved on, traveling away from her. By the time she got to her knees to wave her arms, the craft overhead was gone.

No tears came. Her arms still up, she looked across the way toward the trestle.

In the gap of the beams stood Hawg, holding a helmet like a bucket. He stared right at her in the ditch near the culvert.

Jack Sullivan didn't get much sleep, either. Calls from the local police, the county cops, and then the State Troopers kept him up all night. The Sheriff proved apt at covering the bases and even coordinating a search effort for this killer and missing persons.

He regretted taking on the job of Mayor of the small town then. Certainly, it lavished him with more power – a grip on county affairs, and more pots to poke his fingers at – but this was proving a hassle. Who could've foreseen such a nightmare unfolding? He kept telling himself there had to be a simple explanation for it all. If a deranged killer was butchering people, Jack reasoned it had killed the drug mules Mr. Roberts wanted so badly. But there was no way to know that and it only made matters worse.

Jack swore in his mind many times over it all. What were the chances of some lunatic escaping and slaughtering people in his town?

Doug assured him, "There are no cases of escaped maniacs that I know of. I'll keep looking."

Jack offered him on the phone, "So, maybe some peckerwood up by Godly had a kid go rogue. Ever think of that?"

Godly was a town of yellowhammers. In fact, this was common knowledge as far back as before the First World War.

Doug replied, "We are keeping our eyes open. I'll learn what makes this fucker tick by autopsy, sir."

While Doug White, and of course, his drunken loser of a brother, Andrew, weren't high on his list of favorite folks, that line made Jack smile. Doug was passionate and a good egg. He'd kill the bastard if he caught him and not string matters out with a trial or a media circus from out of town.

"It's a helluva thing, Jack," Doug said with a gentle voice, seldom addressing him in such a way. "If you'd seen the bodies, not just my deputy Alex, but the others, and the bikers at the Green Parrot. You'd shoot the fucker, too."

"Do your best, Douglas. I don't live far away from this either. All BS aside, it has to be done."

When he turned the phone off, Jack cursed the hour. Jack decided to shower and get ready for the day. He let his wife sleep. She needed rest. Though her bout with cervical cancer was a year in the past, Betty still was weaker for the trial. Jack pondered for a moment an old fear of his, that his catting around had brought home the HPV virus and set her illness in motion. For a moment, his world of control tilted and there was something in his stable world he couldn't get a grip on. He squeezed his eyes shut tightly, banishing these thoughts. Betty was his foundation, even if she took longer to put her face on than she used to. Surely, he couldn't have been responsible for her near-death trial. Jack wouldn't allow that his weakness threatened her. His anger rose, boiling that his bad choices could lead to a threat to his son. In any case, he required action. His idle hands needed to act, to make a stab at his world to right it in his mind.

After he turned the coffee on, he thought of Andrew White.

"Mr. Militia, smart mouth, flying a flag upside down on the anniversary of Waco." He ground his teeth and said, "Buddy. Heh. You shit on the wrong guy's car, you dope. I'll award you plenty of time to spend with those kids of yours."

As he showered, he thought of how he would massage Andrew's attendance records to make sure he had a legal basis to fire him that day.

After Hawg finished with Micki, he rolled on his backside by the culvert entrance. Her hindquarters sticking out, he shoved her rump in farther to banish Micki from his sight. Hawg's limbs felt tired and his side ached more. He reached in the tube and ripped her tattered half shirt from her. Hawg then pressed this over his wounded side. He gave a low growl as the pain shot through him again. The wound had started to scab, but the pain troubled him. Hawg always healed fast. He had to get better. He knew who would fix him.

Hawg read the helmet full of biker balls like tealeaves. He then grimaced, his original idea returning to his mind. He'd take the offering to her and hope she'd fix him. Damn the man on her porch. He'd kill him, too. Hawg hated killing something one didn't eat. It was a sin.

The sun would break over the land soon. Hawg saw the helicopters still in the sky. Daylight would bring more men on the ground. His time was short. He had to heal. He had to hide.

Hawg ascended to the road and saw a police car in the cemetery. Someone had staked out his sleeping place. Angered, needing rest, Hawg turned south. Off to his right he smelled water. Though his eyes couldn't pick up the source, his other senses understood a rushing water supply was not far off.

Daylight would bring him trouble, but several miles of timber flecked the landscape around the town. Perhaps this is where the water hid? He pondered this for only a few moments. After he went back to Luella's, Hawg decided to go south and find a place to sleep. These men out across the land were many, but not omnipresent. Like all those from the country, the earth was his friend.

Determined to complete his ideas before he moved to a different sector of the rural area, he set off for Luella's trailer, again.

"I don't know if I feel safe going home," Hux confessed to Roberts as he tied up the boat on the edge of the quarry. "Glad whoever dumped your people from Cicero did it close to the old shed and my Uncle's crash cabin. Funny, in a way."

Roberts looked across the waters at his car and then at the

two rustic cabins set back on the gravel clearing. "You think that thing tracked you to the saloon?"

"I'd bet on it. Pigs have a great sense of that stuff. I wouldn't know how he did it, though. I never saw him behind us."

"Come now, Mr. Huxtable," Roberts said, half admonishing him, but wringing his hands in an attempt to hide his nerves. "That creature cannot be a hybrid."

Rage leaked into his words as Hux shot back, "I don't really care if it's a guy in a costume, man, my pals are just as dead." They walked across the gravel and Hux fished in his pocket for keys. He unlocked the cabin on the right and said. "I intend to crash here a bit if I can. I suggest you do likewise on the couch if you so choose. I gotta rest and reckon you do as well."

Roberts surveyed the modest cabin and said, "I should've just gone back to Chicago."

Hux eyed him as the door closed. "And to tell them what?"

"A giant boar is terrorizing a drug stop off point, so don't fret that delivery that never was paid for."

"Yer a riot."

Roberts sat on the worn-out couch and said, "Not sure what I am at this point. I saw it plain as possible, that thing, so inhuman. I'll carry that with me forever. Still, it doesn't absolve me of my duty to my employers. I will have to call."

Hux nodded. "It was big Ed that screwed ya all. Tell them that. But he died in the bar. This will be big news soon. I don't know how the Mayor will spin it all, but this many people dying bad can't be covered up for long. Even your bosses will know something bad happened in Montrose."

Roberts gawked at the stark walls then his eyes went back to his shaking hands. "Not high on decorations, Mr. Huxtable."

"The maid is out," he joked. "I'm not big on furnishings as this is just a spot to recharge or get laid when I have tail I don't wanna take home. There is a generator out back for the water, but there is surely a flush in the shitter if ya need to use it."

"Thanks."

"I gotta sleep, man."

"How can you with all you've seen?"

Hux shrugged. "Don't know, rightly. I'll lie down and see."

Douglas White went home for a quick shower and breakfast. Before getting under the water, he opened a small pint of Jack Daniels and drank most of it. Once the water hit his face, his body tingled. The words of Big Ed came back to him.

They had sat in the Green Parrot and talked only a few hours ago. Big Ed had sat on his throne, the heavy leather seat he held court in every night. Ed ruled one last time, as he'd sat there, barely alive, missing most of his left leg, bleeding to death...no matter how well it got cinched off by the men who found them all. Amazed that he had lived, Doug heard his story...and even his confession before he died. Doug had known Ed for years and often covered for the big man. Ed was a good egg in general, but never did he realize the things Ed knew...and passed on at the moment of his death. The lapsed Catholic had made a bid for paradise before he died on his throne. Ed had held a pig sticker and stroked it like a rosary. The weapon hadn't even been bloody. Doug assumed this action was for what could've been.

As he dried his hair, Doug thought of how Ed had sat there, ashamed of his sins, but proud of his death. He had wanted Doug to tell his sons that their daddy died fighting, not "running like a bitch like Hux" as he put it.

Doug would tell them. He'd also find a way to crush Hux and his drug line. More plans came to his mind, like how to hang Mayor Sullivan and his connections to Hux, offered up by the dying biker lord.

He thought of his brother. Doug worried about his nephew and hoped the experience didn't damage little Jordan. Though the boy seemed resilient, it would be illogical to assume seeing such things wouldn't bother him down the road.

Unsure of how the day would go, Doug put his hands over his face. He didn't pray. He seldom did, but thought of getting religious again, soon. His thoughts were on his sons and the other children of Montrose. What could he do to protect them? Though tired, he had to give it his all.

"How corny," he said to himself as he mused over his task and could find no path that provided him comfort. Though he didn't know what to do exactly, he'd do as he always did: Follow the straight path and make it work.

After coffee and some ham, he really wanted another drink of whiskey. His wife made him a thermos of coffee and tried to console him. He really wanted a second shot of whiskey. Doug resisted. The day was just starting and he had had no sleep.

When he touched the breast pocket of his fresh shirt, he found his toothpicks and a single cigarette. He felt like a felon for lifting it from Tyler's ear. He didn't smoke it, but never discarded it, either.

Something told him it would be a longer day than the previous one.

Once the morning came, Mr. Solow opened his back door.

The figure of Elias was all that his eyes focused on, standing in his work clothes on the sidewalk.

"Morning, Elias," Mr. Solow said dryly.

"Mornin', sir."

"What do you have to say this fine day?"

Elias looked back at the long barns and said, "I do believe Ms. Rhonda due to have her calf, sir."

Solow nodded. "She's past due. Let's go see, shall we?"

"Yes, sir."

"Beautiful morning, isn't it?"

Elias nodded. "Great day to be alive, sir."

CHAPTER TEN

Endings

Andrew was glad Jordan started playing video games first thing in the morning and didn't seem upset about the previous evening. He was more excited about staying home from school. Andrew called in to work and used up another personal day. Again, the life of his boy mattered more than their numbers. The world seemed clearer now that he had made this choice. His stomach turned a bit at Carol Brandt's attitude on the phone, but part of her bad nature made it easier not to care about work.

Lynne was dressed in a tan suit, beautiful as ever, and said to him, "I'll take Kenny to daycare. It would be better if we had more one on one time with Jordan today."

Andrew agreed and gazed at his younger son, crashing toy trains into his farm play set.

"Old Macdonald had a farm...." Kenny chirped, speaking so clearly for a two-year-old.

Lynne armed up her purse and a leather computer bag before requesting, "Put his shoes on, will you? I'll take this to the car."

As she departed and Andrew scooped up Kenny to put his shoes on, the boy said, "With an oink, oink, here and an oink, oink there...."

After they left, Andrew labored to stop his hands from shaking. He did a lousy job. His eyes focused on the farm set and the playhouse near it. All of the pigs sat at the dinner table in the house. On the cutting block lay the farmer on his side.

Not sure what psychological damage was done to his older son, or if, per his mother's words, the White family even got psychological damage, he drank more coffee. His hands leveled out in a few minutes.

Andrew grabbed the phone, went upstairs, and talked to Lucas about Cassidy. As it turned out, she was reacting the same way as Jordan.

"I'd love to ask him about it more," Andrew said with caution to his friend. "But I don't wanna screw him up, you know?"

Lucas agreed. "Yeah. Cassidy never mentioned it, but she's shying away from the TV and weird animal shows this morning."

Andrew considered the centaurs and bizarre creatures in modern cartoons. "Yeah, I suppose that makes sense. Jordan is having no trouble destroying aliens on the video games, though."

They shared a weak laugh and farewells.

After unlocking the attic, Andrew ducked his head and walked into his storage room. This place was a menagerie of old artifacts: Cases with broken weapons, boxes with uniforms and several battlefield flags Lynne wouldn't let him display in the front room. Since the tight asses in town narced him out and the ATF paid him a visit, Andrew watched where he kept his hoard of weapons. Though his illegal cache was at the cemetery, he kept several hunting rifles and old collector's items here.

He sank to his knees, surrounded by hours of obsession and the fruits of his hobby. "Is it all worth it?" He wondered aloud, considering the tattered Nazi flags, Japanese sabers, Confederate uniforms, and medals under glass. "Spent so much time chasing this stuff to keep it under wraps, what a laugh in the end." He thought of his wife's admonition that he needed to spend more time with his kids than echoes of dead men.

Andrew wrote it off to a leisure pursuit, one that increased as he was demoted at work. He filled his angst over failure in life with guns, with methods of death dealing. Why? Did it make him feel like more of a man? Like it could get him farther? He didn't want to know the answer.

"What good were they when I needed them?" he said,

thinking of how he almost lost his son and not all of these weapons, locked up here, made a damn bit of difference. He could sell them all and not buy his son's life back.

"Dad?" Jordan said from the hallway.

"Yeah?"

"Who are ya talking to?"

Andrew held up the cell phone. "Lucas up the road."

Jordan nodded.

Though he thought it a nice save, Andrew turned to him and said, "How are you doing?"

"Okay," Jordan said simply. "Can we go to the video store later?"

"Sure," Andrew answered, hands folded.

"Dad, do you think they will catch that thing?"

"I reckon so. I hear the choppers out and from what Doug text messaged me, the countryside is crawling with cops. He's bound to turn up somewhere, whoever he is."

As they walked down the steps, Andrew dreaded the meeting with the DCFS advisors later on. Already, his wife called with word from them that Jordan and Cassidy should be evaluated. Granted, that was just logical, considering their experience. Still, he hated interference in his life from any government agency or service. Andrew's attitude toward it had worsened since his experience in the military and other bouts with public officials.

The phone rang and Andrew gave it an irritated look. "Work?" he muttered, reading the caller ID. "Yeah?"

"Mr. White," came the voice of the shift coordinator Carol Brandt. "Mr. Sullivan wants to see you in his office, as soon as possible."

"Doesn't he know what happened to my family last...?"

"He has to see you this morning, Mr. White," her curt voice cut him off. "Bring your badge with you."

The line went dead and Andrew's heart sank.

"Great. The hits keep coming."

Jordan asked, "What is it?"

"I gotta go check in at work about something. You'll probably have to stay at your grandma's for a bit."

They left the attic and Andrew felt his gut turn. Badge. They wanted his security badge. Not that they couldn't deactivate it. It was that bitch in the office's way of letting him know he was fired.

At that point, he had a hard time giving a damn.

Doug really didn't want to go to Luella's when he got the call from the county cop on patrol. When Matt failed to respond to his radio or his cell phone, Doug considered retirement or at least, driving toward Indiana. The feeling of dread in his body grew the closer he drove to the edge of the Solow farm.

Though the area where the bikers met their slaughter at Elias' trailer appeared cleaned up for the most part, a new crime scene existed nearby. Doug was slow to get out of his cruiser, seeing parts of his friend, Matt, all over the deck. When he saw the leather boots standing side by side, one with a shinbone protruding from it, Doug looked away fast and spit the toothpick from his mouth.

"God," a big county cop with reddish hair said to Doug, holding a handkerchief over his mouth. "Something was pissed."

Doug eyed the man, recognizing Kevin Grimes from the early shift. "Something not someone?"

Grimes gestured with the handkerchief, his pale skin turning pink. "No man did that. Look yourself. Matt got ripped apart.

Tears rose to Doug's eyes as he thought about Matt, small town Lothario. How many of the girls in town would lament his passing All of his casual charm and enormous penis couldn't stay the hand of fate, though. Pieces of his friend littered the deck, mostly in a haphazard manner. The boots setting together made him pause again. That tiny bit of order in the bloody chaos disturbed him.

"Matt, you poor bastard," Doug said as he stared Matt in the eye. The head of the police officer stared blankly back from Luella's bench. Gravity pulled blood from the head, turning Matt's face a pallid white under the beam of the light. Both of Matt's arms and one of his thighs lay on the deck. His right hand still held a gun, finger on the trigger.

"Rest of him is inside," Grimes told Doug, sour look on his face.

The sheriff pointed down and said, "Get someone on these tracks. This fucker isn't human." He didn't want to focus on the hooved prints in Matt's blood. He didn't want to see any more. Doug really didn't want to see the fat lady flailed open, either. "Luella inside?"

Grimes shook his head. "She's not here." He appeared relieved by these words.

Doug shared his empty happiness if only for the break in the gore.

The sheriff stepped inside the trailer and looked around a bit for himself. It didn't take long to check the small dwelling. He thought the hallway that connected the rooms was interesting. On the paneled walls hung portraits of John Wayne, Jimmy Stewart, Hank Williams Sr., and Gene Autry. Doug wondered who the pictures were for.

He returned outside and reached for another toothpick in his breast pocket. "What about her dog? This blood all came from Matt?"

"No sign of him, either."

"Huh," he said and knelt by the hand to see if Matt had discharged his weapon. "Isn't that odd?"

Stunned that his cell phone rang, Hux almost pissed himself on the bed. Glad he didn't, he answered the phone. Head back on the pillow, he almost jumped out of his skin as Roberts stood at his door. He listened to the other voice on the line and shut the phone off.

"Who was that on the phone?"

"Sheriff. He needs to speak to me, he says."

Roberts leaned on the doorframe and nodded. "Concerning what?"

Hux admitted, "Not sure, but he didn't sound awful pissy. He ain't got snot on me, so no pressure."

Roberts lobbed him the keys to his car, then returned to the couch as Hux got up and went to the door.

"I'll bring us back some lunch, ok?"

Roberts never acknowledged him as Hux moved and grabbed his leather jacket. He lay on the couch and closed his eyes.

Hux went out back and took a leak before he walked to the boat. Once in the boat moving across the quarry, Hux thought about killing Roberts again. What would one more body in the county matter? Hux remained unsure of that. Still, he held hope that everything could go back to the way it was before this monster came into their midst. He wanted things to go back to the way they were...him nailing dumb chicks, rebuilding engines, screwing off at work, and being a conduit for the dope trade. The cash he'd squirreled away at banks out of state returned to his mind...for they were his eventual escape routes when he knew life in Montrose got too hot.

He killed the engine near the edge and thought of his bike. He so wanted his Harley again. It was always his path to freedom and tranquility

Hux then hatched a plan to go get his bike and hit his locker at work. Screw them for he wouldn't be working today. In his locker, he kept some droplets that would easily take care of Mr. Roberts. He didn't want to go home. Certain his bike was out beside the Green Parrot, he headed toward there in the dope dealer's car. Positive the cops had better things to do last night than impound his ride, he smiled at the idea.

Hux wanted to ride again, he wanted to feel free once more.

When Doug heard the inhuman wail across the Solow property, he grabbed his gun and headed to his car. He called in for back up as he raced around to the main entrance. Officer Grimes had Doug's back as they pulled into Solow's drive. Grimes showed no fear as he emerged from his car with a shotgun and Doug kept his weapon drawn as he stood. In the air was a low wail, coming from the cow barns.

The screams from the barn door echoed awfully, but Doug shook his head at Grimes. "Back me up."

The door to the back barn was slid open. Doug saw a rope knotted around the rusted metal grip on the door. His eyes followed the rope into the barn and to the original point of the scream that wasn't human.

"Jesus wept," Grimes said, grabbing his stomach.

Doug pushed his hat back as he saw Elias, hand on the rope, that terminated around the leg of a calf, partially hanging out of its wailing mother. Solow worked at the point of birth, trying to extract the calf and failing.

"Douglas," Solow shouted when he spotted him. "Help us, for the love of God. Open the door further."

Doug blinked and then focused on the sliding door with some horror. Again, he followed the line of the rope and saw the half-born calf struggle. The wails of the cow nearly drowned out Solow's repeated pleas. Doug returned his gun to its holster and flexed his fingers just before he grabbed the door. He sent Grimes an unsure glance and riveted to the task assigned. Unsure how much weight to apply, so as not to pull the calves' leg out of joint, he used all of his weight, but only made the door inch at a slow clip. When he encountered resistance, he pushed harder and suddenly, the door moved fast. The calf pulled free, bag around it billowing and the cow bleated on. Solow and Elias were laughing, happy the birth was over.

As Elias covered and cleaned up the calf, Solow tended his cow, saying, "Thanks, Douglas."

While he rubbed his hands on his pants, Doug watched Grimes wander away, then lean over. The big Irishman never went sick, though.

Doug said, "Now I know why dairy farming wasn't for me."

As if nothing major happened, Solow tried to get his breath and asked, "What brings you over here, son? Ms. Rhonda appreciates your help."

Doug told the tale of Matt's death and how Luella was gone. This greatly upset Elias, who almost ran out of the barn. Solow told him to stop. Elias hesitated.

"She can't walk too far," Elias said, worry in his voice.

"Crews are coming to search, Elias," Doug promised him.

Still, he wiped at the calf as he said, "I need to go see for myself."

Solow nodded and after Elias finished, he departed them in a hurry.

"This has been a terrible night," Solow lamented, Grimes nodding behind him at his words.

Doug agreed. "Yep. I've had better, sir. I think I may be able to shake a few things out of one of the bikers that got away from this thing or guy we're looking for."

Solow's right eyebrow arched. "Oh?"

"I'd love to beat it out of his ass, but the state gives me shit about that."

Jordan didn't mind his stay at Gramma's. She had good cable television and served him too many snacks. His stomach didn't take to the gummy candy well and he threw up. She made him cereal and he spewed that as well.

"What is it, dear?" she said with care.

Jordan looked around the old widow's home and felt so alone. "I want my Dad."

She sat by him on the couch but he got up fast. "He'll be back soon, honey," she told him.

Jordan didn't mind his gramma's house. The food tasted different, but she bought him toys. So, as his dad said, it all evened out. He worried about his dad.

"Your daddy and that place he works," she said with bitterness in her voice. "It takes up so much of his life."

Jordan hated where his dad worked. He went there once on an open house day. It was vast, loud, and dirty. Jordan thought it was scary and couldn't fathom his father spending half a day there every day. He hated the place for it kept daddy there and not at home.

He swallowed hard and stared at his hands. The right one shook. Jordan sat down and buried his quivering hand under his hip. He thought of the monster, the pig man. They'd said the kids imagined it and it was really a regular man. Jordan frowned at the thought. They'd seen it. It was a pig man.

Jordan's mind shifted and he reflected on something else. He thought about Cassidy and hoped she was doing all right. If she were there with him, he didn't know what he'd say. They had spent a long time last evening, waiting, just hoping Hawg would never come back. She'd cried a great deal. Jordan had wept, but soon that faded in his case. He wondered why that had happened, but he couldn't understand much that day.

He closed his eyes and all he could hear was the cry of Hawg. The monster was real. Jordan had smelled him, felt his rotten breath on his face and stared into his eyes.

Hux parked Roberts' car in the parking lot of the VFW that sat near to the Green Parrot. True enough, the tavern was draped in the yellow bands of a crime scene. A few State troopers and commonly dressed men sporting rubber gloves knelt behind the hitching post.

In the windows of the VFW, a pair of old ladies glared out at the scene. They pointed at Hux as well.

His Harley was over near their scene behind the tavern. There wasn't a really good way to get to it and ride off with no one seeing him. So, deciding on the direct approach, he walked across the street and right up to the first trooper to make eye contact with him. He looked down at himself just before he met the cop and wished he'd had the means to change and clean up for the day.

"Jesus Christ, what went on here?" Hux asked, face long and glaring at the bloody spatters on the side of the bar's façade.

The trooper checked Hux over, read his Harley clothes and said, "Bar is closed today, son."

Hux nodded, curious if the bikers that lost their balls died or not. "Looks like it. Hey, I left my ride out back last night. Care if I go get it?"

The trooper opened his mouth, said nothing, and then gave Hux a long stare. "Why would you do that?"

Hux grinned. "I had a designated driver, pops. That's the law, right?"

"Yes, it is." The trooper looked at the bikes still lined up at the post. He then said to the other trooper, "Rear of this joint a crime scene?"

The younger trooper shook his head and the man said to

Hux, "I don't see any harm in it, really. You were here earlier in the evening?"

"Yeah. I just got a call from Sheriff White to come see him at the Solow farm."

The trooper seemed happy to hear that. "Good. I'll tell him you are on your way."

Hux shook his hand and walked around the bar. Once on his ride again, he felt so much better. He was angry with himself that when the escape happened, he went for Roberts's car fast, as it was an easy escape. He should've gone for his bike.

Now, he thought as he stoked the pipes, to the plant for a visit, then the sheriff, and then, lights out for Mr. Roberts. He grinned for Roberts was genuinely afraid because of what he'd seen. The tough man from the big city was disturbed down deep by the monster and Hux liked that. Hux wondered why the beast had ripped their nuts off and seemingly collected them in a helmet. Was it on purpose? Did the monster seek revenge for something? Hux shook his head, dismissing all of that. The creature was not capable of such feelings, he reasoned. It followed Ed and him out of instinct.

Not worried about Ed fighting a scapegoat coat he made up for him, he figured they could pin the JFK assassination on Ed about then.

Andrew swiped his card and walked into work like any other day, save for he'd called in and was not with the regulars at shift change. Though it didn't feel like the last mile, Andrew felt certain this was it for him. He was surprised his card still worked on the door. His mind raced with fears for his son, and that diluted the other things that could disturb him. If they fired him, he'd get six months of unemployment and a bit of severance. If anything, he'd enjoy a summer off and do field work at harvest time.

Insurance issues and other matters bothered Andrew, but he didn't care about that now. The rattle of the machines and the smell of the plant made him ill. During his lay off a few years ago he had applied for work at various print shops, and the smell of ink had made him nostalgic. Now, it made him sick, a reminder of where he was when Jordan needed him.

When they laid him off before, no one would walk him out, as was company policy. Sure, his demeanor denoted he might take a swing at the one who walked him out or be trouble at the moment of truth, but Andrew did no such thing. He joked later, "I may have to return to this upholstered MEN'S room, so I behaved."

As Andrew walked in, he knew that was a lie. The dick-heads who stabbed him in the back up in the front of the plant stayed away to ensure their safety. Jerks like Lou Lauren and Scott Grady knew the score. While going to jail for battery then seemed like a great idea, now, he wasn't so sure. Frustrated, for he really wanted to crush the front teeth of that asswipe Sullivan, Andrew figured Lynne and the kids needed him free, not in a cage.

"I'll kick his ass another day," Andrew promised himself, unsure if he could hold it together at the moment of dismissal.

He passed through the long path after the entrance, flanked on one side by giant racks full of skid loads and on the other by Plexiglas barriers hemming in the stitching lines. He spotted Della Rodgers from up at the front of the plant, a woman rumored to be in line for Jack Sullivan's job. She wore a baggy top and Andrew wondered how much longer she could hide she was pregnant. He didn't wonder who the father was, though. In this place, he pondered, it was often decided by draft lottery or DNA at the moment of truth. Della shot him a bitter gaze, her attitude so stuck-up she practically walked on the ceiling.

"I hope the kid belongs to Matt Crouch," Andrew said, barely audible. "That'll learn you."

Several people stopped Andrew before he made the open area beyond the stitchers. Hoist drivers stopped and women fixing magazines came over to lament the trouble with Jordan the previous night.

"It's just terrible," Marcia said. She was an older lady nearing sixty who'd helped train Andrew twenty years ago when he was first hired. She could recall him before he grew a beard.

"Jordan's all right," he assured her.

Lena held up a yellow envelope. "Want to donate for Andrea

Ennis? So bad that they found her dead out in the country."

Andrew nodded and fished a couple bucks out of his wallet for the collection. He eyed the pictures of Jordan and Kenny in his billfold and smirked. They'd grown a great deal since that pic was taken.

Brian Miller, a hoist driver who Andrew had gone to high school with, said, "Damn douche bags made you work over last night. They are half responsible, man."

Andrew leaned on the yellow safety rail, waved at the distant offices and said, "What else is new? When they lay off guys who've been here thirty years and then promote some suck ass who has been here three years, what more can you expect out of them?"

Another lady in her fifties, Paula Grimes, stepped over from the stitcher side. While Andrew half smiled at the bad frost job on her hair, he accepted her hug. He'd known her through three marriages, the last ending in cancer. "We're all praying for your little boy, Andrew."

"Thanks, he's a tough one. He'll be ok."

Brian asked, "What are you doin' in here? I figured you'd called in."

Andrew smiled. "I may be in for the last mile, guys."

Marcia blurted, "They'd never fire you after what you've been through."

"Sure they would," Andrew told her. "They're pigs."

Paula's lip jutted out and she looked genuinely sad at the idea of Andrew being fired. "Even pigs have some feelings."

"Ah, it'll be all right," Andrew said and started to cross the big hoist aisle.

Brian dropped his safety glasses down and shook his head. "That's fucked up, man. We heard stories of all these people getting killed."

Andrew watched the women go back to work and said to Brian, "Yeah, messed up."

"Your kid saw this guy, the killer?"

Unsure how he should answer, Andrew nodded.

Brian whispered above the din of machinery, saying, "I heard it's a monster, not just a big dude. That true?"

Andrew opened his mouth, hesitated, and then his eyes followed the path toward the office.

Brian's eyes widened, "Holy shit! It's true!"

Andrew said, "We aren't sure what it is, ok? The kids...." Starting to laugh, Andrew said, "Oh shut the fuck up, Miller. Who's gonna believe you anyway?"

Brian drove off laughing and Andrew turned to face his fate with a half grin.

Jack Sullivan wasn't smiling. He stood at the door to the bindery office, hand on the railing to the steps that led up to his office.

No words were spoken as Jack headed up the steps. Andrew thought he looked like a geek in his cream-colored pants and yellow shirt. A quick glance in the bindery office showed the bitch Carol Brandt behind the desk, smirking in glee at the sight of Andrew passing by. The foreman Debra Johnson also seemed to ooze merriment from her crypt keeper face. He'd never seen either of those women smile before. Now, he didn't feel bad for not giving money when Brandt's mother died a month back. He reckoned folks like her hatched out of garbage anyway. Johnson's husband had passed on last year while watching NASCAR. The devastating loss hadn't softened her up one bit. If anything, she painted her visage with anger and was far more ruthless than ever. These people never cared for his family so why should he have mercy on the memory of theirs?

Andrew paused on the steps, waving at Minh the IT guy in the pressroom. Minh waved back, busily adjusting something at one of the presses' main frames. He'd get Minh his Colt 45 and dynamite later, Andrew thought. May be selling a lot of collectables soon, Andrew mused as he entered Jack's office.

The first thing he noticed was that his office had a window. Only the offices at the opposite end of the plant had windows. Andrew often joked that they refused to let the slaves see the outside world as it would inspire hope. Andrew could see the shallow edges of Injun Creek as it snaked past the plant and trickled under the railway line. He and his father used to fish in Injun Creek farther on up the road from here. Jordan liked to fish, he pondered, as he sat down across from Jack.

"You're probably wondering why I called you in today," Jack said in a momentous voice, his head framed by motivational sayings on the walls.

Andrew wondered which cheap movie Jack Sullivan learned his dialogue from as he replied, "I could never imagine, Jack."

"Call me Mr. Sullivan."

"When I was assistant on the bind line in the early nineties, you used to come fix my strapper. You were good enough to be Jack then." Andrew's eyes noted the tiny picture frames on Jack's desk. His kids or wife? Andrew suddenly didn't give a shit.

"Mr. Sullivan to you," he said as his voice deepened.

Andrew sat back, fingers interlaced behind his head. "So, Jack, get it over with. What do you have to say to me?"

"Always Billy Bad-Ass, to the end, huh?"

"Your father worked with mine on the Norfolk & Western railroad, Jack. How did you get to be such an aristocrat?"

Jack's eyes flared. "That is inaccurate! I expect you to do your job."

Andrew loathed how he talked down to everyone, separating his contractions to sound smarter. "I've always done it. If leaving to look after my kid interfered with your overtime, thems the breaks."

"You are using this to get out of work. I have no sympathy for men like you."

Hand on the knee of his denim jeans, Andrew said, "Did you call me in to brow beat me or did you have a special reason to see me?"

Jack sucked air into his nose, his teeth tight together. "You are part of the problem. You are something I can do without."

"You ever wanna jump, high classed guy, I'm sittin' over here."

Eyes narrowed, Jack snapped, "You would love that, would you not?"

God, Andrew thought, *he sounds like a douche bag.*

Jack went on to say, "You would love me to take a swing and have me arrested."

Andrew mocked his tone and said, "You do not have the balls, Jack Sullivan."

Face full of redness, Jack sat back and slapped a folder of papers on his desk. "I do not need to have them. I have yours. This is your life here and it is over. You copy that, Billy Bad Ass?"

"Thank God. I thought you were gonna ask me to the prom," Andrew stood up fast and Jack's mouth dropped open. The big man towered over Jack's desk and said, "Judgment day will come for all, you bastard, or is that a part of the Mass ya miss every Saturday night when ya go to church before the tavern?"

Jack stood and Andrew felt the fight was on. However, the plant manager didn't swing at Andrew. "I think it is time you left my plant."

Andrew gave a nod, and waited for him to go out the door first.

Covered by the trees that shaded old Injun Creek, Hawg slept for a time. The bark of the Harley's straight pipes nearby roused him from his slumber. Angry, he sat up and looked through the trees.

A quarter mile away sat a yellow structure. The conglomeration of buildings made up one business. Injun Creek ran along side of this structure, so Hawg kept to the trees as the echo of the bike tormented his ears.

It was a familiar sound. Though he couldn't smell the rider, he was certain of his identity. Eyes riveted to the rider as he parked his bike and started to take off his sunglasses, Hawg recognized the biker.

The one that got away.

Hawg never made a sound as he slipped from the tree line and started to cross the parking lot of Ambrose Brothers Printing.

CHAPTER ELEVEN

Rampage

Hux stood at the back doors of the plant, hit the handicapped button to make both doors open and froze. The scent in the area was bad, like rotten fruit or pig shit....

He turned fast and saw Hawg, loping across the parking lot past the giant air conditioning units that only benefited the office areas. Surreal in appearance, clearer due to the sunlight, Hawg was coming for Hux.

His boots wouldn't move at first, so shocked was he by the revelation. This paralysis only lasted a moment and he turned, fleeing down the ramp to the plant's locked inner doors.

Hux ran down the long rug that led to the two inner doors. His badge swipe card hung from his key chain and he slapped this against the security box, never looking down at his actions. He couldn't take his eyes off Hawg as the beast grabbed the handle of one of the swinging outer doors, ducked his head to get inside, then smashed the other glass door as he made room for himself to get in. Hawg's side arm shot made the glass fly down the rug, but didn't appear to break the beast's skin.

How does it know me? He couldn't comprehend it, but felt glee when the security door clicked. Hux yanked the door open as Hawg dropped to all fours and moved down the carpet to the security entrance. The door that unlocked had a hard spring, so it swung open slow on purpose. Hux was through it but unable to pull it shut fast enough. Hawg grabbed the edge of it. Eye to eye with the beast, eyes riveting on the steely tusks as they started to extend, Hux abandoned his struggle.

He stumbled backward down the center aisle of the plant. On his left, the tall racks of skids loomed, full of stock wrapped in plastic and a safety netting so it could never fall onto passersby. To his right lay the stitcher area of the factory, various turns in the production line shielded by Plexiglas. Hux ran down the yellow stripes on the floor, but only for a few steps. He collided with Mary Ann Statler, in the middle of a major gossip session with a trainee Hux didn't recognize. She changed husbands with the decades and often cruised the small town to see whose car from the factory was parked at another's home. Her tales and nose were longer than anyone's Hux could name. He bounced off her and fell against the wooden cabinet where Mary Ann was about to deposit rejected books from the stitcher line.

"Why, Huxtable! Drunk so early again?" she sniped and froze as Hawg's screech filled her ears.

Hawg only saw an obstruction between him and Hux. Her loud scream added to the cacophony of machine noises tormenting the creature. Hawg made a backhanded swipe with his right claw, knocking her jaw out of joint and sending it around the back of her head, but not removing it from her body. The trainee ran and her tongue wagged, a deep howl spitting from her neck. Hux stumbled down the aisle and Hawg sunk his left claw into her cellulite-ridden thigh. With a minor grunt, he pitched Mary Ann toward the line. She landed on the steel spools that fed wire to the stitcher heads. Her askew jaw wasn't there to stop anything and the long bolt at the top of the spool drove through the roof of her mouth, into her sinus area.

Hux heard her screams ebb away, but pushed himself farther on. Mouthy to the last, Hux mused about her as he aimed to get his feet going down the stitcher line. Around the next line walked Paula Grimes, full of shock and wonder at the sight. Hawg's momentum took him past her, his elbow striking her side, sending her careening back into a huge cardboard box full of bad books. She screamed as well, but the creature never stopped to silence her. His red eyes focused on Hux.

Day shift foreman Debra Johnson wasn't so lucky. Her abrasive attitude was in full-on nuke strike mode when she saw everyone leaving their lines to see where the noises had come from. Hux assumed the old woman was out to get counts on the lines and she stepped right behind him, hands on her hips, angry at the world as always.

Hawg wasn't impressed with her attitude. He grabbed her outstretched index finger and snapped it backwards, then angled his head sideways. Her mouth kept working, yet Hux couldn't hear her threats to Hawg as the tusks of the beast poked into her neck and the side of her head, before Hawg's teeth bit into her mouth. Like a twisted kiss, Hawg bonded with her but a moment before drawing away. Blood gouted from her head as Hawg drew back, ripping her face off. She stood for a moment, convulsed, and then dropped like a sack of bones, her life running out on the production floor.

Hawg stepped on her, ribs breaking under his hooves, spitting her blood against the Plexiglas of the next line, still focused on Hux as the biker fought to get his feet to follow each other.

Lena Alsdorf stepped around next, almost running into Hux as he fell on the floor, unable to get his coordination down. She faced Hawg and he dropped low, preparing to extract this small woman with ease via his tusks. His tusks swiped, tearing her sagging breasts loose, snapping her ribs as the steel gouged in fast. The momentum of the savage blow impelled her against the Plexiglas and she sank low, leaving a smear of blood on the sign telling visitors how many days since their last lost time accident.

Around the corner of the same machine ran David Wills. All he could perceive was trouble and he certainly never counted on what he ran into. He saw Lena sink by the glass and couldn't do anything fast enough to stop Hawg from clutching his neck. When this happened, a dip of chewing tobacco spewed out of David's lip. Hawg raised him up and then drove his skull into the nearby glass. David's head pulped on the Plexiglas, leaving a stain of greasy hair, fragmented bone, blood, and brain to dribble down near Lena's extended hand.

Hux backpedaled, then saw Human Relations Specialist Karen Lauren freeze in her pumps behind Hawg. The creature never knew she was there. Unlike the others who happened across him, her open mouth didn't emit a scream. Like all the rest who saw the beast, confusion reigned, and an initial shock stabbed deep. Karen dropped her clipboard and receded back into the stitcher line. Not an ugly woman for over forty, Hux sold coke to her hubby, Lou, who was in charge of Payroll up front.

Hux reached the center hoist aisle and spider-crawled into the open. He saw two hoists approach and hoped they would provide him with cover. On cue, Brian Miller arrived and stopped, eyes wide at the sight of Hawg. He swung his hoist around, preparing to exit the scene as Hux crawled into the open and Hawg stepped past the iron retaining barriers. Miller elevated his forks five feet. His eyes narrowed as if he prepared to charge Hawg.

At that moment, Jimmy arrived from the other direction on his hoist. He drove backward as the hoist drivers were apt to do. Standing on his hoist, reality registered too late. Hawg grabbed him by the buttocks and yanked him free of the moving hoist. Once Jimmy's foot was off the pedal, the hoist stopped cold, but he didn't. Hawg slung him into Montroses, the left one driving through Jimmy's sternum. Jimmy gagged, arms flailing and then went limp. The pack of smokes rolled in Jimmy's shirt stayed put, but his bowels let go all over the concrete production floor.

Hawg made eye contact with Miller, but Hux's scrambling motion up past the next barrier line made the creature switch his attention back to his prey.

Hux turned the corner and scrambled past the bindery office. Again, he fell to the concrete as Hawg took a few strides. The bindery office door opened and out popped the shift coordinator, Carol Brandt. Her face hardly had time to record puzzlement as Hawg shoved her against the retaining pole, snapping her shin in the process. Carol cried out and Hawg up-heaved his right claw. Like a cleaver, it dropped and tore loose the meat of her back, shearing it down to the vertebrae.

Hux crawled by the hallway that led to the restrooms. A few of the guys from the pressroom walked over, stunned by the sight. Gopher saw Hawg and stopped. From out of the MEN'S room stepped Minh, oblivious to all, walking right into Hawg's left leg.

Hawg saw the men from the pressroom, and then Minh. The short man from IT locked eyes with the beast, but didn't move a muscle. Hawg grabbed Minh by the ankles and scooped him up. With a roar, Hawg swung the small man like a bat, bludgeoning the first man from the pressroom. Their heads met and a sickening echo rang in Hux's ears. Gopher backed away, almost falling over the huge paper rolls there to supply the infeed. Hawg twirled Minh around and swiped him down, aiming at Hux's legs. Kicking himself away, Hux avoided the blow, but saw Minh's ruined skull hit the concrete. The sound was hollow, wet, and final. From that impossibly bad wound and the feces splotches on his tan pants, Hux assessed Minh's fate with ease. His profile resembled a gooey fingerprint, scrunched in and filled with lines.

Hux scooted and pushed off the concrete, hard enough to rise up in full. Still, he backpedaled again and Hawg prepared to charge...just as Jack Sullivan descended his stairs, leading Andrew White down. Hux came face to face with Jack. The biker grabbed him by the shoulders and turned him around, putting the plant manager's back to Hawg. He then pushed Jack toward the monster and ran the other way.

Hawg bellowed and dropped both his claws down, chopping at Jack's shoulders. Blood sprang from Jack's yellow shirt and he cried out. Hawg made a stab with his tusks, but Jack turned around, facing his fate by mistake. Hand held out to stop the horror that tore open his back, Jack humped it to flee up the stairs, but Hawg stomped a hoof through Sullivan's leather shoe. Nailed in place, Jack couldn't stop Hawg as he embraced him like a pro wrestler, broke both Sullivan's arms against his body, smashed his ribs until they crushed into his organs...and forced Jack to gape up at Hawg. The beast angled his head down, tusks splitting Jack's head open in a double rut. Both eyebrows and cheeks sliced through. The skull opened and divided into three sections, Hawg broke the embrace.

Hawg looked up the steps at Andrew, but White never went down any further. The beast quickly searched on after Hux and kept moving. Hux saw Andrew slip down the stairs after the creature stepped away. White pulled the fire alarm.

While the sirens went off, Hawg only hesitated a moment. This time slip was long enough for Tonya Harmon to exit the pressroom office and walk past Hux. The biker recalled her, the one he didn't want to bed from the pressroom as she was known as "Herpy Girl" for a good reason. Tonya supplied Hux with a confused expression, looked around as to why the alarms were going off, then stepped into the embrace of Hawg. Hux heard her scream as the creature grabbed her by the thigh and the right arm, but those screams paled in comparison to the ones she uttered when he threw her toward the spinning press infeed rollers. In a defensive pose, she put her hands out, but all this did was offer fuel to be fed through the tight, spinning rolls that only allowed something as thin as paper to pass through. Per their function, Tonya's fingers shredded to grime and her hands crushed back to her forearms before someone hit the STOP button. A large crimson stain spewed up the white rolls of paper that traveled the length of the first units, hitting the inkwells that started to cover the initial plates for images.

Hux stumbled and ran, this time past the doors to the cafeteria as he attempted to get across the pressroom.

Hawg pursued, by his shifting looks and trembling body, he appeared somewhat shaken by the alarms and noises from the presses. None of it stopped him, but it slowed him down.

Earl Gamblin had worked at the company for close to forty years. He never realized today would be his last day at Ambrose Brothers. A head pressman only a year shy of retirement, he walked down the line when he heard the screams from near the lunchroom. A stout man, and no pushover, he couldn't help but freeze up at the sight of the monster. Hawg paid him little mind, only trying to get to Hux as the biker moved on up the main aisle. Earl stood too close to the aisle and Hawg grabbed him by the throat, pulled him up and dropped him over one of the huge paper rolls. Earl's back broke in three places as he landed, and a piece of plaque popped loose around his heart. He was dead before the EMT's arrived.

Hux made it to the doorway at the edge of the pressroom

that led into the ink storage area. Hawg's claws gripped his leather jacket and Hux shed it, much to the anger of the monster. Hux was through the door and ran into the personal assistant to the Pre-Press Department. Scott Grady was a stocky man with ruddy skin. The dress clothes he wore appeared uncomfortable and tight about his bloated throat. When Hux grabbed Scott by the elbow and tossed him toward Hawg, the pressure on his throat was relieved. Adam's apple ripped loose and his body slit open down his abdomen, Scott gagged and grabbed his neck and stomach. Shock spread on his face as he couldn't hold in his intestines or the flood of blood and gore. His jaw worked, his screams caught forever in his neck as Scott fell toward the Cyan inkwell.

Hux took his chance, turned, and ran down the narrow hallway. His boots took him closer to the pre-press department. The roar of Hawg rebounded off the slender hallway. Hux looked back as he ripped open the glass door. Each overhead light blessed Hawg with a momentary halo as he traversed forward, using the carpet for traction. Hux sprinted into the room full of dividers and computer stations.

Pristine, cool, and clean, this environment was unready for such a primal incursion.

A few men in white shirts sipped coffee and talked about how the fire alarm must've been a drill. Della Rodgers walked up and listened to them as they talked. Alarmed by Hux running through, their conversation stunted to a few lines.

"Too bad about Dinsdale," one of the men said as he put his hand in his pocket. "He was such a family man, doting on that wife of his."

All of the men nodded soberly until the loud noises reigned. When the door burst into a thousand pieces of jagged glass, heads popped up from the computer station. Like a group of human gophers, they gaped at Hawg as he ducked through the doorway and stood up. Hawg shielded his eyes from the glowing lights overhead, but parted his fingers to see the figure before him.

Some of the men drinking coffee squealed like girls at play while others pissed their khakis where they stood.

Della Rodgers, controller of scheduling, the one the company had groomed to replace Jack Sullivan someday due to her education, company ties, and diversity record, died next. Hawg dropped down to lope after Hux and rammed right into Della, tusks into her stomach. Instinctively, he rose up, driving his tusks further into her enormous stomach, sending her up in the air and then screaming to the polished floor. Hawg slipped on the slick surface, his hooves unable to get good traction. His eyes saw the same thing Hux beheld...the innards of Della's body, unborn baby and all, spilling out onto the floor.

Hux thought fast, recalled that a nearby dark room for the scanning area had an exit leading out to the main entrance; he bolted for the curtained door. Through the darkness, he saw a reddish glow from developer lights, and saw two figures. Hux panicked at first, but understood the only real threat to him remained behind him. He sprinted across the room, but his right hip slammed into a developing machine, causing him to spin and yell out.

His yell joined the holler of Hawg as the beast ripped the door of the darkroom open, spilling light into the chamber. Hux backed toward the other door, seeing the two other figures clearly in the light. It was Lou Lauren, tall, black haired, looking stunned. His pants to his ankles, he let his cock slip out of Mrs. Annette Moyer, computer analyst...she of the great bosom and teardrop shaped ass. Hux blinked, noting the gray pubic hair of the black-haired man just as Hawg crossed the room and gave him a left-handed chop, shearing off his rather large appendage at the gray pubic locks. As Lou screamed and gushed blood like a super soaker toy, Mrs. Moyer got a clue about what was going on. Hands in the sudden gush of wetness, she exclaimed, "Don't come inside me!" She stared at her red fingers and screamed.

Hux slipped out the door.

The bright lights confused him for a moment, but he was heading toward the wooden door. Beyond this barrier, Hux felt horny for the foyer and reception area. The glassed-in façade of the company looked so inviting beyond his path. Even more inviting were the fire trucks and cop cars outside the tinted glass. Through the wooden door, Hux barely regarded Juanita, the portly receptionist placed on display for all visitors to see. She was a kind lady, but not very good at her job. This kept the illusion high that Ambrose Brothers cared for cultural diversity, no matter how inconvenient it made contacting the plant's switchboard. She hollered at Hux as he charged through, never asking for clearance as he hit the first of two glasses doors that led to the outside world. When he hit the second, the outer most, he found it locked. Eyes afire, he faced Juanita, who locked the door on him. This was a security measure for her to control and she frowned at him, somewhat pleased she stopped his progress.

"Open the door, you stupid bitch!" Hux screamed, slamming his fists on the glass.

Whatever she was going to say never got out as Hawg burst the wooden door from its hinges. The creature took a few steps, then breathed several times as he looked out, seeing the outside world. His head turned toward Juanita as she screamed, but to Hux, Hawg appeared fatigued. Covered in blood and grime, chest heaving, the beast appeared winded.

The creature hunched its back, bent, and vented its bowels over the display cases. These cabinets of wood and glass housed the best product Ambrose Brother's had to offer, the cream of their production efforts. Any customer would've been hard-pressed to see their pristine examples of such labor now, covered in liquid feces.

Juanita screamed. Hux didn't know how she could keep screaming and never take a breath. He turned to see Hawg face her, irritated by her yell and open-mouthed expression. Hawg's eyes glanced at Hux and his tusks protruded, but the screaming woman still drew his ire. Hawg slashed at her, his entire body swiping in Juanita's direction. She pushed away from her desk, still screaming, mouth agape. Hawg's left claw missed her, but the slicing stream of urine that whipped from the end of the monster's penis didn't. The line of fluid bisected her mouth, causing her to stop yelling. Mouth closed, she dropped to her knees and started to choke under her desk. Hawg turned away from her, facing Hux. Again, the beast sucked air and didn't make an initial charge.

whether the beast was tired or not, Hux himself remained trapped. Hux panicked and kicked at the glass to no avail. Outside, the firemen and police exited their vehicles, confused at what went on before their eyes.

"Help me!" Hux screamed and thrashed. "That bitch locked me in with it!"

A few of the cops saw Hawg approaching the first door. The beast spotted them as well. His red eyes scanning the crowd; clearly, he counted up his opposition.

One of the policemen, a young Montrose cop of barely twenty-five years, drew his gun and fired. The shot shattered the main windows, causing a chain reaction to the entire façade.

Hawg shielded his head as the shards started to rain, but leapt through the nearest gap. He landed on the bushes outside. These shrubs hadn't greened up proper to spring just yet, so their thorny ends provided him little cushion as Hawg landed and rolled to the black top parking area.

"Hold it!" one of the cops yelled at the younger policeman, but the kid kept firing.

Hux saw the gun kick but never saw blood appear on Hawg. The creature roared and sprinted away from the vehicles, toward the long reeds that fenced in Injun Creek. As the door opened, Hux heard a splash in the waters beyond the lot.

"What in the hell was that?" the young cop exclaimed, gun shaking in his hand.

The older officer zeroed in on Hux and asked in a steady voice, "Yeah, Hux, just what the hell was that?"

"It knows me," he said dryly. "That thing came after me...I don't know...why...it didn't care about anything but...." Choosing his words more carefully, Hux said, "I don't know anything man. I just came to work to get smokes from my locker."

The cop leered at him. "You can buy smokes anywhere, Huxtable."

"Am I under arrest?" Hux asked as more people started to run out of the main entrance.

"No, but you better not stray too far until we understand what's going on."

Hux nodded. "I gotcha. Still, I need some smokes."

The cops never stopped Hux as he started to walk around the other side of the plant, opposite the creek. This way, he navigated the rail lines and then loading docks. No one stopped Hux as the plant was in a state of panic. All he could think of was getting to his Harley and getting away.

CHAPTER TWELVE

Aftermath-2

Doug washed his face in Mr. Solow's sink, rubbing deep into the corners of his eyes to get what felt like boulders out. Sleep. God, he'd kill for sleep. He wiped his face on a dish-towel and gave the farmer a sheepish look. Solow just waved it off with a grin and turned toward the refrigerator. Doug's cell phone rang and he saw who it was via the ID. Surprise spread over Doug's face.

"That's odd. Hello Reverend Wingler."

"Sheriff," the curt voice popped back. "Is there any news on my daughter's whereabouts?"

"How did you get this number?"

The minister's voice was rough, full of power as he said quickly, "Never you mind, for the Lord provides."

Provides the county sheriff's cell number? Doug couldn't help but smile at his own weary jest.

"Reverend, if there was any news, you and your wife would be the first ones I call."

"I have to trust that all is being done to find my Micole."

"Go out around Montrose and look, sir. We're canvass-ing the countryside for many things. If you know of any place where she'd stay, let me know."

"I have three sons and one daughter," Wingler told Doug, his voice still in the throes of serious sermon bile. "I shan't lose her. If she dies, I wouldn't want her blood on your hands."

The line went dead and Doug put his phone away. He stared at his hands and rinsed them off again.

He then gladly accepted the glass of iced tea the farmer offered him, and the seat in his living room. Solow took a glass of tea himself, lit up a smoke and sat in his recliner. The scent of the smoke drove Doug wild, but he said nothing about it.

"Thanks, Mr. Solow."

"Thank you for your help, Douglas. You always were a good boy."

Not insulted by his words over his youth, Doug looked at the pictures on the walls and said, "No problem, sir. That birthing deal was an easy task compared to my last couple days."

"Sure is a terrible thing, son, all this death. It was wonderful to see life again."

Doug grunted in agreement, then glanced at the pictures, some tiny-framed photos, all black and white, fading away from sunlight and age. Others truly were even older from their yellowed edges. These pictures were group shots of military regiments. Others appeared to be family gatherings, perhaps picnics or reunions.

"I cannot fathom where Luella would've gotten to," Doug shook his head. "That man, that thing or whatever it is, if it killed her, she can't be far."

A look of distress spread over Solow's face. "Poor lady, such a hard life she had to end in that way." He took out a red handkerchief and rubbed his nose. Solow then flicked ashes from his cigarette and said, "I did all I could to make her comfortable, you know? I sure tried."

"Mr. Solow," Doug said gently. "I hate to pry, but I want to ask you this. I don't need to know for any official case thing, I just want to."

Solow sipped his tea and shrugged. "Go on."

"What was the connection to you and Luella Goodkind? Was she an old friend, what?"

Solow smirked and took a drag on his smoke. "Ah, you wonder if she was an old lover of mine? Nasty of you, Douglas, but nothing so blue, young man. Luella was my half-sister, made by my ol' daddy when he strayed from the pure ways once in Baton Rouge."

"Oh."

"Since her appearance and dubious past were somewhat off putting to the locals here, she never bothered saying it and I never shared. It was our own business."

Doug nodded. "I see."

"You young people tell too much of your private business. Was at the laundromat mat once and heard tell this gal starts blabbing about having an ovary blow out. For the luvva God, Douglas, can't anything be private anymore?"

"That's true, sir. Thank you for telling me."

Solow shrugged. "Anything I can do to help you. Still, we better get to searching for her with the others, I think. My legs aren't as young as yours no more. I need a few more minute's rest."

Doug took out a toothpick and replied, "Sure. I was supposed to see that biker Huxtable out here soon. I wonder where he's got to?"

Mr. Roberts wondered the same thing. He awoke from his sleep in the abandoned cabin and sat up with a start. Seldom one to leave himself exposed or in a weakened position, he cursed his foolishness.

"Abandoned in the godforsaken boondocks," said Roberts.

Up on his feet, Roberts peered from the window of the cabin out on the waters of the quarry. The boat was gone outside and no car sat in the distance.

"Damn peckerwood fuck," Roberts cursed Hux. "I'll find another connection. Fool." He looked at the edges of the quarry and wondered how easy it would be to climb to the top of those huge bluffs and walk back to his car. "When we sailed over, it looked like an impossible task, hence the safety of this spot, aye Hux?"

He sat on the worn couch again and contemplated his next move. His fingers drummed on his left pocket, where his wound-up garrote lived. Not wanting to have to strangle the big biker, he reached down to his ankle and took out his small automatic that hid there. Finger stroking it, he replaced it in its spot, knowing he'd have to wait for Hux to return.

"You are shit, Mr. Huxtable, but can I find another turd to

polish so easily in this shit pile of a town?"

Unsure if he should kill Hux immediately on his return or not, Roberts trembled at the memory of the creature they'd seen. Though humanoid, it looked like a monster from a fifties drive in film. Oh, better make up, Roberts noted, for the seething beast was like nothing a cheesy studio could vomit out fast. The multiple pectoral muscles and nipples, that memory made him pause. That and the metallic tusks.

"How is that possible?" Roberts said to no one. He took a few steps and picked up a book off a pile of novels. "A book on spanking? Tender Bottoms. What a joke, but typical." He dropped the book and paused at what passed for a kitchen area. A card table, a few dirty folding chairs and a threadbare lawn chair served as furniture there. He found no refrigerator, but two long plastic coolers sat against the wall. Upon opening one, only two beers swam in the dank water.

He got up and went to the small toilet room. Hux said there was one flush in it. Roberts urinated and thought on how scaled down this place was for a cabin. He searched around and found no fishing paraphernalia, just extra sheets, some condoms, batteries, and lubricants.

"Predictable," Roberts remarked. "You are easy enough to understand, stupid rube, perhaps easy enough to control in the end." Nostrils flaring, he said, "Mice. At least it isn't rats." The image of Hawg crossed his mind. The tusks, the mouth, the teeth. "Are you bringing back childhood fears of rats?" he wondered to the images in his mind. The hovel in the south side of Chicago he grew up in bled into his mind, mainly the night a rat nibbled on his back as he slept.

His mind spun, banishing that memory and he lay back down, not wanting to sleep, but surrendering to the arms of it nonetheless.

Micki awoke in the concrete tube. It wasn't that she heard the choppers fade away and the cop sirens peter out, it was the sensation of tiny legs in her ear canal. Micki screamed and wrangled to bat at her ear, but the culvert prevented the motion. She could reach her ear, but forgot where she was. Micki inserted her right pinkie and reamed out her ear. Tears of joy sprang to her eyes as she lucked out, snagging and removing the insect. Alarm set in and she had to get out of the tube. Backing out as fast as she could, Micki flailed with her legs in the open air. Though her pain was so great, she fell face down into the grass of the ditch. Her thirst great, she licked up the muddy water there, anything to quench her desire.

It took her several minutes, but she stood up by the mouth of the round opening. She was so hungry. When she stretched out, her body protested, but a rush came over Micki. This made her feel somewhat better. Micki's thoughts ran somewhat lucid, she tried to stand straighter, but could only hunch over. She staggered a few steps in the ditch line and then started an agonizing crawl up the embankment to the shoulder of Route 66.

Her mind burned and thought that if a car hit her, maybe that would bring an end to her suffering. No vehicles passed as she stumbled across the highway. She could hear cars in the distance, but they were on Interstate 55. As she wobbled, Micki fell down the other side of the ditch and stepped up onto the disused section of Route 66. The state closed these lanes to facilitate less maintenance. She plummeted and laid on this double lane set, trying to get her bearings.

She then turned over and looked into the greenery beyond.

Jesus looked back at her.

At first, she was excited, but then started to weep again, for Jesus was made of stone.

After he pulled the fire alarm, Andrew saw Hawg march on through the plant. There was nothing he could do. He had no gun or weapon, nor would his death matter if he punched the beast.

Andrew looked down on the floor at the file strewn about. The bloody remains of Jack Sullivan forever ruined Andrew's dismissal papers. He stared down the way at the shift coordinator Carol Brandt. He realized she and maybe Deb Johnson were the only other people who knew about his dismissal. Andrew shook his head violently, ashamed that he thought of such a thing when so many were hurt.

He started down the way, but soon saw the path of destruction Hawg made. The dead, the dying, the injured filled the aisle and the areas nearby. He saw Minh and stopped cold. Down on his knees, he turned his friend over. It was a waste of time, as his skull was smaller in size than usual and he was long gone.

"Damn, damn, damn," Andrew said and laid him down gently.

Way off this path Andrew saw people huddled by machinery, hiding. He was tempted to tell them to get out, to run away, but he didn't know where Hawg was. Not willing to send anyone to their deaths, he headed toward the back door of the factory.

Andrew paused before he hit the stitcher line area and thought about Jack Sullivan and how he died so fast. He just let it happen. Was it only because he couldn't have stopped Hawg and would've died himself? Andrew understood he wouldn't have died to save that man, who was so vindictive he'd tried to fire him over petty nonsense in the middle of a family tragedy. He couldn't make himself sorry that he'd seen the inside of Jack's skull.

It would have taken Andrew a while to get through the plant, even if he had gone another route to avoid the apparent bloodbath route. He felt so sorry for the fallen, for friends he had made twenty years ago when he came to work there. Through the rack he saw Lena Alsdorf, thick glasses gone, her eyes still open, face frozen forever. Wilma, on her knees in the blood, hair stuck to her tear stained face, cursing anyone who tried to stop her from covering up Lena's body.

Most of it made him feel numb, as if it was a crazy film, not reality.

All that proved important was Jordan and getting back to him. These people didn't matter, he told himself, no matter how close they all were. Blood is what mattered, family. He wished he could shut out the wails of the crying and the screams of the hysterical ones on the production floor.

Many had fled the back of the plant and meandered in the parking lot. Several escaped in cars or were in the process of adding to such an exodus when Andrew departed. As he walked to his truck, he saw Hux, slipping down the side of the building toward the line of bikes.

Andrew broke off his path and headed toward Hux. The biker saw him coming and said, "Easy man. I didn't mean to...."

"You fucker!" Andrew raged and stopped short of striking him. "What was all that? You led that thing here?"

"I didn't know it followed me!"

"Yeah sure," Andrew sneered, his hand on the throttle of Hux's Harley.

Hux exclaimed, "On my mother's life, Andrew. That thing... it knew me...followed me here."

"How? That's fucking silly! Could it smell you that well?"

Confused, Hux shook his head, then looked down at his Harley. "My bike. The damned thing knows me by my bike."

"What?!"

"The straight pipes, the cylinder missing at times. The fucker knows me. He wants me. I escaped him. It jumped back into Injun Creek."

"Well, what the fuck are you gonna do about that?"

"I dunno man."

Andrew frowned. "This is the answer for you, Hux. You want me to spell it out for you? The cops can't find it or get that thing. It wants you, it knows you and can find you, by the sound of your Harley. That means, we know how to get it into the open."

Hux rubbed his rump and asked. "What are you saying? Are you saying we gotta trap it or get it?"

"I don't know what I'm saying. This has to stop before my kids get it, or, if that doesn't grab ya enough, *you* get it."

Hux nodded, watching as the people filed out the back door of the plant. None seemed to be in a mad rush, though. "What do we do?"

Andrew shook his head. "It's nearby right? How did you get away from it?"

"Cops and firemen out front. It jumped in the creek like I said. It ran from the guns."

Both looked toward the creek and then each other. "You fire up your hog and its curtains for us."

"What do I do?"

"Come with me. We have to figure this out."

Hawg ran the edges of the creek until it emptied into the Vermillion River. His body glided through the loam and toward the opposite bank. The current was weak so Hawg swam against it for several minutes. A white walking bridge stretched over the river at one point. He paused and glanced at the green grassy area near this bridge's edge. Eyes focused, Hawg picked up a series of grave markers far off. This wasn't where he had slept before, but it almost looked familiar.

Out of the water and trotting on all fours, Hawg passed through the park. He didn't see anyone nearby, however across the river he saw a few old men walking. They missed him as he approached the border of the graveyard. In the park he saw smaller structures made for children. Hawg stopped to sniff a tiny barn door on a steel post. His knuckles nudged it and the door swung around, creaking. He could smell children, but none were there. He sensed old women as well. Old, dried up sows left their scent everywhere.

Near a rusty slide, a concrete drinking fountain drew his attention, only because a pool of water gathered at its base. Down to all fours, he prepared to drink this still water until he saw his reflection. He'd seen himself before, but thought of the children who played here and his own toys back in the round barn. He was not like them. Then again, they weren't like him, either.

A yard-high wrought iron fence was all that kept Hawg out of the graveyard. He eyed the spikes on top and showed them respect. Hawg easily conquered this obstruction by grabbing in-between the spikes and soon, he ran among the tombstones. He needed rest. As he tried to find a place to sleep, he eyed the boxy crypts, reminding him of the stall he slept in at the other grave-yard. It was snug and inviting.

Hawg wanted to go home. He had to. Soon. Responsibilities awaited him but he was too weary to return. The elusive biker caused him to feel anger, such rage that he wasn't used to, down on the farm. He felt pain in his body. That was alien on the farm as well.

The faces and folks Hawg slew in the factory skipped across his mind, but they didn't stick. After all, he reasoned, they were all pigs.

Hawg traipsed on, his legs weary, until he saw a crypt greenish with age. The pillars out front denoted a colonial style, and the word over the iron gates on the entrance drilled into his brain.

SOLOW.

Andrew glanced at the implements in the bed of his truck and then at Hux. They stood in the biker's driveway, loading in more materials. "We really need to call my brother about this idea."

"Are the cops going to go for this scheme?"

"May not hurt to have some more guns around if we really can get this thing trapped."

Hux pondered that for a moment. *I want to kill Hawg*, he thought, *not the cops. How do I shake this asshole to get what I want done?*

"Weren't you supposed to go get your kid?"

Andrew swore. "Shit, your right. Still, we should contact Doug. Listen to the sirens. This town is gonna go crazy once it all hits the fan. There won't be any more shielding the story."

Hux nodded with vigor. "Gimme a minute to figure all this out, all right? We aren't even sure what we're doing just yet."

Andrew dropped the truck into reverse and they backed into the street. "I'll feel better once Jordan is close to me. I need to call my wife."

"You saw it up close, Andy?"

Andrew nodded once as he drove. "I saw it kill Jack Sullivan right in front of me. Pig man indeed, huh?"

Hux raised his eyebrows. "Jack bought the farm? Shame."

Andrew shot Hux an acidic look. "I won't shed any tears, but I thought you two were tight."

"He's an asshole."

"Not anymore."

"What was it? What did it look like to you?"

Andrew's thumb tapped the wheel. "I can see why the kids thought it was a pig man, but, damn, that's what they invented the word monster for. It was a guy, I'm sure of it, but damn, the metal horns or whatever? Christ. I wouldn't begin to guess what it really is. I'm sorry I doubted Jordan, though."

CHAPTER THIRTEEN

Setting Traps

Nothing like this had ever happened in Montrose, of course. The witnesses to the rampage at the factory varied from older workers who told their stories with sober words to younger, eclectic employees who told stammering confessions that exaggerated the events.

There was no one in the Mayor's office or answering his phone to hold back a tide of inquiries. Once a few emails and calls started to make the rounds, reporters dispatched from Peoria, seventy miles away.

Sheriff White came to town, passing Andrew and Hux as he entered the plant through the rear employee entrance. Doug didn't want to accept the reality of the call to Ambrose Brothers. Some of his worst fears made vivid, he soldiered on. The ambulance services of Montrose and the neighboring hamlets of Odell, Fairbury, and Chenoa offered up their services. It was a mess and the county coroner, Porter Loring, stood just inside the rear entrance of the plant.

"Getting tired of seeing you, Porter," Doug said to him as they walked down the ramp to the ruined key entry doors.

The aged man spoke with his usual upbeat prose. "Ah, but it's not quite midday and life goes on. Since the plant manager is among the dead, no one wanted to make hard choices for the factory."

Doug blinked. "Oh?"

"Some foolish woman in prep wanted to keep the factory running, aside from the affected areas. How is that for a company woman?"

"My brother is right, by God. Dickheads do run this place."

Loring delivered a pat on the shoulder. "I took the liberty of speaking for you, saying I needed space for a crime scene and things had better wind down for the day. I assume that is fine, yes?"

Doug walked the aisle with Porter, past the body of the woman with no jaw impaled on the spool. He couldn't recall her first name, but Porter lamented her fourth husband's loss. "They have good death benefits here," Doug commented.

Porter imparted a wry expression and moved on, saying, "Volunteers, the local police and rescue squads are doing a wonderful job on this. The clean-up will be speedy if the aftermath deranged."

Doug cleared his throat and said, "I heard the tales already. A giant pig man? C'mon, Porter. You've been to the circus and seen the damned elephants. That's all bullshit talk."

"Of course it is, but...." his voice weakened as he pointed at the injuries to the shift foreman. "I don't think a normal man has done this. If so, whatever weapon he used was quite effective. Goodness, there will be no tidying up her for an open casket wake."

"Well, the security cameras will tell the tale, once and for all, right?"

Loring nodded. "Yes, I'd thought of that. Get ready for a real show, Sheriff."

But when Doug asked the foreman on duty about such tapes, they gave him blank looks and directed him elsewhere. He questioned the bindery specialist, Stan Vernon. He also provided him a vacant stare and informed Doug he was presently there to fix the mail heads and plastic wrap feeders. At last, he cornered Mrs. Lauren from Human Relations. Her manner was uneasy, for the entire cast of the dead hadn't been announced yet.

"Certainly, I can take you to where that is supposed to be," she said with a lighthearted laugh. "But you will be disappointed."

"What? Are you going to say the tapes are gone?"

"No," Mrs. Lauren confessed, hands in the air. "The cameras

are dummies. They have a red light that blinks, but are not connected to a real security system. That costs money. The supervisors and planning committee deemed it a bad expense."

"Christ," Doug said and buried his face in his hands for a moment.

"I saw it, up very close," she told him, eyes wide, head bobbing. "I can repeat what I told the officers."

"And that is?"

She said in a low, almost whispered voice, "It wasn't human, Sheriff. It was a foot taller than you. I know your family are big men, but this monster was a giant. It was all fleshy, pinkish, but had blood and brown stuff all over its body. It stank so I can guess what that was, really. The eyes..." she paused, blood draining from her face as Doug read her earnest recollection. "...they were red, inhuman, almost albino in nature. Its mouth was full of teeth, but not like a shark. It had these horns." She forked her fingers and curled them out from her jowls. "They seemed to move as he moved."

"He?"

She shrugged. "It was bare-assed, Sheriff and I know a man when I see one naked. It was not normal, the thingy, almost twisted and swinging."

Doug nodded and started to turn away.

"It had a bandage," she said with a meek voice.

He faced her again and Mrs. Lauren placed a hand to her side.

"Right there?"

"Yes. Isn't that peculiar?"

Doug turned again, wondering who would patch up such a thing.

Andrew sat down beside Jordan on the couch. Lynne's grandmother's home was modest and very tidy, even if the front porch and living area had been converted to a children's play area in later years. As they watched Cartoon Network, Andrew lamented that Lynne's grandfather built the home they sat in after World War Two. An excellent carpenter, Andrew thought of the bomb shelter in an antechamber of the basement the old man installed. He missed that guy and wasn't ashamed to recall shedding tears at this funeral six years ago.

"So, how long will this take?" Jordan said, playing his Gameboy and using the television show for a soundtrack.

"A couple hours," Andrew assured him. "There was some bad stuff going on in town today, out at the place where daddy works."

"Bad things?" His brown eyes looked up at his father. "Was it the pig-man?"

Andrew hesitated, knew it was too late to lie convincingly, and said, "Yeah, it was him, all right."

Jordan stared at his game again and said, "Lucky you weren't there when he was, huh?"

Andrew closed his eyes and could smell the creature Hux called Hawg. The strong odor of a swine had been in the air, but the awful scent of a sweaty man, rancid meat and mildewed water had wafted off the beast. It was something he'd never forget.

Eyes open, Andrew said, "Yeah, lucky me. I saw it, but the thing was past me."

"You saw him?"

Andrew smiled. "You were right, son. It sure looks like a pig-man. Well, I have to go help Uncle Doug and the police. You see, there may be a way to track the pig-man."

Jordan froze and said, "You all aren't planning to fight him, are you?"

"Nope, daddy isn't stupid. We plan to trap it."

Jordan blinked, he reached out to grab Andrew's flannel shirtsleeve. "You should kill it, dad, not capture it."

He gave his son a pat on the shoulder and said, "I don't think what we have in mind will be too healthy for it."

The game went on and Jordan said, "He's a pig, dad. Mr. Solow kills pigs all the time. The Bible says there's no sin in that."

When Andrew returned to his truck, he sat behind the wheel and exhaled.

Hux gave him a sideways look. "What?"

"I know you have kids, but have nothing to do with them,"

Andrew said shortly. "I'm not worried about hurting your feelings today, all right?"

Hux shrugged and gazed down the street at the manicured lawns. "I got fixed so as not to have any more. No skin off my ass, pal."

As he adjusted the cuffs on his shirt, Andrew continued. "You worry on how they deal with things, at least I do. I see kids come to school from messed up families. Hell, why else do you think we get so many shitty employees in the plant?"

"What are ya getting' at?"

"My son is more rational than us."

"He's a kid," Hux shrugged, eyes never blinking. "They accept things better than us jaded asswipes of the world."

Andrew started the truck, but never put it in gear yet. "Do you think my brother is going to accept your plan?"

"I doubt it."

Hux was correct.

When they departed the house and Andrew called Doug, the sheriff was not pleased at the call he received.

Andrew closed his phone and Hux stated, "He sounded thrilled."

"I think his exact words were, 'are you fucking kidding me? Leave this to the professionals.'"

Hux gave a nod. "I gotcha. The professionals are getting folks killed."

"I know."

"If you want out, tell me, Andrew. I want this thing dead. You got kids and a good life. I got money and pussy, that's it." Hux sounded logical and calculating as he spoke. "That fucking Hawg has gotta die. He will follow me if I root him out. I can trap him. If you want to scoot, be my guest."

They drove a few blocks before Andrew answered. "I can arm you up better. I have a stash of very bad things."

"I figured you did."

"This fucking Hawg isn't worth either of us dying over."

"Agreed. But drop me over by the VFW. I have some things to get straight."

Andrew grunted in agreement. He thought that this way

he'd not have to show Hux where his cache was at. "Meet me at the cemetery on 66. I think your idea about the pit is a good one."

Hux peered into the bed of the truck and then out at the small town as the houses passed by. Hux hoped the idea was as good as it looked in his brain.

Elias walked to the door of Luella Goodkind's trailer. It stood open, wind rattling the busted screen in the outer door. The old man could smell coffee inside, fresh. He stepped in and saw the automatic coffee maker probably performed its function on a timer. Elias chose his steps carefully and walked into the kitchen. He looked at the living room, torn apart, loveseat flipped over, and reached for a coffee cup. After he filled the mug, he unplugged the coffee machine.

"Lord, girl, it's all for the best."

"Get out of there, Elias," a deep voice called from the outside of the trailer.

Elias almost dropped the mug, but held it level as he returned to the doorway. Mr. Solow stood just off the deck.

"There's nothing we can do to change it now."

"Never saw you come out here, sir."

"I never walk this far on a given day. Then again, you never need to be reminded of your duties." Solow turned away, thrust his hands in his overalls pockets and whistled at his golden retriever. The dog bounded out of the higher grasses behind the trailer.

"It's been a bad couple days, sir," Elias confessed and stepped down from the deck. He took off his straw hat and wiped his brow.

Solow kept walking as he said, "Been a bad world for some time, Elias. The Lord purifies at times. Come along now. We have more work to do."

"Yes, sir," Elias said and sipped the coffee. It was cold.

But when they reached the main house yard, Deputy Grimes was waiting.

"I need to speak with Elias," Grimes told Solow. "There's been a really bad incident in town and several people have died."

Mr. Solow let his hands dangle by his sides. "That a fact? So sorry to hear. What kind of incident?"

"Sheriff wants to see if Elias' memory has improved since last night."

Andrew stood at the edge of the freshly dug grave not twenty yards from his family crypt. Though the locale was deserted, abandoned by even the cops waiting for Hawg to return, Andrew felt as if he wasn't alone.

"Graveyards will do that," he said to no one as he eyed the backhoe left by the workers. He walked to the edge of the fresh grave. Near the top of the grave, he read the tombstone marker. "Andrea's parents. Damn. They are still alive." Again, he looked at the fresh spot, set off to the side from the main two lots.

Since no one was in the graves and vaults hadn't been installed yet, Andrew fired up the backhoe and started to dig them out farther. He'd used a machine like this many times while clearing land for his neighbors and landscaping back by his silo. It didn't take him long to widen the grave to triple its intended size. He never worried about discovery as Andrew wagered he was the least of anyone's worries this day.

While Andrew worked, an elderly lady drove through the graveyard. The woman crept at a snail's pace. She exited her car, left some flowers on a marker, and waved at Andrew. He waved back and kept working. She departed, thinking him doing honest work, so he finished up his labor.

"Deeper than six feet, but you're a tall piggy, aren't ya?" he said, peering into the pit. He left the end of the digger down in the hole and climbed off the machine. "Time to play Tarzan," he joked as he walked over and opened the bed of his truck.

Unsure how he'd explain his actions if discovered, Andrew went about his work of jamming the sharp implements into the soft dirt at the bottom of the pit. Sure, he was surprised at how many long knives Hux had on hand, but added to his own corn knives, disk blades, stunted steel posts, hedge trimmers, and railroad spikes, the grave appeared ready to embrace a tiger or at least, a mutant pig man.

Andrew took great care not to fall backward onto the bed

of nails he'd created as he climbed out on the backhoe arm. He then walked over to his family crypt, swore about the broken doors, and patted the two stone coffins. After he unlocked the lids, Andrew slid the left one to the side and let the reflected sunlight show him what he needed.

"Concussion grenades and a few flashes, for a start," he said with a wry smile. "Then, something a tad more sinister." He reached down and pulled up a couple hand grenades, taped tight. He set these down and eyed the claymores. Unsure if these would be the best to use on this occasion, he let them be. Then again, he reasoned and looked across the expanse of the yard, they may come in handy if....

Andrew turned, back in the rear of the crypt, and gazed out onto the graveyard.

"What if he won't go into the hole?" he said to no one. "What if he won't do as we wanted?"

Nose irritated, he turned his eyes down and saw the brown leftovers on the floor, deposited by Hawg.

Eyes scanning the crypt, Andrew shuddered. "He likes it in here, doesn't he?"

Once Hux returned to Mr. Roberts' car, he broke out into laughter. He thought of the dealer from Chi-town, out at the quarry, probably waking up with no means of escape. Oh sure, the guy could walk out, but he was waiting for him to return. Hux didn't know what to do about Roberts. Oh, he knew what he had to do, but was unsure of when to do it. The mass killing made it all too real for him. He had to run. This was all over now. There was no going back to his regular life.

When he swung by his house, a state trooper's car was there. Hux kept right on going, cursing the fact that most of his weapons were still there. He'd palmed a tiny automatic when picking up materials with Andrew earlier, but that was chicken feed.

Though he kept his cool when he saw the trooper, Hux's innards panicked the further he drove away. He decided on a destination, Ambrose Brothers. Sure, there would be cops around, but it was a spread-out spot and what he desired most was in the lot. His plot to skip town flared in his mind often, but he'd need his bike and stashes of cash from his place. He'd return after dark and slip into his house.

Plus, there was a better stash hidden on his bike. He needed a toot to screw down his courage. His plan unfolding in his mind, a thrill bubbled out over his body.

Hux drove the car to the backside railway line seldom used by the plant. It was the same one that he'd snuck down earlier. He parked the car, pocketed the keys, and jogged down the side of the building. When he drew near the dock doors, he passed by a few of the hoist operators out for a smoke.

"What the fuck are you doing out here, Hux?" one of them raged. "I heard tell you are responsible for all of this."

"Aw, that's bullshit."

"They said that thing, whatever it was, chased you through the plant. What's up with that?"

Hux wanted to get past them, but sensed their ire rising.

"What do I got to do with any of it? So what?"

"All of them people died and the pigs wanna talk to you. What are you doing out here?"

Hux reached into his leather jacket and took out the small automatic. Both men glared at the weapon and stopped their advance. Hux never pointed it at them, he just checked to see if it was loaded and the safety was in place.

With a casual voice, Hux said, "I gotta get going, boys, now step off."

As he passed by, the younger man said, "You fucker, didn't you sleep with Andrea Ennis once or twice? Doesn't it matter to you that she's dead?"

"I fucked her, I never slept with her. Another dumb assed girl with crack in her brain. Life's a bitch."

Hux walked away from them and then started to jog again. He recalled her well. Sure, he was sorry she was dead. She liked it in the can and swallowed. Not many did. He would've scored that with her again.

Once out in the open, Hux slithered down the line of cars parked on the far side of the plant. In the distance, he saw the rescue vehicles clustered around the entrance. Bold in his move, he walked to his Harley and climbed on. When he fired up the engine, the straight pipes barked. Though certain many eyes were on him, Hux looked only at the exit of the parking lot. He thought he heard voices shouting as he pulled away, but couldn't be certain.

While he rode, Hux worked on getting his head straight. He tried to banish the fear that the beast would rise up behind any bush or garbage can due to his bike. Though just running away seemed like a great idea, the hurt in his insides refused to let him take that path. Hawg had to die. He'd hunt him, ferret him out and lead him back to the cemetery. First, he had to get his head together, then he'd call Andrew and tell him his plan.

But God, he thought, it felt good to ride again.

"Drew, don't do anything foolish now."

Lynne's voice on Andrew's borrowed cell was serious as a judge. Her tone usually was, he reasoned. He laughed and eyed the brick of explosive in his hand. "Hon, I'd never do something like that."

"Just leave this to the police."

"I will."

"Did you hear the official story on what happened? It's hilarious!"

Andrew took a breath. "No, what did they say?"

Lynne never hid the amusement in her voice as she said, "Doug says an armed maniac ran amok in Ambrose Brothers today. The sheriff sounded sober on the radio when he said it was a big man dressed in a Halloween costume, probably of their own design. The man is still at large."

"Jesus wept."

"Drew, it was no costume, was it?"

Andrew fell silent for a few moments. "No, hon, it wasn't."

"I'm glad you called."

Andrew sat down the brick of explosives and picked up several wires. He said, "I love you, Lynne."

"I love you, too. I wonder if you are still fired."

"I think everyone who knew may be gone. I'll worry about that tomorrow."

"I think they have bigger troubles than you at the plant right now."

"Yup."

They talked a bit more and told each other they loved each other once again. He swallowed hard as he closed the phone.

Lynne was his rock and his life, everything to him. She tolerated his silly hobbies and attitude, because she saw under his skin. She was a bright girl, and Andrew was her only lover, ever. She shamed him and never knew it, with her even devotion to God, family, and education. No matter how weird life got, she was there to support him, literally and figuratively. He had to protect her, no matter what.

"Now, for Plan B," he said quietly and reached into the stone coffin.

Micki crawled in the bushes on her belly. The pain to her privates seemed like a natural part of her existence and the scrapes to her small breasts faded fast. Her collarbones were ruined and she couldn't understand how her arms ever worked as well as they did.

Her eyes focused on the tall man inside the crypt. He was swearing, walking in and out, and then reaching into the big coffins.

She studied him for a long time, thinking him a grave robber. Then she watched as he stretched a wire across the entrance to the crypt. Not understanding him, she stared, fascinated.

Micki shuddered every so often, so tired, so hungry, but overall, she felt good in the graveyard. She was already dead, after all, so this was her place to be. Here in the bushes, with the stone image of Jesus looking over her, arms spread wide, she felt better than she had in days.

When the stone head turned and then gazed down at her, she couldn't find the will to breathe any more.

With a voice to rival any Hollywood over-the-top actor, the mouth of the stone Jesus said, "If you bring forth what is within you, what you have will save you."

Micki coughed, remembering to breath. She wanted to speak, but found no words.

However, Jesus had more to tell her.

"What you do not have within you will kill you."

The voice was not threatening, forceful nor angry. The tenor of the words, though, carried authority and kindness. The words washed over her face as pure as water.

"Woman, why have you come out to the countryside? To see a reed shaken in the wind? To see a man dressed in sackcloth, unlike your leaders in soft clothes? They cannot understand truth." The voice grew stronger and said, "The Kingdom of Heaven is inside you, woman. It is outside you and all over. I am with you always and have never left you. Split a piece of wood and I am there. Lift up a stone, and you will find me there."

Micki folded her hands and put her head to the earth.

Hawg awoke at the rumble of the Harley's straight pipes. The sound cut out fast. Hawg wondered if he dreamed it, but soon, the air held a scent, a human odor he recognized.

The creature pulled from the Solow crypt and started a slow crawl to where the smell originated. Head in the stunted bushes, he peered across the Vermillion River at the biker in the children's park, deserted save for the longhaired man he sought. Hawg watched him at a picnic table. The biker faced down on the table, held a rolled-up dollar to his nostril and inhaled. This man sniffed his nose many times, then repeated his actions with the tube.

A high-pitched whine cut the air and Hawg flinched. He saw the biker reach in belt pocket and pull out a silver object. This thing opened up and the biker spoke into it.

"Yeah, Andrew. I'm about ready to go Hawg hunting. Sure, I'll start a cruise around. It may be hairy as the cops are after me but they don't scare me none no more. Yeah, questioning and all that. Explosives? Sweet. I knew ya would come through, pal. All right. I ain't yer pal after all."

Hawg saw no more reason to wait. He would cross the river and get after this fool. When he splashed into the river, the biker turned to face him. Eyes wide, the biker said into the phone, "Jesus Christ! It's here in the park! I gotta go!"

The man was on his mount by the time Hawg swam the river.

Still, the biker never fled. He faced Hawg at a distance and sneered, "Never knew pigs could swim. Come get me, you ugly fuck." The man's hand rested on the tank of his ride.

The bike roared to life and the man on it pointed his arm at Hawg. Above the engine sound, Hawg heard three loud pops. But he felt no pain as he charged.

CHAPTER FOURTEEN

Quarry and Pursuit

Andrew wasn't as mechanically inclined as his siblings, but he understood explosives. It didn't take genius to light a fuse, but it did require some knowledge to rig up a timer and wire it to an explosive device. This day's activity didn't require any sort of timers, but rigging the trip wires to explosives, that would make Andrew sweat a bit. He did his work diligently, double-checking all of his leads.

He took a few guns out of the crypt before he started plotting the destruction of his collection. Two converted machine guns and two sawed off shotguns, replete with ammo, along with a couple automatic pistols with laser sights lay in a case outside the tomb. Several grenades, both the kind to stun, flash, and eviscerate, joined the guns. These would be for Hawg's welcoming if need be. He planned to rig a couple of aged claymore mines up in the pit as well. He handled these plate-shaped devices with great care as he tilted them against the crypt next door to his own.

He returned to his task, wiping his brow as he assembled the explosive charges in neat rows. Andrew carried the lids of the caskets outside. He'd want maximum effect, that's why he started stacking the charges away from the stone side where they'd make their initial blast. The bricks of plastic explosives would more than tear the crypt to kingdom come. Every so often, his fingers trembled and Andrew told himself this was only a just in case scenario. If he went to jail for his illegal weapons now, he reasoned, that'd be a chump change charge compared with destroying the giant pig man.

"Wish you could see it, Jordan," he said with a grin, then wiped sweat from his eyebrows. "But better you don't, I suppose."

Andrew stepped outside and called his brother again. He got the answering line, but never left a voice mail. Andrew hated to do that. Impersonal or no, he wouldn't beg his brother for his approval. This was all on Hux and him. That idea sounded bad in Andrew's head. He hated the alliance they'd struck up so fast, but there was nothing else to do at the time. Hux could deliver the beast. Sure, there was a chance Hux would never show and this exercise would be for naught. Andrew decided to worry on that later.

Mouth dry, Andrew walked in a circle, hoping he and Hux weren't morons for trying this. He then thought of calling Lucas Ellington, inviting him over for the festivities. No, this had to work this way, for them alone. If he died, well, there was no reason to make Cassidy fatherless, too.

Andrew looked into the crypt at the limp wire over the entrance. He'd set it secure once he was ready, Andrew reckoned. Suddenly, the image of Hawg missing the wire altogether or seeing it, struck him.

"Need a remote," he said, and started to search for wire to rig up a hand-held back-up to the trip wire. "Damn, not enough wire. Wonder if I got time to get home and back here?"

Andrew turned his head up at the sky, and his eyes rested on the crypt next to his. The styled name SOLOW rested in his mind. While he knew that Mr. Solow's parents were buried in town at South Side Cemetery, this crypt stood for his grandparents and him, yet there were two empty slots. He never noted it before, but they were for Solow and someone named SISTER.

"Solow," Andrew mumbled, staring at his truck.

Micki watched the tall man, could even hear him swear as he climbed back into his truck. The engine came to life and the vehicle jerked as it sped from the cemetery. Her heart fell as he went. She saw his guns and felt safer with him around. Surely, Micki thought, he'd not take her like the beast had done. She glanced down at her ruined sex and sobbed, thinking no man would want her again after this was over.

Slowly, she crawled from her hiding place with Jesus. After a few attempts to stand upright failed, Micki was content to take steps hunched over. Like something semi-human, she made her way to the crypt where the tall man had worked. Aside from the coffin lids outside on the ground, and the ruined gate to the sepulcher, nothing seemed amiss. Her bleary eyes snapped into focus, seeing the wire on the floor of the crypt entrance. She couldn't see inside the small spot from where Micki stood, nor was she about to enter such a place guarded by the wire.

She gazed at the lawn around the area and saw no evidence of the man being there. Micki recalled him removing a great deal of materials from the crypt, but these must've gone with him into his truck.

Micki walked away from the crypt, steadied herself on the brown edifice labeled SOLOW and then started across the yard again. Her route different, she became disoriented, only wanting to return to the hiding place where Jesus loomed to protect her.

Suddenly, the ground opened up to swallow her. She teetered on the brink of a gaping black void, then slipped, but fell to her bare buttocks on the edge. Her feet dangled into oblivion…no, there was a bottom. On closer inspection, she saw the jagged edges of death that were the pit's teeth.

When she pulled her legs from the pit, Micki pulled her knees to her breasts and tried to cry, yet no tears would come.

Hux sped across town as fast as he could open up the bike. Hawg was in pursuit, and he half laughed at the contest. There wasn't any way the beast would catch him, he reasoned. Then again, he couldn't get over how he'd fired at the thing point blank and managed to miss. The other projection knife under his light had failed to launch as well.

The beast showed great determination, its gait comical in his rear mirrors, but steady. When they traveled down an old brick side street, Hawg grew closer, getting better traction off the small cracks. However, on the open blacktop, the monster slipped often, much to Hux's glee. He wondered how far the thing would go before it tired.

Hux took the route out of the south side of town, intending to loop around and make Route 66 out beyond the REC PLEX diamonds. He planned to start the progression back to the graveyard, but never knew if the beast would follow him that far. He had to play for time and make sure the beast stayed with him.

Once in the open country, Hux swore Hawg moved faster. Still, the thing couldn't catch him on the Harley. He navigated the straight section of the rural area and suddenly realized, one more section over was the quarry where he left Roberts.

Hux slowed and came to a full stop at the stop sign. He turned and looked at Hawg and let it get close to him. The creature slowed, unsure of the biker's intent. Hawg stopped full, took many breaths, and glared at Hux.

"C'mon, big boy," Hux said. "You got rid of one problem for me. Let's see how ya do this time."

Doug White had experienced better days. His life as a small-town sheriff was never boring, but what happened in Montrose would've challenged the mayor of a metropolis.

"Gotta hand it to the staff, Porter," he told the old Medical Examiner as they loaded the last of the bodies from the massacre. "Everyone kept it together and did their job."

Porter's brow furrowed. "I expected no less, Sheriff. We've seen highway accidents before and these young ones here are trained well. My task is easy, taking care of the dead. Lots of margin for error there. However, your job, that is one I wouldn't desire."

Doug nodded, taking his hat off and running his left hand through his hair. "You're right there, Porter."

Hand to his hip, the older man asked, "No word on this monstrosity yet?"

"This area is vast, Porter. All the cops, troopers and hunters that are out looking around, still nothing. There's a fourteen-point buck that eluded our hunts last winter, so anything is possible."

"Do you think this monster is moving on, leaving our area?"

Doug scratched his neck. "No. I hadn't counted on that. See, this thing chased Hux through here for a reason. I reckon it has a beef with some locals, after the attack on the bikers. Whatever the answer, it is just out of my reach."

"Odd that it appeared out of nowhere," Porter noted, index finger tapping his lips. "Surely it is a deranged person of some sort."

"That I have no doubt."

Porter folded his hands and smirked. "One wearing steel horns?"

"Lots of crazy folks out there, sir. It may be a helmet of some kind."

"Crazy? Don't I know it. Usually, they kill themselves on drugs and end up on my table. This is a new factor. I'd hate to have your task of figuring out where a pig man would come from around here."

Doug watched the old man walk to his car and then turned his head to the east. The sheriff's mind was on the victims, on backcountry roads, spots no one traveled really. He thought of where Genesis died, the trail of where he ate Buddy, vomited on Jack Sullivan's Buick...went to the cemetery and slept in the crypt that belonged to their family...next to the Solow crypt. The creature killed the bikers and not Elias, he pondered, and his own man Alex, not Mr. Solow.

"Good God," he breathed, not wanting to accept the obvious.

When Andrew pulled into his driveway, he glanced toward the Solow place. Never a nervous man, he felt icy tingles across his shoulders. Swift to shrug off these feelings, Andrew focused on matters at hand. He climbed out of his truck and tried Hux on the phone. No answer. He stopped for a moment, wondering if this was a fool's errand, but something inside drove him on. Andrew could feel it coming closer. He could feel the beast nearby as surely as if it breathed on his neck.

After he slid the door to his shed open, he carefully navigated the path to his toolboxes through kid's bikes, toddler push cars, and weed whackers. He grabbed more wire and a pair of handgrips to act as triggers for his plan. A fresh wave of shivers flooded his body again and he swore.

"Damn, I need a drink." Halfway to the house, he stopped and headed for his truck. "Naw, fuck that. All I need is to get a DUI on top of transporting weapons grade nitrates."

Once out on the road, he again pondered Solow's house. It was suddenly so obvious to him. If he confronted the old man, what would he say? Andrew shook his head, thinking himself a fool.

But as he turned out and headed back across the roads leading to the cemetery, he saw a police cruiser heading toward the Solow farm.

Hux's mind worked fast, spurred forward by the drug in his system. Part of him said to head back to the cemetery, but another piece of his heart refused to let the problem of Mr. Roberts go.

"That seedy fucker will never let this one die now," Hux said. Sure, the dealer was very upset which is why he let Hux bring him out here. Roberts was a snake and would soon shed the skin of fear. He'd go back to his slithery ways and Hux would be screwed.

A plan was born, a risky one, a drug soaked one, but a sketch Hux thought he could execute.

Still, the beast pursued him, seemingly relentless in its hunt. It followed Hux all the way down the pastoral road that led to the quarry entrance. Hux saw a few trucks pass them and their brake lights pop on once they figured out they couldn't identify what ran behind him. None of these vehicles turned to go after them, though.

Hux gauged Hawg's speed, never letting him get too close, and sped up to cede himself time for his plan. He placed a large gap between them before he reached the edge of the waters that aimed toward the abandoned cabins. As he pulled up and killed his bike, Hux drew out his cell phone, noted a call from Andrew, and then hit the button for Roberts as he got in the boat.

Eyes back as he started the engine, he saw Hawg run into view, pause, suck air in and stare at the man in the boat.

The boat went forward and Hux feigned terror as Roberts answered. "Christ it's after me! Get ready!"

"What? Where have you been, you shitter? I...what is going on?"

"The monster, Hawg, it's on my ass!"

The sound of ruffled curtains came over the line. "Damn, you led it here?"

"I don't think it can cross the open water...oh God, I think it can!"

Hux still had a huge lead on the beast as Hawg slipped into the water. He was nearly to the other side as Hawg floundered at first, but then started swimming. Roberts emerged from the cabin, cell to his ear. He slowly dropped his hand as his mouth popped open.

Roberts drew his pistol, stared at Hawg and remarked, "Look at that sonofabitch go. My word..."

Hux docked his boat and pulled it to the rocky shore. He leapt out, gun in hand and joined Roberts. For a few moments, he too was transfixed at the sight of Hawg. The beast had no problem swimming across the deep waters of the quarry. Like a weird variation of a dog paddle, the thing carried on, eyes on them.

Roberts face still registered astonishment as he said, "We better get inside."

Hux looked down at Robert's hand, gun pointed in Hawg's general direction.

As he reached out and plucked the weapon from Roberts' hand, Hux shot him in the foot. Roberts cried out and Hux shoulder blocked him, sending him rolling on the rocky shore.

"Damn you...I...." Roberts wailed in confusion as Hawg drew close to the shore.

Hux stood in the open door. "He's run a long way, man. He's hungry. Hawg wants me, but blood is in the air now."

Roberts grabbed at his wounded foot, but started to scramble back toward the cabin door. Up on his feet, he soon collapsed, unable to run.

Hawg rose up out of the water. He appeared cleaner than before to Hux, pinker than he recalled. Water drizzled from

Hawg's tusks as he roared, looking at the biker over the bloody man at his hooves. Muscles flexing, the beast meant business and was ready to spring forward.

Hux leveled both guns at him.

Hawg hesitated, his red eyes widening.

"You comprehend just fine, don't ya?" Hux said in a loud voice. "I won't miss so close." Then again, he mused to himself, he thought that in the park the distance was sufficient.

Roberts screamed at Hux, "Shoot it! For chrissake! Shoot!"

Hawg looked down at the bloody man and his nostrils widened. Spit fell in droplets from his maw just before Hawg lowered his head. Hawg bolted forward fast, sinking his teeth in Roberts' ankle. By the cracking sound in the air, Hux expected the appendage to come off, but Hawg wrenched his head back to the side, moving Roberts body a yard in the gravel. One claw down on Robert's knee for leverage, the creature made a move at Hux. The biker stepped back into the cabin and slammed the door shut. He heard the knee break and Roberts's scream out just before the door shut. Hawg's weight slammed into the door, but it held. Hux quickly dropped a bar over the door. He fired through the door with each gun, doing a mock gunslinger action from gun to gun.

Hawg never impacted on the door again, but Hux could hear him rage outside. The cry wasn't one of pain. Hux banked on frustration and also gambled the beast would turn back to Roberts. By the screams out of the man from Cicero, Hux was correct.

Hux slid up the side window by the toilet and dived out, head first. He hoped his timing was good as he slammed himself into the side of the cabin. Roberts' screams became worse and Hux bolted for the boat. He didn't want to check back, but he had to reassure himself that Hawg was busy enough. If he wasn't, he prayed the guns would do the job this time.

Boots in the boat, Hux nearly capsized the tiny vessel as he sat down. Guns still in his hands, he saw that Hawg went to work on Roberts and the drug dealer was still alive…but Hux didn't understand how. Hawg's left knee pinned one of Robert's legs down while he'd split open his guts with his tusks. Hawg had the long intestines out and found it difficult to dislodge them from his tusks. All the while, Roberts screamed in agony, his insides up and out for him to see, his other leg broken and bent backward.

While the screams kept going, Hux said," Die, already, fer God's sake, die!"

Hux put down the guns and yanked the cord on the engine. It failed to start, but Hux yanked a few more times. Again, no life from the engine. He grabbed up the oars and started to row like mad. He was about a quarter of the way across when Roberts stopped screaming.

Hawg stood up, chewing, and swiping the guts away from their entanglement. Still sucking air, the creature seemed vexed. Hux kept rowing as the beast sliced down with its claws and then dropped to rut in the gaping flesh of the drug dealer. Thankful for its hunger, Hux glanced over his shoulder at his bike. God, it looked beautiful. He had to reach it. He pulled on the engine cord and it barked to life. Hux practically came as he directed the boat forward.

Halfway to his target, Hux saw Hawg stand again. He never wiped the grisly dinner from his mouth or face. He squared his shoulders toward Hux and…smiled?!

Hux felt pressure on his bladder as he pressed on quickly, confident he'd make it, but uneasy at the horrific sight all the same.

When Hawg plunged into the water and started to swim faster than before, Hux nearly pissed his pants at the sight. As he started to row to supplement the craft's speed, he recalled reading that during Hurricane Katrina that no hogs had died on farms, that they swam to higher ground.

Hux was near to the edge when he dropped the oars, reached down, grabbed his gun, and fired at Hawg a few times. The bullets never came close, but they made the creature pause. Hux heaved on, and pushed the boat back to the shore. He grabbed up both guns, tripped and fell on his face on the rocky edge. He rolled and fired blind in the direction of Hawg. He lost Roberts' pistol in the roll, but got to his feet and faltered in his steps to his bike.

Leg over his Harley, Hux saw Hawg nearing the edge of the quarry. He fired up the engine and smiled, feeling safe at last.

Hawg climbed out of the water, but never made a line toward him. Instead, the creature grabbed the front of the small boat. Hux filled with fear and twisted the throttle. His back tire swung on the rocky surface as he turned to go. Sure enough, Hawg slung the boat at him. The exploit was awkward, close to a side arm volley, but it nearly hit him head on. The glancing shot struck his rear tire. Hux fishtailed and almost lost control. A rider for years, he quickly recovered and headed out.

In his mirrors, Hawg was coming for him.

Hux turned and headed toward Route 66.

Mr. Solow held a fence post as Elias twisted wire around the metal loop imbedded in its top. Perspiration sprang on Elias' face as he worked the mesh around the pole, making certain it was secure. Elias looked at Mr. Solow as the Sheriff's car drove onto the gravel lane of the main house. Mr. Solow didn't turn to face him, though, only focusing on the post. Soon, he looked at the round barn near where they worked, then at the space where no pasture had ever existed.

"Make sure this is secure, Elias," Solow told him, fishing a red handkerchief from his overall's side pocket. He stepped away from the pen, erected around the western edge of the round barn, and waved to Doug White.

"Mr. Solow, I need to speak with you," Doug called out, not returning his wave.

Solow rubbed his face and then wiped his nose on the handkerchief. "Sure thing, sheriff. Since that brief talk Grimes had had with Elias earlier, I thought this was over on our part."

"I don't think so."

"I hope Grimes's wife is all right."

"Paula survived what happened in the plant," Doug said coldly.

"That's good."

"We better go inside," Doug said with a bitter voice, eyes on Elias.

With a nod, Solow started walking toward the house.

Once on the porch, Doug looked back to Elias and said to the farmer, "You need to hire younger help."

"Elias is still a good man, Sheriff. Iced tea?"

"No, I'm good. I suppose getting rid of Elias would be like firing family, huh?" He followed the farmer into the living room and added, "But he isn't quite family, is he?"

Solow groaned a bit as he sat down, and then sipped some tea he'd poured himself. "No, not quite family."

CHAPTER FIFTEEN

Family

Andrew sat in his truck, engine off. The minutes were nearly up as he spoke into Wilma's phone.

"Jordan, Mommy will get you in a while. Daddy has some more things to do."

"But I want you to come get me," Jordan said, not quite pleading, but insisting.

"After a while, we'll all be together. Just watch out for your little brother and your Mommy, for Daddy, all right?"

"Okay," Jordan replied fast, but seemed to want to talk more. "Dad...."

"Yeah?"

"When will you be home? Will it be safe from the pig-man? Are you going to kill it?"

Andrew swallowed and closed his eyes. He climbed out of his truck and said, "I'll be home later, Jordan. I think we won't have to worry on the pig-man any more after tonight."

"Is Uncle Doug going to shoot him?"

Andrew couldn't help but smile. "Maybe a lot worse. I'll let you know. But remember what I said. Watch out for Kenny and Mommy, always."

"Okay, Dad."

"Love you, Jordan."

"Love you, too," the boy said and the line went off.

Andrew called Hux again, but received no answer. He then squinted at the phone, seeing there was a text message from the biker.

ON THE WAY. COMING IN HOT.

"Some message," Andrew mused, wondering how he texted him on the bike. "Carefully."

Suddenly warm, he shed his flannel shirt and deposited it in the truck. Andrew took the wires, grips, and extra explosives to the crypt. On the way, he could've sworn he smelled something, raw, primal, and female.

"I need to drink more," he chided himself. Andrew looked at the sun and judged they had a few hours of daylight left.

He stepped over the loose wire and climbed into the crypt.

The journey to Route 66 was less than a mile and Hux had to cross the railway line. His heart flipped for a moment, afraid he'd be trapped at the warning lights. Luck was with him and he crossed over the tracks and stopped, awaiting Hawg.

The creature emerged on the high tracks, looking down at him on the Route. Though he could see the beast breathing, the creature didn't appear winded.

"That's a good bastard, keep coming," Hux muttered, thumb working his phone.

Hawg didn't make a straight bee line for Hux. Instead, he leapt into the ditch and made a guess where Hux would be driving.

Not expecting such a move, Hux dropped his phone and hit the throttle hard.

Hawg loomed on the roadside, parallel to him. Unable to grab the gun off hand, worried only to keep the bike steady, Hux held on for his life and kicked the bike in the ass. Their eyes met and the look of primal anger in Hawg stabbed into Hux's mind. The bike accelerated, besting the beast. Hawg fell behind, but swiped at the rear tire of the cycle. Hux's entire body felt like ice as the bump hit home. The blow glanced off and Hux started to thank God, something he seldom did. He checked over his shoulder and then checked his mirrors. Sure enough, the monster remained after him.

If he was successful, Hux promised God to get religious very soon.

Montrose appeared before them, spreading out with a

trailer park on one side, a large recreation Complex for base-
ball diamonds on the other, all in the back yard of the State
Penitentiary. Hux didn't know if the creature would follow him
all the way past and a few more miles to the cemetery. Then
again, he'd have never believed the creature would do what it
did in the factory.

In small towns, word gets around fast. It didn't take long for
phone calls, text messages and camera phone shots of the dead
to circulate, or in a few bad cases, end up online. Added to what
happened at the Green parrot the night before, word went wild
all over town.

While Porter Loring affected a fine clean up, the tales of
the biker bar massacre and other deaths ran rampant. The city
council stepped in as the Mayor couldn't answer questions. The
Chief of Police sought to quell fears and synchronize efforts
with the State Police. The local National Guard Unit, put on
notice earlier, was then called up for another night of searching.

Though the eyewitnesses from Ambrose Brothers swore the
thing wasn't human, the official word was it was a deranged
maniac of some sort. The only images of Hawg that a few people got on their phones were too pixilated to be clear.

The chief of police soberly mentioned a few missing maniacs from Indiana that could be to blame. He named Wilbur
Ferguson, the Mud Lick strangler, who'd escaped custody a year
ago and was presumed dead in a car crash. He also alluded to
Bubba Ray Armstrong, the Kirkwood, Missouri cannibal who
had escaped from a mental home months before.

Some accepted, but many knew the truth. What could they
do with such knowledge, though? The story spread and many
demanded action.

Reverend Wingler did what most ministers did during
troubled times. He prayed. In this case, he prayed loudly near
the flag outside Ambrose Brother's rear entrance. Someone had
lowered the flag to half-staff and a hundred people still hung
around the parking area, many unsure of what to do; several
stragglers from work refused to leave. The cameras from the
Peoria and Bloomington News caught the scenes and that of

Wingler showing up, swept back gray hair, looking pristine in his coal gray suit, as he stood under the flag and offered prayers.

Some of the most fervent drunks and drug users at the plant bowed their heads, dutifully following his powerful request.

"Let this not be business as usual in the case of tragedy," Wingler stated in a loud voice. "We all find God at the same time, too late."

No one objected to the prayers, not even the wanna-be hippies and proud atheists in the bindery. Some of the older employees recalled when they were allowed to pray before pot-luck Christmas luncheons. That practice was forbidden in the name of diversity.

"We need to hold our loved ones tight to our hearts this night. Thank God they were spared from the evil of the Devil. The wiles of Satan are all over and have lulled us into a stupor, where once confronted with a minion of Hell, all we could do was fall. This land is full of such evil. God will judge America for the way it condones this pagan lifestyle. What else has America done to bring the judgment of God? We have put the god of self in front of the God of the highest Heaven. We have embraced all forms of sexual deviancy and hedonism for which God destroyed Sodom and Gomorrah. We have become a sec-ular humanist cesspool where nothing is right or wrong. We forget the words of God, much less the physical Word of God. We are losing this country to alcoholism, to drugs, prostitution, AIDS, and abortion. We are tortured by the sins of murder, rape, incest, and hate. Is there an answer for America? YES! It is not a government grant! It is not more classes, or sensitivity training! The solution for this nation is a return to the preaching of the Word of God! A return to the Word of God, where we learn of Jesus Christ, who was crucified for the redemption of your sins! A government grant cannot rid your life of the Devil, but the sacrificial blood of Jesus Christ can change your life, your mind, and the destiny of your eternal soul! This book is the two-edged sword of truth that convicts your dark heart! This book is what tells you how to live and why to live a good life. This book is Jesus Christ on paper, pure and simple! Who is Jesus Christ to you? Was he just a good guy? No, he was not! Some of you say he was a great spiritual leader. No, he was not! He didn't claim to merely preach the truth but he claimed to be The Truth! He is either Lord, or a liar. If there is no absolute truth in your life, you are living a lie. If there is no absolute right or wrong, you are living a delusion. If some over-educated fool comes up and tells you there is no God, Jesus didn't exist, or we came from apes...tell them that if ignorance could be sold by the pound, they could buy the universe!"

His voice rolled and his flaring eyes stabbed at the members of management who watched him with bleary eyes.

As Wingler went into the invocation, Karen Laurens suddenly screamed out in terror. Porter Loring held his arm around her and delivered the sad news about her husband. Wingler went on preaching and it added to the surreal picture as Karen sank to the pavement. The drama helped a few younger men take a knee by Reverend Wingler and to promise to dispense with their sins and take on the blood of Christ. Wingler gave sympathetic looks to the weeping Mrs. Laurens and her consoling friend, Annette Moyer. The preacher wasn't aware that Ms. Moyer's panties were still damp with the blood and semen from Lou Lauren, but it didn't matter. They needed saved, dirty pants or no.

A car parked near where several police stood and an ambulance took on another body. The new arrival was Betty Sullivan, holding the hand of Jack Jr. She spoke with Porter Loring, nodded, and turned her face from the crowd. She turned to look at the flag, then at Wingler. Betty had a single tear on the left side of her face. That was it. That was all there would be.

Already, human nature took over. A few of the men talked of who would get Earl Gamblin's pressman job.

Brian Miller argued with the police insisting that a monster threw Jimmy Mans into the forks of his hoist.

The television crews bore witness to it all, filming many wild tales and testimonies.

Elias hummed a song as he poured kerosene on his burning pile. The spot where he dispatched trash items or old branches was an area of field tiles spread in a tiny mound. Several years of burning had never diminished the mound beyond its original state. A few bags of trash, some green wood now ready to go, and a few old shingles joined the object Elias held in his left hand. Once the fire blazed, he looked at the helmet one last time, read the inner writing that denoted it belonged to a man named DOUBLE D.

The helmet went on the fire.

"What's on your mind, Sheriff?"

Doug's gaze held steady on Mr. Solow as he gripped the band of his hat in his hands and asked, "Is Hawg from your place? What do you know about him?"

"That's a direct question, I like that," Mr. Solow chuckled. "You have a name for this escaped maniac now? Hawg? Radio said it is some Hoosier serial killer."

"Oh, the chief has to tell folks something. He's fulla shit. I like you, sir, and always have. I've known you my entire life. You and my Pa went way back. If he'd have ever talked ill of you, I'd have suspected you right away. But Pa liked you a great deal. You two were friends. That carries a lot with me."

"Suspect me of what?" Solow asked, face blank. "I've been open about my farm and your boys have searched all of it for a clue to this fellow and his rampages."

"Why didn't he kill you?"

Solow took another drink. "Just lucky, I suppose."

"Wonder why he chose to lay in a crypt beside the Solow one at the cemetery?"

"Ah, but not *in* the Solow one, son. You are fishing, Douglas. I cannot blame you. You have your hands full and the weight of the world on your ass."

Doug's face soured. "I can't pin any of this to you, sir, but I'm not stupid. Please don't treat me as such and lie to me. Be honest with me."

Solow's face grew grim. "I'm too old for prison, young man. And you are right in that you cannot tie this Hawg thing to me. I'm an old hog farmer, nothing more. On the stand, I could get senile really fast. I could even spin a great tale of how I was on board the *USS Eldridge* during that famous Philadelphia

Experiment. Ya know, I ain't been right since, or that is what I could say. I wonder what such things as electromagnetic radiation and gravity tests do to one's DNA, huh? They'd think me crazy or a curiosity. I don't care what the lynch mob might say, you have no case against me."

"You are a religious man, right? I sure can't stop by for rhubarb and not hear a sermon from your tapes."

"What is your point?"

"How can you justify lying or doing this if you are such a religious man?"

"Doing what? Keeping and tending animals? Get to the point, Douglas."

"What is he, Mr. Solow?"

Solow drank again. "Can you understand it? Can you grasp what I have done with no thought? You are a father. What would you do if you had a child with Downs Syndrome? Put them in that home in Dwight and forget them? Would you do your damnedest to keep close and care for them? It's a sad thing when one creates something the world can do without. But no God fearin' man would hate their own kinfolk. That's just asinine."

"Your son? How?"

"No one is perfect, Douglas. I'm sorry for all of this, but the will of God goes as it must. You see, I used to think God was making me serve a penance for my past sins. The Catholics are good for that, but us Fundamentalists, we know that's hogwash."

"Yes."

"Jesus died for our sins. However, I wrestle if I was earnest enough in my confession for my transgressions."

"I don't follow you."

"I used to think the Voodoo priestess I banged in New Orleans way back when cursed me. She died when I was on top of her. Freak thing, ya know? I used to blame the affair I had in the fifties with the Indian Shaman's wife, but I wasn't exclusive to her privates. Hell, that Shaman was shootin' blanks. All of her kids came from others, or so I reckon. I know he got the electric chair for strangling her back just before Kennedy got assassinated. Always wondered if that was bad karma, but the blood of Jesus is supposed to trump all that, right?"

"Mr. Solow...."

"Heck, I used to wonder if God was pissed that I used to love to get a gal in the backside. That was against his laws major, you know? Maybe it was the test on the *USS Eldridge*, who knows? Though no scientist, I reckon it had something to do with me crossing up with Luella, my half-sister. Paying off the sins of drunken stupidity, that's a good mantra, as the hippies call it. It was an accident, a freak happening, and she is poisoned by the curse of my evil or the twisted means of bad science."

"All right. But it's loose. How did it happen?"

"Got ahold of a snatch full of bad drugs, I wager. It's a long story you don't want to hear, son, but suffice it to say, I reckon he'll be back in time."

"What makes you so sure?"

"He's threatened and feels those close to home were threatened. It's all about blood and family, Douglas. Yours, mine, and ours."

"I see."

"Are you going to take me away?"

Douglas stood up. "I don't know what to do with you, to be honest. You ought to feel great, all of those dead people on your mind."

"I feel nothing of the sort, Douglas. The world is full of predators and prey. Those people are weak. The weak deserve what they get. Hawg is strong. He'll come home someday."

"I'll be waiting."

Solow nodded. "That's your job, Sheriff."

"Hawg killed Luella. How's that make you feel?"

The old man swallowed. "It was her time."

CHAPTER SIXTEEN

Primed

Hawg kept his velocity fixed, and straight on down the edge of Route 66. His claws and hooves took better to the earth near the ditches, aiding in his long strides. The paved road was a place for machines and men who were slaves to them. Hawg loved the earth, deep and pure. It would help him to reach his goal.

He also hungered for the fool on the bike, meat in general, and more gilt. Though the run through the country winded him, Hawg learned so much about himself. His endurance seemed to grow the longer he ran. Never before had Hawg experienced such independence. His tempo, ever balanced, seemed to be less tiring the longer he ran, so Hawg kept to it.

The walls of the town loomed again and Hawg felt fear inside his stomach. He hated town and all of its fences, walls, and rattling noise. It was better to be close to the earth. Soon, he would be back home with family and his own blood. After this fool died, it would be as it was in years past, only better.

Hawg saw the biker grin when he looked over his shoulder. The fool really thought he could escape him or trick him into something dire. Hawg knew better. Hawg could smell the biker's fear, big enough to walk over a lake on.

His own terror subsided as they trekked down 66 as it snaked through the edges of Montrose. The side of the road offered him great cover and few even noted him until they'd passed by. Hawg heard a few wheels screech and then the crash of metal and glass. He continued on, nearing what smelled like a sewage disposal plant on the cracking Route.

A man on a bicycle crossed the highway and aimed straight at Hawg. Never slackening his pace, Hawg charged on, braining the rider with a swipe of his right claw. The bike rolled a bit as the rider fell, dead by the side of the road.

Hawg carried on, hungry and burning inside.

If he didn't slay and eat the balls of this idiot, it was really of no matter. Hawg had plenty of time. His mouth turned up in what passed for a smile.

Unlike Hawg, humans couldn't live forever....

"This little piggy went to market...." Andrew said to himself and smiled as he twisted the last wire onto the end of his hand-held trigger. He lay this on the head of the right-side coffin. He looked in each sepulcher, noted the rows of plastic explosives wired together, the bottles of nitro and the dynamite primed and ready. Curious if the conglomeration would have the whiplash effect he planned, Andrew gazed down as he stepped forward, seeing the wire across the entrance to the tomb. Above the floor several inches, the trip wire held the initial trigger. He looped up a long line of cable and took the hand-held trigger with him out the door. Carefully, he pushed the ruined gate open farther. "And that little piggy is gonna go wee, wee, wee all the fucking way home."

He hated this moment, for now he had to wait on Hux. There wasn't much to do save to kill time. Andrew put down the gripper and walked halfway to his truck.

Andrew walked over to his father's grave. The wildflowers left by Jordan and Cassidy made him smile.

"Well, Pa, here's to you. Zero hour and the battle is ready to be fought." Overhead, a plane zoomed and slanted. He hadn't seen many of the crews out searching around since the disaster at Ambrose Brothers. Most of the cops and helicopters were focused on Montrose and the areas near to it. Eyes down, he said, "Wish me luck, Dad. Be seeing you soon."

Andrew thought of the war and death his father experienced. It was nothing like he had planned out today, of course. "You being the hero made me into a collector?" Andrew said to the wind. "Probably, but who fucking cares? I'm comfortable with who I am." He looked toward Montrose and heard the thump of chopper blades. "I guess."

He saw a looming statue of Jesus over by the bushes. He'd seen it before, many times, but walked over to it, hands on his hips.

"Well, just you and me Lord, huh? What have you got in store for me this afternoon? Do I get to see you face to face or not?"

Fear tripped up Andrew's arms and settled on his head when he heard a dull moan from the statue. His fear faded as he looked down, seeing a pair of eyes glaring at him from the weeds just under the brush.

Remembering his guns were back in the truck, Andrew swallowed hard and said, "Who is it?"

Again, came a tearful moan.

Down on his haunches, Andrew pulled the bushes apart.

The face was brutal, bruised, covered with dried mud and probably blood. The eyes never blinked and glowed under the greasy strains of butterscotch colored hair that dangled in her face.

"I won't hurt you," Andrew said gently. "Everything is all right."

He lied, for as she unfolded from the bushes, and he saw her ruined flesh, Andrew felt like a big fibber. They were leading the thing that did this to her back to this location.

She seemed familiar, but he couldn't place her face. Perhaps one of the temps at work in the previous summer. So many came and went, he couldn't get a handle on them. This one had a cross tattooed on her backside above her ass-crack...three of them in fact, like Calvary.

"Micki?" Andrew said and her eyes burst into tears.

Hux slowed going through the edge of town. He checked over his shoulder many times, worried Hawg would catch him. Visions of the beast ripping him to pieces, leaving him alive as he ate him like Mr. Roberts, tugged at the edges of Hux's coke fueled mind. Still, the thrill of the chase buoyed him on.

He thought of the guns on his body and the knives in his boots. He'd never go down without a fight. Hux promised himself he'd die fighting that thing. It had to die. It had to leave this earth, badly. Hux wanted to hear it scream in pain.

Hux kept those things at bay in his mind as he plotted his escape from Montrose. After this thing was dead, he'd get gone fast. He'd go to his storage places, get his cache of cash, sneak into his house, gather what he treasured, and hit the road. First, he would go to the Sturgis area as friends there would hide him. Then, across the Badlands to more friends, maybe in Sparks, Nevada.

Still, the angst inside twisted at him. He would try to drink or to smoke it away, but the death of the creature had to be the exorcism for it. For what it had done to him, for the violation and the twisted feelings all over his body, Hawg had to die at his hand. On the seat, his ass ached, a reminder of Hawg's touch. Ever since, his manhood randomly refused to stiffen. His mind was elsewhere, not on trim or booze, but on that feeling. Hawg's death would bring it all back.

Mr. Solow hadn't felt like cooking, so he microwaved some leftover pork chops. He lamented that a dinner of soda pop, pork chops, bread, and potato chips wasn't the healthiest spread on earth, but he was long since past worrying over his health. A diet wasn't in his future plans.

He showered, donned fresh clothes, and poured himself a glass of homemade wine. Though never one to get really drunk, Mr. Solow enjoyed the nightly drink. It put him in the mood for sleep.

Eyes on the afternoon paper, he grimaced. Though the paper went to press too late to include the morning slaughter at Ambrose Brothers, the paper contained stories about the bodies found the night before at the tavern and at the corner of his property. His head felt hot as he read the lines, but no word of a monster made the papers. Many thought it was the work of a gang, probably over drugs. Alex's death was mentioned, but its details proved vague and unclear if he died with the bikers... just that he was killed.

"People talk," he mumbled, and knew survivors at Ambrose Brothers would tell the tale. Would they be believed? He didn't care. There was no connection to him. His words to Sheriff White? "Who listens to crazy old men?"

He folded the paper over and dropped it beside the couch. Solow scanned his wall of tapes and settled in on a topic. He inserted the tape in the stereo, refilled his wine glass and sat down.

"I'm glad that you all came out on this fine spring evening. This week, we remember the passion, the death, and resurrection of our Lord Jesus Christ. If you don't know him as your savior, if you have never experienced his powerful love, then you will before I am through this evening. Love is a powerful thing, but sometimes one forgets one's true love. I heard of a man in Texas who didn't kiss his wife for ten years, and then shot a man who did." There was a pause as laughter rolled in the stadium.

There was a knock on the screen door and Solow recognized Elias' touch. The old man entered, unbidden, and poured himself some wine in a coffee mug.

"Thanks for joining me," Mr. Solow said as he offered to refill the mug Elias had drained fast.

"No sir, just one for me. I got to keep a clear head."

"Oh?"

"I think tonight's the night."

Solow nodded. "Praise the Lord."

"This is my personal Bible that I use when writing my sermons. I received it from a chaplain when I was in Vietnam. As you can see, both of us have seen better days. I don't use this Bible any longer when I preach for the lettering is very small. I have reached the age when curiosity is greater than vanity. But I do use this particular Bible to find things fast. This book is well worn, well thumbed, full of underlines and notes in the margins. This is the book that responds to the touch of my fingers, for the pages roll almost immediately to the book, chapter and verse I'm trying to locate. Although it's worn out and beat up, it's still good. Still very good. But is the word of God still good and relevant in America today? The same thing that was wrong in this

world two thousand years ago is still wrong with this planet today. The thing that was wrong seven thousand years ago is still wrong with this world in Chicago, Illinois. It is sin! The equivalent factor that coiled up in the garden and made Eve fall from grace is the same thing that makes a young man shoot his fellow students today! It is what makes a mother drown her children, it is what makes a father cheat on his wife and bring home AIDS. It is what makes children turn to darkness and away from light. It is sin and it still flows from the original source-- from the prince of darkness himself."

Doug was outside the office of the chief of police when Reverend Wingler caught up to him. Unable to escape in his car fast enough, Doug stood touching the car like it was the nirvana and he drew strength from its avenue of escape.

"I know you are a busy man, Sheriff," Wingler said, face taut and eyes in full brimstone pulpit threat mode. "Any word on my daughter?"

"We have no reports of Micki or any sightings of her. The troopers and volunteers are combing the countryside and all avenues will be pursued."

Teeth barely able to part, Reverend Wingler snapped, "I don't think she's dead, Sheriff. She's probably passed out in the house of one of those biker bastards you refuse to lock up."

"One has to commit a crime to be locked up, Reverend."

"Mr. White, Sheriff, you have always been an amiable enough fellow," his tone softened, but Doug sensed the viper ready to strike. "But if I didn't know any better, I'd think you are turning a blind eye to the drug trade in this town."

Hand on his car becoming a fist, Doug replied, "Is that so? That's a serious accusation, sir, beyond worry over your daughter. Micki has a juvie record longer than both of my arms, and how many times have I returned her to you, drunk, behind the wheel, and not charged her?"

Wingler grimaced. "Yes, I know...."

"I can bend so far, sir, and try to be a good man. But we are doing all we can to find her. I have my hands full today, but rest assured, sir, I will do my best to find her."

"It's that damnable Huxtable, he's the culprit," Wingler said with cinders in his words. "She is obsessed with that man, far too old for her. He has her hooked on something, keeps her coming back."

Doug nodded. "Hux is a bad man and is also wanted for questioning. I'll get him today."

"I heard tell of a beast on the loose, a giant pig-man. How preposterous is that?"

Doug shrugged. "I've not seen any such thing."

"But some have, and they have believed."

"Sometimes, folks want to believe really bad. The worse it is, the more they want it to be so."

Wingler was about to speak when a city cruiser pulled up and shouted at Doug, "Sheriff! Trouble at Bob & Jodi's Tavern uptown!"

"That's news?" Doug retorted. "Can't you handle it?"

"You better come along."

Doug looked at the minister and said, "Gotta go, Reverend."

"I'll pray for you," Wingler said flatly.

Doug turned the key in his ignition and said, "I need it."

Not bothering to be coy about his arrival, Doug turned on his cherries and parked in the street outside the line of parked cars. Out in the open air, he donned his hat and listened to the ravings filtering out of the open door.

"This shit is getting better and better," he muttered and delivered the city cops tart looks as he walked to the door.

Bob & Jodi's was an establishment frequented by younger drinkers in Montrose. Older folks went down the street to *Sherman's* or to the country and western establishment *Woody's*; druggies and folks of color to *Sadie's* down the other way by the dry cleaners, bikers to the *Green Parrot* on the edge of town, respectable folks to the *Pub* near the library.

The bar ran along the left wall of the tavern while the right side held numerous small tables better for standing at than sitting. Various stuffed heads of elk, deer and other critters lined the wall out of reach. They didn't fit with the clientele, but the owner, Bob Fanchie, was too lazy to take them down. Bob was Andrew's age and Doug was acquainted with him from various arrests at the tavern. Fanchie stood behind the bar, hands on the counter, and nodded at the man on the floor clinging to the CD jukebox.

Fanchie said, "Gopher came in after they let them out of work, got plowed on gin and shots. No different than any other day, other than today he started fights and mouthed off too much. Now, well, I didn't know what else to do. This crazy stuff is gonna get out all over, Doug."

Normally, this wasn't such a personal event to rate a cameo by the county sheriff. But this wasn't a normal day in Montrose.

"Fucking monster, killed them all," the man blubbered, huge buckteeth popping from his mouth as his eyes suddenly lit on the Sheriff. "Your brother was there! I saw him on the stairs when the thing butchered Jack Sullivan!"

"Calm down, Gopher," Doug said with a gentle tone. "Let's get you home."

"Where's safe anymore?" he wailed, tears streaming from bloodshot eyes, knuckles still white on the jukebox. "Can I be safe in my bed seeing that big monster in my dreams? Yeah, I said it! You heard me good. It wasn't a man at all. I saw it and will never quit saying it."

"Calm down, Gopher," Doug said insistently, hands on his gun belt.

"This ain't Russia! I'll tell 'em all, drunk or sober, what I saw until my dyin' day. Not everyone who saw it is a drunk, Sheriff! Your brother saw it, he pulled the fire alarm after it killed Jack Sullivan!"

Doug reached down and yanked Gopher up by his forearms. "You need to sleep this off."

"It ain't gonna be that easy," Gopher whimpered, eyes closed, tears streaming.

"What's going on, Sheriff?" Fanchie asked, fingers drumming on the bar. Several patrons looked at Doug with listless faces, as if they all spoke with the owner.

The thump from the sky drove into Hawg's spine as he ran after Hux. While cars screeched to a stop at a series of stoplights, letting them pass through, Hawg stopped a hundred yards beyond. Although his breath returned to him fast, he saw the chopper overhead, blades spinning. He saw the biker's back light flare as he slowed; aware Hawg no longer pursued him.

Hawg scanned the nearby subdivision and greenery that hemmed in these two-story homes. The chopper drew closer as did cars with flashing lights. The bushes and trees called to him. He darted off Route 66, and soon discovered this greenery was a thin barrier against the outside world. His mind worked fast, swiftly abandoning any thoughts of peace and solace in these environs.

As the chopper lowered, Hawg felt the wind of the spinning blades. He loathed the sensation it parceled to his body. The chopper bobbed up and down and Hawg saw the door slide open on the side. Surely, they endeavored to make him skittish by this machine. Though he hated it, he didn't fear it. Hawg scanned the long hedge and the home beyond. The flashing cars closed in and the biker changed his course in the distance.

Hawg leapt over the short hedge like a stallion, and into the back yard of an elderly lady. He skidded to a stop near the edge of an empty rectangle of concrete. The old woman sat in a wicker chair, coffee on a glass table, newspaper in her hand. The radio on the table spoke, but Hawg didn't pay any attention to it. Her eyes blinked and the old woman made no sudden exit, not even when the chopper lowered and grew closer to her back yard.

Hawg gawked up at the chopper and bellowed. With the side door open, he saw the man in a dark uniform stare at him. He could smell the man's terror, even if he held a long weapon in his hands. Hawg seized the edges of the table, but then thought better of his plan. He looked at the house and saw something higher up that appealed to him.

The woman never screamed as Hawg left her and jumped onto the wooden latticework on the side of the house. He climbed several feet before it broke, sending him crashing back to the lawn. Angry with himself, Hawg jumped high, grabbing the gutter of the porch. He then pulled himself up to the roof of the small side porch before repeating this motion on the main roof of the house.

Unsure why the fool in the chopper hadn't shot at him yet, Hawg closed in on his prey. His hooves skidded on the shingles, but he stabbed in, getting good footing. The screams of the flashing cars drew close as the first cracks echoed from the chopper. Hawg felt the heat of the shot as the man missed him. The chopper bobbed, up and down, not wanting to get close enough for the beast to leap at them. Hawg understood they'd keep a fair distance. That's why he grabbed the small satellite dish and ripped it from its moorings.

He saw the horror in the face of the shooter above him just before Hawg twisted in his motion. Hawg heaved the dish like a disk, aiming not at the man, but at the swirling blades over his head. The wobbling path of the satellite dish struck true, up near to the focal point of the swirling blades.

Like a hovering kite yanked by a child, the chopper jerked, twisted around and sputtered. The man with the rifle fell out of the rising machine and landed over the peak of the house. The chopper didn't stay up long. With a single low scraping sound, the machine coughed, rose up and fell like a stone. It crashed beyond the hedge and into the back yard of the next home, taking out a glassed-in porch in the process.

Hawg exalted his arms and roared, staring for a moment at the man lying across the peak of the home, facing up. The man never budged as Hawg drew nearer to him on the roof. Only the man's eyes moved as Hawg took hold of him.

When he glared over the side of the house, several flashing vehicles entered the driveway. Hawg flicked the man off the house with a casual action of his claws, sending the paralyzed body onto the top of a flashing SUV. Hawg expected the windows to break from the man's impact, but was disappointed. With a sigh, Hawg leapt off the roof and landed where he planned...on the stomach of the man he had just heaved off the roof. The guts and spine of this trooper cushioned the hooves as his body crashed into the roof of the Montrose police SUV. Glass shattered and the roof bent in from Hawg's impact. Cart wheeling off the SUV, Hawg's tusks drew in as the arm extended from the driver's side of the SUV. Tusks out of the way, Hawg quickly bit into the forearm of the policeman aiming at

him. The gun went off, but the bullets only injured trees. Hawg
tore loose the meat from the bone, chewing and savoring a fast
meal. So hungry from his run, he wished he had time to gorge
himself, but this would not be the case. The walls closed in and
too many sirens screamed close. Hawg bolted back the way he
came, happy he had eluded the flying machine. He glanced at
the wreckage of that thing, smoking in the yard next to the old
woman, who still sat with a paper on her lap, watching.

Hawg sprinted in the ditch beside the Route and was a
few hundred yards away before his ears picked up the uneven
bark of the biker. When Hawg jumped up the side of the road,
the biker came into view. He saw him on the edge of the highway, looking at the commotion in the distance. Hawg heard his
cry and felt his terror as he saw him again. The bike's wheels
screamed and the machine swung around.

Hawg went after him as the city receded. He would have
him. Before the day was done, Hawg would see him die.

Andrew retrieved the guns, the flannel shirt, and a bottle of
water from his truck. Micki Wingler, he mused. The smart-
mouthed, wild-assed preacher's daughter. Who woulda thunk
it? With a few shop rags from the truck, he cleaned off her bru-
talized face, and then offered her the water and the rags to try
to regulate herself.

She gulped the water, spit some out, and then drank it slowly.

After she put the shirt on, Micki clung to Andrew. He held
her as gently as he could, for as she embraced him, she cried. All
of it came out, the story about being left for dead by her lover,
one she never named, and then the beast attacking her, over and
over.

"I have to call you some help," he said, no longer caring
about the plot to kill Hawg.

She looked at the stone markers, then at the tiny one that
popped out of the ground. This read BABY and made her cry
out, "God, don't let me be carrying that thing's kid."

"It'll all be okay now," Andrew assured her, not caring if he
lied. "But I gotta call the ambulance. I don't care what the plan
is with Hux."

"Hux?" she spat the word. Lips quivering and eyes widening, Micki demanded, "What do you mean?"

Andrew held Wilma's phone, but never pressed any buttons as he said, "Hux and I are trapping this damned thing, this rotten Hawg, here. He's leading it back here right now. We gotta go."

Before he pressed a button, Micki leapt from his side and started to run. She screamed, full of terror at the idea of Hawg returning.

Unfortunately, she ran right toward the pit.

He was up fast and pursued. Right about then, he was glad he didn't plant the claymores in the graveyard randomly as he first thought. Andrew shouted for her to stop but she never did. Her steps were short and uneven, though. Micki's body in so much pain, her flight didn't last long, but she made the edge of the pit as Andrew leapt to catch her. He grabbed Micki's thighs as she went to rush over the edge. She hung over the expanse, in his grasp, staring into the oblivion offered by the knives, implements, and explosive charges spread all around. A spider web of thin wires crisscrossed the opening at about the height of the tallest blade, ensuring that Hawg would trip the grenades Andrew had rigged up in the pit.

Andrew yanked her close, pulling her out of the hole. "Don't do that again, you hear me? None of this is easy for me, either."

She wailed, hands grabbing at Andrew's t-shirt. "Can't let it get me again. Never, ever again."

"I won't. We gotta go...." his voice trailed off as his head rose. Micki's did too, her eyes blinked once, tears ready to fall.

They heard the sound of straight pipes up the highway and slowing near them. They both comprehended that Hux was coming in fast.

When the Harley shifted, they also heard a steady set of grunts. A ripple of terror traveled across Micki's body, akin to one shaking out a rug.

Eyes set on the direction of the entrance, Andrew mumbled, "They're here."

CHAPTER SEVENTEEN

Reckoning

When the reverberation of the Harley echoed out across the expansive graveyard, letting them know Hux's literal arrival was moments away, Doug pulled Micki back toward the set of crypts.

"C'mon, we have to get back away from here." But once he had Micki to her feet, Andrew ran to his truck. Determined to do the act alone, he pulled out a long roll of greenish canvas. As he ran back toward the trap, Andrew let it unravel behind him. Micki grabbed the edge of the tarp and got in line with his plan. Hurriedly, they pulled the cover over the top of the pit.

"That won't fool anyone," she said in a mousy voice as Andrew took her by the forearm and pulled her away from the area.

"It doesn't have to, but it's close enough for jazz." Andrew unhanded her as he saw Micki wince to his touch. "Sorry, I never meant to...." But he waved at her fast, pointing between the crypts of his family and that of Mr. Solow. "Hux sounds like he's revving up at the entrance, goading the Hawg in."

"Hux...." she said as they stepped around to the backside of the crypts. Her eyes looked toward the sound as if she could see what transpired many yards away. She then stared at Andrew. "What are you doing?"

On his knees, Andrew opened a couple long cases. He took out a semi-automatic machine gun, checked its ammo, and then tossed it between the crypts. He then took up another machine gun, did an ammo check, and slung it over his right shoulder.

He stuffed a small revolver in the back of his pants and then made sure the sawed-off shotguns were ready.

"If I'm going to die," Andrew said with a smile, holding up two hand grenades. "It isn't going to be pretty. I've spent a lifetime gathering up this stuff and playing soldier, sweetheart. Now, it's time to fuckin' fight."

While Micki wrung her hands, she looked back at the direction the roar came from. "Give me a gun."

Andrew focused on her face, then looked at her shaky hands.

The bellow of the beast resounded in their ears and she screamed, "You have to give me a gun! I'll kill myself before I let that thing have me again."

Andrew took a sawed-off shotgun, showed her where the safety was, and instructed her to get in-between the crypts. "Get in, hon. I'll go along the outside side. I doubt Hawg can fit into the gap. If he tries, just blow his fucking face off."

She nodded, squatted down and grabbed Andrew's arm as he started to back away from her. "You afraid?"

Andrew half smiled and winked. "Shittin' my pants, sweetheart. I'll change later."

He crept around the side of the Solow crypt like he was out on maneuvers again. As the Harley roared, obviously in motion, Andrew wondered if he unconsciously put himself away from the high explosives in his own crypt. He stepped out, scooped up the trigger switch grip and started to back up for cover.

Andrew stopped for a moment as he saw Hux swing around into view in the distance. The ass end of his Harley fishtailed, but the biker was clearly grinning as he acted. Not twenty yards behind him, leapt Hawg into view, moving on all fours. Up on hind legs for a moment, the beast bellowed and dropped down, in hot pursuit of the laughing biker.

Andrew shook for a moment, enough to rattle his teeth, but screwed down his courage. He knelt beside the crypt, and brought down the machine gun from his shoulder. "Come get some, schvine-hundt," Andrew grunted, using his German grandmother's expression for pig-dog.

Hux howled like a wild man as he weaved on and off the gravel path in the larger part of the graveyard. Hawg kept after him, following the course Hux took. At one point, the beast mounted up on a huge brown stone and took a sprawling leap. Hux never knew the creature nearly caught him. Hawg missed, spun, but set his hooves to running and was back to the pursuit, relentless.

Andrew sank back as they both passed near to where they hid. Hawg never looked at the pickup truck as they raced past the tarp-covered pit.

"They missed it," he heard Micki exclaim.

"Shush over there, for God's sake," Andrew yelled as Hux looped around the other end of the graveyard. "Hux knows what he's doing."

Hawg planted his back feet and stood, trying to pivot and cut off Hux as he turned and started his track through the cemetery once more. Hux had to lean back to avoid the claw that swiped at him, but his laughter filled the air along with the roar of his cycle and the anger of the beast. Again, the pursuit was on.

"Hux," Andrew heard Micki say.

Andrew didn't know why she was muttering the name over there, and hoped she wouldn't expose them before the trap was sprung. As Hux rumbled back toward the tarp, Andrew had a vision of the beast getting after Micki between the crypts. Maybe she is what they needed, for he'd have no trouble shooting the creature if his head was in-between the crypts.

Hux thundered on, making right for the edge of the tarp. He couldn't open it up all the way in the close quarters of the cemetery, but seemed to relish the challenge of dodging the stones and controlling the metal monster between his legs.

Hawg was right behind him, only a couple of yards away.

Andrew leveled his machine gun, wishing he had a clear shot at Hawg and his machine gun was more accurate.

Micki lowered her shotgun just as they neared the tarp.

She pulled both triggers.

While such a gun couldn't kill much of anything at such a distance, the spray from the barrels hit its target full on.

The left side of Hux's face turned to a bloody mess and his arm jerked up, off the break on the handlebars to hold on his exiting scalp. His speed increased and the bike wobbled before it wrenched with a fatal twist. The bike jerked, corkscrewed down and sent its rider airborne, ass over elbows, and straight onto the green tarp.

The Harley twirled over and Hawg pulled up from his pursuit, slowed, and then stopped. He watched the biker fly through the air and hit the canvas covering. Hux screamed as he fell into the pit, then his loud voice shunted. A sudden cry went out, but it was wet, bubbly, and weak. Then, Andrew's handiwork with the wires came home to roost. A series of small explosions sent Hawg to his backside as fire and debris leapt out of the trap. Shards of the implements, dirt, and pieces of Hux belched from the ground in the ejecta cloud from the explosions. Andrew swore he saw a hand and a ponytail leap up and fall.

Andrew watched. He could do nothing else. He saw Hawg turn from his backside, adjust his tail, and then cautiously creep toward the edge of the pit. Hawg sniffed the edges of the crater, peered in, and smelled more. The sunlight off Hawg's tusks made Andrew want to piss his pants.

Then, Hawg rose up and looked right at him. Red eyes scanning, Andrew figured Hawg spotted Micki in the crypts. She was so dead, he thought, having used up her shots on Hux.

Andrew brought the gun up and squeezed the trigger. His spray of bullets from the magazine struck all around Hawg, but he soon nailed the beast at last. Hawg dropped down, but only to run. Blood had sprung from the creature's right hip, left upper pectoral muscle and his left forearm. The beast moved forward, but not at Andrew directly.

As Andrew stepped out from the crypt, he aimed better and fired again. Another stream of bullets hit near Hawg, then struck home, a few slugs causing founts of blood to spatter away from the creature's right shin and the left side of his face. Andrew paused, pleased that he thought he took Hawg's left ear off. That moment allowed Hawg to complete his mission. He grabbed the tiny marker in the ground, the one labeled BABY and ripped it up. Hawg kept in motion, slicing away from Andrew and the bullets, Hawg launched the stone marker at him. The object came in like a fastball. Andrew tried to move, but the marker deflected off his left forearm.

Pain shot through his body and he could hardly close his left hand. Unsure if the projectile broke his arm, he grabbed a flash grenade off the ground. The beast corrected his path and came right at Andrew. Grenade between his legs, Andrew yanked the pin and lobbed it. No sooner did the grenade hit the ground than it exploded into a brilliant glow. Hawg was going so fast, he screamed at this irritation and at the concussion of the flash grenade on his lower body. This shock was all that saved Andrew from an impact with the beast. He sidestepped the creature and then shoulder-rolled into the grass.

Hawg shook his head, eyes blinking because he came up empty handed. He sucked air fast, showing his weariness from the run, but still Hawg seethed power and strength. Blood ran from the creature from many spots, but it didn't seem to stop his resolve. He squared up, ready to charge Andrew as the man stepped into the open away from the front of the crypts.

"Hey, fucker!" Micki screamed and threw the flannel shirt into the face of the beast. "Come get me!"

Andrew and Hawg both wore stunned looks that Micki had stepped out of her safe position to confuse the creature. A tense moment passed as she waved her arms in the air, still not far from the gap between the crypts. She took a few steps away, giggled, grabbed her filthy breasts, and hopped into the White family crypt.

Surprised she got over the trip wire, Andrew yelled, "No, Micki! Get the hell out of there!"

Hawg took a step after her, but looked down at Andrew, eyes narrowing. Andrew could figure the beast's plans. Certain Hawg could kill him and fuck her later, Andrew reached back for his revolver. He struggled to hold the pistol with his left hand and fire the machine gun with his right. Hawg leapt, swatted the machine gun away, and looked down at Andrew's left hand.

The gun dropped from his hand. This motion distracted the beast for a moment. The open left hand grabbed Hawg's right wrist and pain shot through Andrew's forearm. Hawg never had time to comprehend the use of leverage as Andrew slammed a boot to the beast's groin and put everything he had into a right uppercut. Andrew's fist struck Hawg in the solar plexus. The beast wobbled from the shot to his testicles, but the blow from Andrew to his midsection didn't faze him much.

Hawg lowered his tusks, trying to expose Andrew's brain to the world, but the man chose that second to release Hawg and drop down to the ground. Enraged, Hawg grabbed up Andrew in a bear hug and squeezed, turning around to face the Solow crypt. Andrew felt agony in his ribs, figuring a few cracked and a couple broke as the beast slammed him into the bars of the Solow crypt. Andrew melted down, like a puppet in need of a hand up its ass.

Head lowered, Hawg sniffed him, glanced toward the other crypt for a moment, but when he looked back, Andrew had moved close and was near his face. Holding one tusk with his left hand, Andrew stuck his thumb in the bloody hole on the side of Hawg's head where his ear used to be. The pain was so severe, Hawg stood and roared, casting Andrew to the ground a few yards away. On all fours, Andrew crawled in front of his family crypt. Eyes on the sawed off shot gun Micki had used, he grabbed the barrel.

Bent over, Hawg held the side of his head and faced Andrew. On his knees, Andrew swung the shotgun down like a bludgeon, nailing the swinging penis of the beast. Again, rage filled the creature and it swung down, connecting with Andrew's right shoulder. He thought his arm came off at the shoulder joint at the guillotine move, but it clearly only dislocated. It'd happened when in the service once and after a bar fight up by South Willy. Andrew rolled on the ground, pain blazing in his body, understanding the use of his right arm was pretty restricted.

Head low, tusks ready to strike Andrew's spine, Hawg didn't expect the wrought iron gate of the White family crypt to pop open and connect with his face. More out of surprise than discomfort, Hawg stood fast and backed away, shaking his head to clear it from the shock of the blow.

Andrew spider crawled, and Hawg's eyes followed him. The beast then looked into the crypt as Andrew grabbed up the revolver he had dropped. He fell to his ass, pain from his shoulder so bad Andrew cried out in a horrid sob.

Hawg saw Micki, legs spread, taunting him to get her. At last, the beast could wait no more and did go at the crypt. Andrew knew full well the blast from the crypt would probably kill all of them at this distance, so he aimed to get up and run. Andrew fell badly again, crying out in pain.

Hawg hit the entrance to the crypt, body on the trip wire. Nothing happened.

Andrew cursed and fired twice from the ground. The bullets struck near Hawg's legs, enough to get his attention and his upper torso out of the crypt.

Again, the beast squared its shoulders and faced Andrew. The girl slipped a hand out of the crypt behind Hawg and started to reel in a wire that trailed off toward the Solow crypt. As Hawg's nose flared, he turned to watch her actions, Andrew fired again. This time, the bullet hit Hawg in the center of his chest. Hawg turned back to Andrew, then looked down at his sternum. Blood bubbled out of the hole, and the creature blinked. Red eyes forward, it dropped down on all fours, ready to strike.

"Christ help me," Andrew said as he aimed at its face and squeezed two more shots off. Hawg charged, twisting his face, both bullets deflecting off the tusks. "Aww shit," Andrew said as the raging beast was on top of him. Face to face, saliva ran down Hawg's mouth and through the cleft in his chin.

"Hey baby," Micki shouted as Hawg had Andrew down, ready to drop his tusks onto his face. She swung a leg out on the gate, exposing her bloody, ruined vagina to Hawg. "Suuuewwwie!!!" In her right hand was the handgrip trigger. Her left hand ran over her belly, near to where the wound to her crotch began.

Drool ran off Hawg's tusks and into Andrew's face. He held his breath and the beast pulled off him, snapping his left collarbone as he rose up. Between Hawg's legs, Andrew saw the twisted penis bounded, ready for what was next.

Micki giggled like a teasing girl and stepped back into the crypt.

Hawg started after her.

Andrew rolled onto his hands and knees, breath getting short. He started to crawl away and then get to his feet, but he just couldn't push off the ground with his ruined arms to do it. His ears picked up the sound of the gate clanging as it opened and Hawg's growl of desire.

"Please God," Andrew said and crawled as fast as he could toward the bushes. "Help me."

The echo of Hawg's howl came to his ears clear enough. Andrew could tell the thing was deep in the crypt as another sound replaced his wail. A high-pitched sound, like air escaping, sliced the area as the contents of the coffins exploded. Andrew felt the concussion of the blast and turned to see the crypt fragment into a ball of fire. He thought he heard the creature scream but it may have been a trick in his mind. The sound popped his ears and sent a spray of debris at him in the bushes. Such was the force of the discharge that Andrew saw something great and gray falling toward him. At first, he thought it was the dislodged ceiling of the crypt or a hunk of the decimated coffins. Alas, it was very benign and landed over the top of him, shielding him from the raining debris that did fall. Arms around him, taking the large hunk of concrete as it fragmented on impact. Andrew sighed at his savior's sacrifice.

It was only Jesus, protecting him from the blast. More materials fell down, even one of the bars from the gate. Jesus took an ass whupping and never yielded as the materials rained on.

He looked toward the crypt, and saw no trace of Hawg or Micki.

Face to face with the Lord, Andrew started laughing. He hoped someone searching would find him. Soon, his laughter stopped and darkness covered him.

CHAPTER EIGHTEEN

Afterwards...

Andrew's eyes filled with blazing light. If not for the pain in his arms and chest, he'd have thought himself dead. Though his ears rang in the aftermath of the explosion, he could discern the thump and twirl of the helicopter blades overhead. In another moment, his brother's face obscured the light from the sky. He hoped God didn't look like Doug. His ego couldn't take that.

"C'mon, little brother, be alive," Doug said in a fatigued, gloomy voice.

"Hey," Andrew mumbled, teeth then clenched and tears rolling from his eyes. "Holy Christ, this hurts. What's happening, bro?"

Doug laughed and wiped tears from his own eyes. "Guys, c'mere, will you?" he barked to a number of police nearby. "Help me get this damned statue off him."

While the men removed the stone cover from Andrew, the injured man said in a feeble voice, "Easy with the Lord, Doug. He's busted his ass to take care of me today."

"You're delirious, Andy. Lie still and be quiet."

EMT's flanked Andrew and started to feel for vitals. When one grabbed for a pulse, Andrew cried out, loud. His eyes blazing at the man who gripped him, Andrew said no more.

"Easy fellas," Doug snapped. "He's been through a great deal."

Andrew relayed, "My left forearm is busted, I think. Right shoulder is dislocated, maybe separated bad, I dunno. Ribs are messed up." He gasped for air as they started to put oxygen on him. "I'm twenty yards of bad road."

Doug motioned toward flashing lights that filled the grave-yard. These lights and the spotlights from the police cars illuminated an area where night had fallen. "We'll get you all fixed up, real good. Hang in there, brother."

The chief of police loomed near Doug, looked down at Andrew, and then at the smoking ruin of the crypt. "This ought to be good."

Doug fired him a disagreeable look. "Get off my ass, chief."

"He's dead," Andrew muttered as the EMT adjusted the tubes to his nose. "Hawg is dead. The killer is gone."

As the EMT's checked Andrew's vitals and attempted to get a stretcher in close to where he lay, the Chief looked at Doug with doubting eyes.

"Your brother blew up the killer? Is that what he is trying to say? You better get this straight, hoss."

Doug turned mean, spitting out, "Get off his ass, too, Chief. You wanted to bust him so bad for having guns, well, who stopped this damned killer in the town? The militia guy you hated so much."

Not that anyone noted it, but Andrew muttered, "I didn't kill Hawg."

The chief frowned, glanced at Andrew and then said to Doug, "I don't want to arrest him, Sheriff, I just want to know what I am supposed to tell the State Troopers and reporters. This has long since passed being a local matter. I've been taking calls all day from people talking of a killer pig man."

"Great," Doug sighed, staring at the partially ruined Solow crypt.

The Chief knelt by Andrew and said, "Was it a pig man, Mr. White? Tell me what you saw."

Andrew looked at his brother and then the chief. He blinked and noticed the chief eyed his injuries closely. "He was a big bastard, freaky, man. Probably some in-bred piece of trash. Hawg musta been seven feet tall."

"Hawg?" the chief said, confused.

"That's what he called himself," Andrew lied as the men started to lift him on the gurney.

"He was blown up with that crypt?" the chief questioned him further.

"Yeah...him and...." Andrew's voice trailed off and his head lay back on the pillow. "God, it hurts...all over."

The chief backed away and Doug leaned over, saying, "That's enough for now. Rest up, man."

"Gotta tell Reverend Wingler...." Andrew murmured, trying to wave his hands. "Gotta tell him his daughter...did the right thing...in the end...."

Andrew closed his eyes and passed out.

The EMT situated to Andrew's left strapped him in and they started to take him toward the ambulance.

More cars arrived as Doug walked to the smoking ruin of the crypt. Whatever was in the blast Andrew generated pulverized the innards of the crypt. Pieces of the ceiling and outer walls had flipped out onto the grass, but whatever was inside was no more. He thought he could see a rib-bone, but couldn't tell for certain.

He then eyed the damaged sepulchers next door.

"Damn," deputy Grimes said to him as he pointed. "Look at that. Mr. Solow will be pissed."

Doug saw how the wall of the Solow crypt that faced the destruction lay in pieces, as did the stone coverings for the coffins inside. The aged wooden containers ripped open in the blast. A body in a black suit hung out of its casing, right arm half chopped free in the detonation. Doug marveled at how well preserved this figure was and squinted at it in amazement. He shown his light in the death box and said, "Wonder what year he died in? He isn't quite bones."

"What do you mean?" Grimes asked and pointed again. "What are them bones then? Oh, Jesus!"

As reality dawned on the deputy, Doug took a closer look.

Under the main coffin lay two smaller spaces reserved for miniature burials. Inside these fractured spots were the exposed skeletons of tiny figures, no larger than newborn infants. Doug saw the twisted remains of the Solow babies, not really made awful by the blast, but born into a freakish existence. To the casual eye, they looked like babies, but Doug saw their limbs were longer, and the jaws more canine...and a tiny set of tusks protruded from the baby bodies' mouths.

Doug stood and said, "I want this area taped off. I will deal with Mr. Solow and will make sure someone comes out to make this right for us all. Now, get to it! Back off, everyone."

He walked over to the chief, who said, "Well?"

"An unknown killer of freakish appearance was slain by an eccentric local gun collector out here in the cemetery. He trapped him here and blew him up."

"That's the story?" the chief wondered, eyebrow raised.

"That's what we will go with for now."

Grimes ran a hand through his red hair as he stood by Hux's overturned bike. He stared into the pit and shown his light inside the hole. "Sheriff? Something is wrong over here. Look."

They stood by the lip of the trap, their lights not showing much but ruined metal and mud, but Doug's beam stopped on a leather boot. A shinbone hung out of it.

"Looks like Andrew blew up more than a killer, aye?" the chief asked, gazing between the two men.

Doug looked down at the bike. "That's Huxtable's ride. For all we know, Hux was in with the killer. It was Hux everyone saw the killer after in Ambrose Brother's, right? Well, maybe there's a connection. Looks like Hux met a bad end."

The chief sniffed at the hole and let his beam rest on charred wires. "I think your brother built an awfully big trap for a biker. Mighty big indeed, no?"

Doug stepped away from them as he saw Lynne, Jordan, and Kenny slip through the line of police and head to the ambulance. Andrew stirred on the gurney as Lynne shed tears at the sight of him.

"Hi hon, what's for dinner?" he said with a remote voice.

"Andrew White, if you don't get better, I'll kill you," she said smiling through her tears.

"Nag, nag, nag...." Andrew smiled weakly.

"Daddy," Jordan said pointedly. "The cops say you killed the monster, you killed Hawg."

Andrew paused, looked at his brother and then the chief of

police. "Yeah, I killed Hawg. I saw he was dead, real good, you savvy?"

Jordan's face lit up, excited about the news.

Andrew went on, saying, "I told you, your daddy is the bogeyman." His voice grew weaker as he declared, "Don't mess with the bogeyman, son." He took a breath and strength returned to his tone as he said to Jordan, "Hawg will never scare you again, you hear?"

Jordan nodded fast. "Never again, dad."

Andrew then said, "Daddy said he'd always be there for you, son. I'll always protect you."

The boy gazed across the cemetery at the ruins of the crypt.

"Looks like we have to get a new place to get buried in," Jordan said with a smile.

Andrew let his head roll back. "It's all right, son. You can put dead people anywhere."

Doug White turned the key in the ignition of his cruiser and looked at the passenger's seat. His right hand fumbled in the folds of his brother's flannel shirt. His hand rose up so he could see what lay inside this covering.

To the naked eye, these items might appear to be gnarled horseshoes, or hunks of steel bent asunder.

Doug covered them up again and headed out for the country. His hand still on the fabric, it touched something under the bundle. His fingers held up the square piece of cardboard, so tiny, he barely recalled how it came to be in his squad car. The tiny book of matches read "Green Parrot" and was stained with Big Ed's blood.

He didn't look forward to seeing Mr. Solow, but he figured it might be the last time they ever spoke. Tired, Doug decided this task better left for morning. Yes, that's what he would do. Sleep first. Well, first he'd kiss his wife and kids.

Tonight, he told himself, he'd sleep like the dead.

EPILOGUE

Elias shooed the last of the hogs out of the round barn and into the morning light. They ran like a swarm of insects out into the large fenced-in area. They seemed content enough to sprint down past the cow barn by the barrier he and Mr. Solow erected in the past days. Though never a place for these hogs before, Mr. Solow thought it best if they enclosed the yard around Hawg's former abode. The open space around the barn did look strange if one wanted to make a case for it. Why have such a grand barn for pigs and no run outside? The feeding pigs served another purpose. The police were less likely to cross a yard of hog waller than clean grass. Plus, they'd already checked the round barn the other day. Oddly enough, Elias recalled, they pronounced it clean.

He gazed up at the main house, at the police nodding their heads to Mr. Solow, making notes on their pads. His reassurances would have to suffice. The old man was an excellent actor, pillar of the rural community and all. The police could not tie anything to them, nor were they even suspicious, but he was sure Andrew White was, all the same. Just because Hawg looked piggish was no reason to suspect the local pig farmer. Solow played the good citizen, humoring them, handing out more iced tea to those with Sheriff White. That Irishman Grimes could drink an ocean, he mused. Plus, from what Elias heard about Hawg's demise in the graveyard, there wasn't enough of him to make a proper cured ham. Elias worried about DNA. He didn't know much about it other than what he read in the papers. He reckoned some fool would do tests on the pieces of Hawg, but no one would ever think to DNA test the beast against a sample of Mr. Solow. There was no correlation and the idea was preposterous.

Elias smiled and said aloud, "Ain't it?"

Mr. Solow seemed to focus on the other officers with Douglas White. The Sheriff stood back, arms folded, not saying anything as Grimes did much of the talking. Elias saw that Mr. Solow held something under his arm, a wadded-up piece of cloth, perhaps a piece of plaid material? He would ask later what that was all about. Doug White seemed at ease, smoking a cigarette as if nothing was wrong in the world.

He closed the big door of the round barn. Elias looked up to the rafters where the chains used to hang. Those were at the bottom of the quarry along with the car of the dope-heads from Cicero. He walked back behind the bales where Hawg used to sleep. Elias imparted a forlorn look at the two empty bales that used to flank the big creature as he slept. He missed Hawg. Though spirited, Hawg was tame until the drug mule made him feral. Elias sighed, knowing it was a matter of time before the beast got loose. It was a blessing from God that his existence never led back to them.

Soon, things would calm down and soon, everything would be like it was, after a fashion.

As he stepped behind the bales into a long stall, Elias saw another blessing from God. Beams of light snuck in from cracks in the boards, making dust motes dance around the scene like a halo.

The massive form that lay on the hay dominated the stall. The stench from the sow wasn't anything out of the ordinary, nor was the sound of a half dozen suckling pigs at her many teats. Elias frowned deep as he noted the mouth of the sow, bulged wide as she engorged herself on one of the babies. The tiny back legs of this piglet wriggled a few times before falling limp. Elias cursed himself for not being on top of things earlier. He bent over and grabbed two of the babes. He pulled them from their feeding. Angered by the action, the sow reached for two of the other babes. Still chewing on the one in her mouth, her motions never came near him, but groped into the air.

"Now, now, Luella, you know that ain't the way," Elias told

the huge mother as she chomped on the piglet.

Luella held a baby in each hand, trying to keep them from Elias. One slipped free and never fled its mother's touch. Only interested in feeding more, the babe returned to its teat, as blind to its danger as its mother was for all time.

Elias looked at the piglets in his hands and then down at the feeding babes. They were longer and thicker of limb than normal piglets. Then again, their mother possessed more breasts than a regular woman. Once Luella bit the piglet's head off, she pulled the torso down and chewed. The cruelty in her face was not like any expression Elias had ever seen from his neighbor. After chewing for a few moments, her look darkened and Luella stopped her motions. With no words, she spat at Elias, depositing a glob of scarlet on the old man's left rubber boot. Still holding the two babes, Elias squinted at the object spat. Amid the bloody mass that resembled uncooked ham were two curved objects. Elias thought them tiny bones, the rudimentary beginnings of tusks. However, the dim lights of the barn showed these to be colored white, like the bones they were.

With a sigh, Elias walked from the stall and held up the two squealing babies in the superior light. He stared at the one in his right hand and said, "You are littler than the rest, a runt for sure."

Unlike his siblings, Runt had shiny steel tusks protruding around its tiny snout.

About the Author

Award winning author STEVEN L. SHREWSBURY lives and works in Central Illinois. He writes hardcore sword & sorcery and horror novels. Twenty of his novels have been published, including BEYOND NIGHT, BORN OF SWORDS, WITHIN, OVERKILL, PHILISTINE, HELL BILLY, THRALL, BLOOD & STEEL, STRONGER THAN DEATH, HAWG, TORMENTOR and GODFORSAKEN. His horror/western series includes BAD MAGICK, LAST MAN SCREAMING, MOJO HAND and the forthcoming ALONG COME EVEING. He has collaborated with Brian Keene on the works KING OF THE BASTARDS , THRONE OF THE BASTARDS and the forthcoming CURSE OF THE BASTARDS and Peter Welmerink on the Viking saga BEDLAM UNLEASHED. A big fan of books, history, guns, the occult, religion and sports, he tries to seek out brightness in the world, wherever it may hide.

OTHER BOOKS BY STEVEN L. SHREWSBURY

Curious about other Crossroad Press books?
Stop by our site:
http://store.crossroadpress.com
We offer quality writing
in digital, audio, and print formats.

www.ingramcontent.com/pod-product-compliance
Lightning Source LLC
Chambersburg PA
CBHW050037180626
46810CB00002B/770